Star Trails Tetralogy

THE TERRA DEBACLE

Prisoners at Area 51

Marcha Fox

Kalliope Rising Press
Burnet, Texas

Kalliope Rising Press
P.O. Box 23
Burnet, Texas 78611

Copyright © 2016 by Marcha Fox
First Printing 2017
Cover and interior design by the author
Stock photos copyright license 123RF.com

ISBN-10:0-9980789-4-8
ISBN-13:978-0-9980789-4-6

Publisher's Cataloging-In-Publication Data
(Prepared by The Donohue Group, Inc.)

Names: Fox, Marcha.
Title: The terra debacle : prisoners at Area 51 / Marcha Fox.
Description: Burnet, Texas : Kalliope Rising Press, [2016] | Series: Star trails tetralogy | Interest age level: 14 and up. | Summary: "Thyron is a flora peda telepathis on an adventure gone terribly wrong. The bad decision of a human girl and her maniacal robot companion (chronicled in Star Trails Tetralogy Volume II, A Dark of Endless Days) has stranded them on Earth, where his botanical cousins face horrible fates ranging from consumption by herbivores to brutal annihilation for use as building material. After capture, Thyron is transported to Area 51, where NASA scientist, Gabe Greenley, studies his every move. Will Thyron's newly discovered psychic powers be enough to save him?"-- Provided by publisher.
Identifiers: ISBN 978-0-9980789-4-6 | ISBN 0-9980789-4-8 | ISBN 978-0-9980789-5-3 (ebook)
Subjects: LCSH: Plants--Juvenile fiction. | Telepathy--Juvenile fiction. | Extraterrestrial beings--Research--Juvenile fiction. | Environmental degradation--Juvenile fiction. | Earth (Planet)--Juvenile fiction. | CYAC: Plants--Fiction. | Telepathy--Fiction. | Extraterrestrial beings--Research--Fiction. | Environmental degradation--Fiction. | Earth (Planet)--Fiction. | LCGFT: Science fiction.
Classification: LCC PZ7.1.F69 Te 2016 PS3606.O9 (print) | LCC PZ7.1.F69 (ebook) | DDC [Fic] 813/.6--dc23

Star Trails Tetralogy
by Marcha Fox

Beyond the Hidden Sky
A Dark of Endless Days
A Psilent Place Below
Refractions of Frozen Time
The Star Trails Compendium
The Star Trails Tetralogy Box Set
The Sapphiran Agenda (Short Story)

Explore the Star Trails Universe at StarTrailsSaga.com

PREFACE

Research into the possibility of consciousness in the plant world is one of science's most exciting frontiers. The 1970s classic, *The Secret Life of Plants: A Fascinating Account of the Physical, Emotional and Spiritual Relations Between Plants and Man* by Peter Tompkins and Christopher Bird, is but one of several books on the subject. The PBS documentary, *What Plants Talk About,* is another fascinating investigation into plant sentience.

This possibility has, of course, been explored fictitiously in such stories as *Little Shop of Horrors* with the infamous Audrey, and more recently in a movie, *Guardians of the Galaxy,* with Groot. It is my hope that Thyron, the protagonist in this story whose adventures continue in *The Star Trails Tetralogy*, will eventually join their prestigious ranks.

It appears to me that certain attributes of mind, as it occurs in man, are common to plants.

—William Lauder Lindsay
Physician & Botanist
1876

CHAPTER ONE

Onboard Impounded UFO
Hill Air Force Base
Ogden, Utah
May 30, 1978
0104 Mountain Daylight Time/0704 Greenwich Mean Time

Thyron hunkered down in the *Cerulean Nimrod's* circular lower deck, cilia on his divided leaves standing on end. The girl, Creena, had failed to heed his warnings, instead listening to that horrific mechanical herbicidal ag-robot/monster, AG4MI. Both had left the ship, a huge mistake, leaving him onboard alone in a very precarious position.

Prior to Creena, all he'd known about humans was that they were omnivorous. As a *flora peda telepathis*, more commonly known as a telepathic walking plant, he was a potential meal item, which was bad. Then the girl came along, whom his instincts declared he could trust. Yet, the current situation brought that into serious question. Consumption clearly wasn't the only threat humans represented.

Oh, no. He shuddered with a protoplasmic sigh, boughs stiffening. A boarding party was on the way.

Oddly enough, the incoming human hoard lacked electronic sensing devices, but their intent was clear—search the spacecraft for anything of value. If they were hungry, he'd be at even greater risk, though what he detected was fear and excitement, not aggression. That was good, but nonetheless, he'd learned the hard way that trusting humans seldom ended well, current situation a strong case in point.

Heavy boots tromping up the spaceship's ramp confirmed their captors had arrived—at least six, only one psi-sensitive. Whether that was good or bad was too soon to tell.

Footsteps paused when they reached where the ship's levels split. He shrunk lower, broadcasting an omni-directional message to proceed to the flight deck above. They did; he released an oxygenated sigh of relief.

He focused back on the vehicle's sprawling living area, its sleek interior disgustingly sterile. Where could he hide? Bench seating was open underneath, electronics and appliances integrated with the bulkheads. Sleeping cylls with stowage lockers below rimmed the perimeter, the latter the only possibility. He knew they'd search each one—as they were doing above deck, based on the racket—but at this point there were no other options. On average, he stood a half-meter tall, but could extend or compress his limbs substantially. He shuffled to the nearest one, its location less visible behind the refrigerator, then extended a shoot and depressed the actuator. The door yielded, then closed automatically after he crawled inside.

Light gone, his photosystems shifted to internal maintenance. Motor cells relaxed, tunicate covering that protected his orb-like visual sensors wilted like botanical eyelids. Stress combined with Terra's inferior atmosphere had already downgraded his usual poetic syntax to the unremarkable diction of humans. He fought the desire to snooze, using energy reserves to psi-sense the intruders' actions.

Before long, footsteps descended the ramp. He sent another psi-directed message, but it went unheeded; lockers whooshed open, expressions of disappointment following. Most were empty, the Sapphirans as well as Creena and the 'troid not possessing the ship long enough to clutter it up.

A shout of discovery indicated they'd found the bench stowage where their entertainment media were stored.

"Hey, Sarge! Should we take these back to the colonel?" one asked.

"No. Leave 'em. Could be dangerous," another replied. "We're lookin' for lifeforms. Let the tech crew handle it."

Thyron rolled his eyes and emitted a protoplasmic chuckle. Game cartridges dangerous? The planet's abysmal technology rating was clearly an overstatement.

The bench lid lowered; more hatches opened, then slammed shut. The invaders drew closer. A hand grabbed the handle; panic spiked. Thyron focused his will on the latch and jammed the mechanism.

"What's wrong?" someone asked.

"This one's stuck. Give me something to pry it open."

Using the last of his stored energy, Thyron concentrated on the door's composite structure, securing it to the locker's frame with an unbreachable atomic bond.

Scratching sounds, pounding, then words of frustration related to excrement. Had someone's excitement caused an issue?

"What's this thing made outta, anyway?" a man grumbled.

"That's what they intend to find out at Nellis. Leave it be 'til we check with the CO. Before we do any damage, we need to know how far he wants to go to open it up. Could be booby-trapped."

Fading footsteps confirmed the party's departure, but fear remained. Even if he had enough energy to reverse the weld, where would he go? This couldn't be happening. This was not where his quest for enlightenment was supposed to lead. He was a prisoner, both he and his progeny doomed forever!

Dissonant feedback from the spacetime continuum arrested his dismal thoughts. *No. Don't panic. Low frequency vibrations attract unfortunate outcomes. This apparent catastrophe is but a minor disturbance. There are no coincidences. Trust in fate's wisdom.*

With luck, Creena would negotiate a truce and be back in short order. Surely she'd find him via a few mental pings, and the 'troid could undoubtedly breach the material, hopefully without toasting him in the process. Then they could repair the craft and be on their way.

Cosmic waves of reassurance responded to his energy shift; thus assured, his leaves closed and wilted, Thyron yielding to a dark botanical slumber.

CHAPTER TWO

Onboard Impounded UFO
Hill AFB
Ogden, Utah
May 30, 1978
0317 MDT/0917 GMT

When a strong energy source struck the locker's exterior, Thyron woke up, disoriented. He had no idea how much time had passed, but a small infrared spot glowed on the door. Hopefully the 'troid. How did it know where he was? No matter, soon he'd be free. A tongue of blue fire breached it moments later, threatening to singe his branches. He shrunk back, watching it trace out a square that hugged the door's perimeter.

The flame retreated; a blunt instrument followed and pried the piece loose. Light flooded his niche, petioles instinctively turning his leaves toward the opening so photosynthesis could resume. Expecting to see Creena and the 'troid, he emitted a flaunal gasp when the person scrutinizing him was not the girl, but a stocky, dark-skinned man wearing goggles and a helmet emblazoned with the letters *MP*. The soldier's eyes widened, rimming irises the color of iron-rich dirt with white, reminding him of an annular eclipse. Thyron peered back cautiously through his leaves, keeping his eyes hidden.

"Hey, take a look at this!" the man stated, beckoning to another likewise clothed in a dull, unhealthy shade of green.

Again he didn't sense hunger, only curiosity coupled with mild anxiety. Apparently, humans on this world were well-fed. Good.

"Reminds me of a plant my mother had once," commented the second man, a much fairer version of his companion. "But what would it be doing on a UFO, all locked up like that?"

"Yeah. Exactly. Like it was hidden in there or somethin'. Plus, I swear, it *moved,*" the darker one stated.

"Think it's dangerous, Sarge? Maybe poisonous?"

"I don't know. Probably not. Just looks like a bunch of leaves. They have a funny shape, though. Kinda reminds me of the NBC peacock. So let's see what we've got." The darker one donned a pair of heavy gloves and reached inside.

Thyron stiffened as the soldier lifted him out, having never been handled by a human before. His bipedal nodes retracted against his bulbous body, partly for protection and partly to disguise the fact he had feet. Mobility, combined with visual sensors that closely resembled eyes in both appearance and function, would be a dead giveaway he wasn't a typical plant. He lowered his nodes slowly to maintain his balance, then reached out with his mind as the man called Sarge set him on the floor. A medley of thoughts issued from the other, whose psignature indicated he was mildly psi-sensitive.

"What d'ya think? Should we box it up?" the fair one asked.

"Anything unsecured is supposed to be. But, since it's alive, maybe not. We need the bio guys to take a look. It apparently doesn't mind the dark. Weird, for a plant."

"Yeah. My mother used to store seeds and bulbs in the basement. Or that red flowered Christmas plant. Needed to be in the dark before it would flower, which was pretty weird."

"Weird is right. Like this entire thing. Sure would be cool to go for a ride, eh?"

The other laughed. "I don't know, Sarge. I'd probably puke."

"You get air sick?"

"Yeah. Bad."

"Dude! What're ya doin' in the Air Force?"

Another chuckle. "Better'n being shot," he said, mood turning solemn. "High school buddy of mine was drafted. Got stuck in an infantry battalion over in 'Nam. Got killed last year. Puking now and then's sure better'n that."

An unfamiliar frequency issued from the speaker, followed by a similar response from the other. Thyron had never felt anything quite like it before, receptors on alert, foliage shifting for another cautious peek.

"Sorry, man," the dark one replied, hand on the other's shoulder. "That must've been tough."

"Yeah."

The emanations continued, Thyron absorbing and analyzing the men's auras for meaning. Psibrations that indicated fear and anger were familiar based on his experience with the Sapphirans, the subhuman pygmies who occupied his native planet. Humans were more complex, not only in intelligence, but another essence which so far had been undefinable. Creena had introduced a few more—loneliness and sorrow—which related to being separated from her family. These emissions were in a similar yet slightly different range.

As he opened up his sensors to more fully discern their meaning, his energy level dropped, as it did when he was light-deprived. His boughs drooped, foliage wilting as the meaning of sadness, loss, and grief registered on his psyche, at which he instinctively radiated an empathic pulse in response.

The lighter-skinned guy was staring at him, hard.

"There's something about that thing that gives me the creeps," he said. "It almost feels like he's listening. Watching. Or something."

"Hmmmm. Looks like it wilted a little, too. I'll radio the CO and tell him so he can find someone who knows something about plants," the dark one replied, frowning as he stepped away to talk into a portable communications device.

Meanwhile, the fair one kept staring, blue eyes dilated with caution. Thyron cloaked his thoughts and stood perfectly still, deciding further contact was a bad idea.

"They're working on it," the other man reported, clipping the comm-device to his belt as he joined the other staring, respective brows furrowed with caution.

CHAPTER THREE

Private Residence
Apollo Park Townhomes
Clear Lake City, Texas
May 30, 1978
0538 Central Daylight Time/1038 GMT

Gabe Greenley's eyes snapped open, blissful shades of sleep decimated by the raucous ring of the phone. He bolted upright as adrenaline fired, ungodly hour of 5:38 AM glaring from his nightstand. Then, as expected, Francesca's muffled voice came from down the hall, confirming she'd answered it.

He sighed and lay back down, heart racing. He loved his niece dearly, not so much her fiancé, who couldn't get the concept he lived three timezones to the east. For the past semester she'd had an early class at Rice University, so was usually up by now; leaving at o'dark-thirty was the only way to beat Houston's commuter traffic on the Gulf Freeway. School was out, however, which her beloved had obviously forgotten. Amazing she wasn't reminding him in no uncertain terms, courtesy of her Latin temper.

Gabe rolled his eyes and turned over, trying to get comfortable again. It took all of seven minutes to reach his office in Building 37 at NASA's Johnson Space Center, giving him another three hours of precious sleep. Furthermore, as a civil servant, it wasn't like he had to clock in. He closed his eyes, turned over, and had barely gotten settled when a few taps sounded on his door.

"Uncle Gabe?" his niece said softly. "Call for you."

He sat up, blinking hard. At this hour? Seriously?

"Thanks, got it," he replied, clearing his throat as he turned on the lamp, then picked up the phone.

"Hello. Greenley here."

"Dr. Gabriel Greenley?"

"Yeah." He sensed movement and looked up, his pet parrots, Larry and Loretta, on their usual perch above the blinds, giving looks only birds could achieve at the predawn disturbance.

"This is Colonel Milton Jenkins, base commander at Hill Air Force Base in Ogden, Utah. I was referred to you by someone you've worked with in the past."

Okay, 5:38 in Houston meant 4:38 in Utah. What on Earth could justify such a call? And from an Air Force Base? Surely this was some sort of bad joke.

"Someone referred you to me? And who might that be?"

"Sorry, I'm not supposed to say. Listen, I apologize for calling at this hour, but we have a situation here and need your assistance. You're an astrobiologist with clearance who specializes in botany, correct?"

"Last I checked," Gabe replied.

"Last I checked, last I checked," mimicked Larry.

"Was that an echo?" Jenkins asked, voice inflected with suspicion.

Gabe cringed, knowing interference, clicks, and echoes were unwelcome on secured lines. "No, no, it was on my end," he said, waving the bird to silence.

"Is someone there?"

"No, it's just my bird. My pet parrot."

"Oh. It's not going to be a security risk, is it?"

"No, of course not." He frowned, having never considered the possibility before.

"Course not, course not," chanted Larry, always more talkative than Loretta, who'd tucked her head beneath her wing and gone back to sleep.

"Shhhhh!" Gabe admonished, hand over the receiver.

"Well, here's the situation. We had an incident here around oh-one hundred," Jenkins went on. "I can't talk about it on the phone, but we have some sort of plant or something here we need an expert's opinion on, if you catch my meaning."

It took a few seconds for the man's words to register through the still dissipating fog of heavy sleep.

Whoa! he thought, swinging his feet to the floor. *Could it be?*

"Did this specimen arrive in a rather, uh, unconventional way?" he asked.

"Roger that," the colonel replied.

"Can you give me a size estimate?"

"A couple feet tall, probably weighs ten or twelve pounds. How soon do you think you can get here?"

"I don't know. I'll check the schedule out of Hobby and get there as fast as I can."

"Great. When you have your flight information, call me back. 801-555-2307. Someone'll pick you up in Salt Lake. Let me know."

"I'll just rent a car, Colonel. Hold on, I need a pencil and paper."

"Colonel paper, colonel paper," Larry mocked, flying down to land on the lampshade.

Gabe swatted him away, but the bird refused to move, instead tightening his talons' grip, flaming red feathered head cocked as his human dug through his nightstand. Finding a pen but no paper, he grabbed Sidney Sheldon's *Bloodline* instead, planning to write the number on the dust jacket, then opening it up when the pen failed on the slick paper.

"What was that number again?"

"801-555-2307."

"Okay. Got it," he said, scrawling it inside. "See you, hopefully, by this afternoon."

He set the phone back in the cradle and stood up, absorbing what had just happened. He stretched, smiling, then elevated the blinds, dawn bleaching the horizon beyond his second story window. He didn't see many sunrises, but this one was indeed glorious, Mercury in the eastern sky smiling back.

With what promised to be an exciting day, he pulled on the khakis he'd worn the day before, shrugged into a clean short-sleeved button-down from his closet, donned a fresh pair of socks, and yanked on his shoes. He'd just trimmed his beard the day before, which would have to do.

The NASA travel coordinator wouldn't be in for a couple hours, so he went downstairs, greeting his profusion of tropical houseplants along the way to his kitchen, where he started a pot of private label Brazilian coffee. Next he grabbed the unwieldy Houston phone book from a cupboard, looked up the number, and called Southwest Airlines. Anything going from Hobby to Salt Lake? Nope—tail end of a holiday weekend, lots of graduations, all flights booked. Great. Did he want to fly stand-by for one at 4 PM with a six-hour layover in Phoenix? Nope, forget that.

He hung up and called Delta. A direct flight to SLC departed from Intercon at 11:30 CDT and arrived 1:50 MDT. Cost three times as much as Southworst with their cattle-class seating, but Uncle Sam was picking up the tab, so it didn't matter. He'd have to drive to the big airport across town, but had no doubt it would be worth it.

After calling Jenkins back, he chuckled to himself, realizing he could have gone back to bed, except now he was too pumped to sleep. Thus, he slammed the rest of his coffee, packed, left a note for Francesca, watered his plants and bid them good-bye, then checked in at work, where he signed out an environmentally controlled vivarium that he'd designed and built, hoping for just such an occasion.

Before leaving, he gave the Director of Life Sciences a confidential heads-up—UFOs officially weren't supposed to exist, so they were picky about such things, even at NASA. Heading for his green S-10 Blazer in the parking lot, he knew his colleagues could put two and two together; an astrobiologist checking out an ECV, then disappearing for a while, wasn't exactly rocket science. He grinned, knowing how jealous they'd be.

He dodged the construction-sponsored barrel race down I-45 toward IAH, pondering what lay ahead. Twenty-eight years as a botanist, five at NASA—perhaps finally, at fifty-three, what he'd been waiting for since earning his PhD at Purdue would come to pass. He'd always felt someday he'd be part of something incredible.

Holy guacamole, he thought. *This may finally be it.*

CHAPTER FOUR

Onboard Impounded UFO
Hill AFB
Ogden, Utah
May 30, 1978
1445 MDT/2045 GMT

Thyron sat perfectly still on the bench occupying the *Cerulean Nimrod's* lower deck, the very spot where he'd tromped the 'troid in a tysa game during their recent journey; one of his most cherished moments of botanical victory. That association was fading rapidly, however, as a bearded man with dark brown hair streaked with shoots of grey scrutinized him with curious green eyes.

"Clearly it's a botanical lifeform," the man stated to a small cluster of uniformed humans, then removed a small light source from one of many pockets in his tan jacket.

Invisible behind his carefully arranged leaves, Thyron rolled his botanical eyes. Lifeform, indeed. Classifying these people as morons was far too generous.

"Strange," the man went on.. "It looks like an *oxalis palmifrons - gigantea* hybrid, a type of wood sorrel quite common in Brazil. South Africa and Mexico, too, as I recall. I wonder if it was brought here or harvested? They're known to have medicinal properties, which could make them of interest."

"What do you suggest we do with it, Doctor Greenley?" asked an older soldier of considerable rank, judging by the cluster of decorative ribbons and dangling metallic ornaments on his chest. His uniform, unlike the others, was a shade of blue, similar in color to coagulated Sapphiran blood.

"We need to secure the specimen in a sealed unit to assure its safe arrival at the Nellis lab, Colonel. It looks rather hardy, but we don't know what its heat tolerance is, which could be exceeded during the trip across the desert. Furthermore, it shouldn't be exposed to contaminants like molds, fungi, bacteria, and such, which could prove lethal. Hopefully, that hasn't already occurred."

"Yeah, I know," the colonel grumbled, expression grim. "We were so taken back, we jumped in without proper precautions. It's not like we have an SOP, at least around here. We usually send in a specially trained detachment for this kind of thing. By the time I checked the manual, it was too late. I'm sure I'll hear plenty about it from my superiors. At least so far no one's gotten sick."

"Spilt milk, Colonel Jenkins. Fortunately, I brought along an ECV."

"A what?"

"Environmentally controlled vivarium—an isolation chamber. To protect it from the environment, at least from this point on. Designed and built it myself, but on loan from NASA's Astrobiology Branch."

"Great. Let's do it. We need to get this thing off the tarmac. A crane's on its way to load it up on an eighteen wheeler so we can get it out of sight until departure tonight."

Greenley removed a notched strip of metal from one of his pockets and handed it to the nearest soldier with hair the color of deciduous leaves after a frost. "Here's the key to my rental car, airman. It's in the back seat. Two of you should be able to handle it."

Airman? Thyron thought. *Odd. He didn't look as if he could fly.*

"While your men retrieve the ECV, I'm going to take a sample to study in the astrobionics lab when I get back to Houston. Then I'll be able to determine conclusively whether it's native or extraterrestrial."

Thyron gasped as the botanist reached into another pocket and extracted a cutting device. *Take a sample?*

Instantaneously, an ancestral defense mechanism lurking in his DNA activated. Thyron froze, having never experienced anything quite like it before. His cytoplasm tingled as deep within his primary bulb potassium transmuted to sulfur that bonded with two oxygen molecules, forming sulfur dioxide. Fortunately, the burning sensation tipped him off before it combined with water being drawn from his leaves, allowing him to stop the process before it emitted a toxic cloud of gaseous sulfuric acid, injuring and possibly killing everyone within ten meters.

The mental concentration required to perform this humane action to shut it down, however, prevented him from cloaking his thoughts. As soon as it escaped, all he could do was hope that no one within range was psi-sensitive enough to pick it up.

No such luck. The botanist's eyes widened and jaw dropped, hand gripping the cutting device frozen in midair.

"What's wrong, Dr. Greenley?" Jenkins asked, stepping closer. "Are you all right?"

The scientist closed his mouth, blinked a few times, then turned in the officer's direction. "Holy guacamole! It just refused! Rather adamantly, in fact. I swear! To be exact, I had the distinct impression it said, *Like hell you will.*"

Several more mouths fell open amid chuckles of disbelief.

"What's that smell?" one of the airmen asked.

"Well, it wasn't me," the scientist stated. "Whatever this species is, Colonel Jenkins, I suspect it's intelligent, perhaps highly so, and possibly dangerous." He shook his head, muttering, "Too bad Backster isn't here to see this," which earned even more mystified expressions.

Greenley dismounted from the bench, narrowing his eyes as he returned the obnoxious tool to his jacket's breast pocket, then stared at Thyron with elevated suspicion.

"I've seen thousands of botanical species, from the tropics to Antarctica, from the Andes to the depths of the Mariana Trench," he said. "But this specimen's unlike anything I've ever encountered, anywhere on Planet Earth."

The colonel took a deep breath and blew out his cheeks. "Yeah. If it's a talking plant, I'd say that's intuitively obvious, Dr. Greenley. Intuitively obvious."

CHAPTER FIVE

Onboard Impounded UFO
Hill AFB
Ogden, Utah
May 30, 1978
1503 MDT/2103 GMT

The approaching racket announced the arrival of two airmen carrying the ECV, a cylindrical, transparent container somewhat taller than Thyron, who perused it with trepidation. Not only was he a prisoner, he was about to be confined like one. If he were a rooted species it would be one thing, but as one with mobility, claustrophobia, another new sensation, promptly bloomed.

Another man held a separate, smaller box, apparently heavy, judging by his strained expression. Greenley released the clamps securing the chamber's lid and set it aside. Thyron stiffened when the man donned gloves; then once again, human hands closed around his primary bulb.

The botanist set him inside, tucked in a few stray leaves and branches, then replaced the lid. After that, he peeled off the gloves and secured them in a transparent bag, then beckoned the airman closer so he could unwind a cable on the side of the smaller box. Thyron scoped it out, noting it contained a chemical energy storage device. After connecting the cable to the chamber, the man activated the unit, causing the interior lighting to flicker on and a fan in the lid to hum to life.

The inflow lacked particulates, implying filtration, while vibrations beneath Thyron's bipedal nodes indicated a ventilation fan was maintaining the unit's pressure, probably through another filter. Which would conveniently protect them from his no-longer-covert defense system.

"There," Greenley stated. "The battery should last at least twenty-four hours before it'll need to be recharged. Now I just need about a gallon of water to top off the humidifier."

An airman radioed the request, another arriving a short time later with a jug, which Greenley emptied into an opening in the unit's lid. Moments later, a fine mist floated from another inlet, carrying welcome moisture.

Luxuriating in the circulating air, Thyron let his leaves blow free, absently revealing his orb-like visual sensors. The gaze of all human eyes descended upon him, several open-mouthed with horrified disbelief as everyone but the botanist backed away.

"Well, well, well," Greenley stated, his own eyes wide. He leaned forward to inspect Thyron more closely, hand pensively stroking his beard. "Will you look at that?"

"Here's lookin' at ya, kid," Jenkins muttered, expression frozen with apoplectic shock.

"Well. This certainly changes a few things," Greenley stated. "I think I should deliver this specimen personally."

"You're cleared for base access?" the colonel asked, surprised.

"Special Access, Q level. Wouldn't be here if I weren't. Been there before. Twice." The man smiled. "There aren't that many astrobiologists, you know."

"Perfect. Then you'd better ride with the convoy transporting the, uh, bogey," Jenkins stated. "Not exactly luxury accommodations, but definitely more secure than a private vehicle."

"Right," Greenley agreed. "I'll turn in the rental car, then go back to the Holiday Inn to grab a bite and a few hours' sleep before we leave. I assume you'll guard the specimen until then. Any problems, don't hesitate to call."

"Roger that," Jenkins replied. "We'll get it boxed up and ready to go. I'll notify Nellis you're coming and have someone pick you up at oh-two-hundred."

After the scientist left, Jenkins ordered his minions to cover the ECV with a tarp, then instructions where to take it. As they fetched the needed materials, the man folded his arms and gave Thyron a final, lingering look, psimissions saturated with fascination, curiosity, and disbelief, shaking his head when he finally left.

The two airmen charged with moving him kept throwing suspicious glances in his direction, but Thyron's gaze held fast. Where were they taking him? And why? With Greenley going along, no telling what would happen. He never should have let that thought escape, lost control of his defenses, much less shown his eyes.

As they covered the chamber, he shuddered with trepidation as he pondered what his fate might be. He switched to remote viewing as the pair transported him from the *Cerulean Nimrod,* across an open expanse beneath Terra's glaring sun, to a nearby hangar, where they set him down with several large boxes toward the back in an area further secured by fencing constructed from heavy gauge wire.

A short time later two others arrived, measured the chamber, then quickly constructed a box similar to the others to contain it. As he was lowered within its depths, Thyron hyper-photosynthesized with horror—he was surrounded by material that had once been the living tissue of a very unfortunate tree. His villous leaves tingled with revulsion as he sensed screams emanating from the wood's coarse grain, his mind assaulted by the vision of it being murdered in its prime—cut down, stripped of its bark, then mutilated to suit the demented purposes of humans.

A series of loud, concussive bangs secured the lid, echoes rebounding throughout the metal building. Moments later, the vibrations ceased and silence resumed.

From outside, shouting and the groan of heavy equipment filled the cavernous building, accompanied by the wheeze of what he recognized from his spaceflight experience as hydraulic systems. Curious, he extended his psi-ceptors beyond the hangar, where the activity was taking place.

A huge boom was hoisting the *Cerulean Nimrod* onto a blunt-nosed ground vehicle disguised as vegetation, judging by the different shades of green and tan blotching its exterior. Several men manually guided the dangling spacecraft into place on the platform behind its heavily reinforced cab, secured it with chains, then covered it with a tarp. As the hangar doors crept apart, someone climbed inside the vehicle and started the engine, which emitted a loud, rhythmic rumble and belched dark, noxious fumes from a vertical metal pipe as it backed inside, an airman directing the operation with red handheld lamps.

When it stopped a few meters away, the men used a smaller wheeled device to lift and load the boxes next to Thyron's onto the trailer behind the *Cerulean Nimrod*; he was next. Once in place, they chained everything down amidst a cacophony of more squeaks, bangs, and scraping sounds, then covered it all with another tarp.

When that was done, everyone left except two helmeted MPs. The pair took up stations just outside the open door, weapons slung over their shoulders while they engaged in muffled conversation. One removed a small human-finger-sized cylindrical roll of vegetal materials from a package in one of his pockets, then offered one to the other, after which he lit the bundle with a tiny flame and began to inhale the smoldering vapors, emanating considerable pleasure as he did so.

Thyron gasped, horrified. He'd felt fear vicariously, but never experienced it personally before. Now it gripped him at a visceral, limb chilling level as he considered the many ways people on this dreadful world tortured vegetation. Would they do the same to him? He shuddered with the realization he was probably about to find out.

CHAPTER SIX

Hangar 18
Hill AFB
Ogden, Utah
May 31, 1978
0308 MDT/0908 GMT

Thyron awoke with a start. What was that horrible noise? It shook everything, even the hangar itself, racket forcing the humans' voices to peak amplitude. He turned the light back on so he could photosynthesize, then psied beyond the container to see what was going on.

A quick assessment revealed the disturbance originated with the transport vehicle. Great. Wherever they were taking him, it was going to be a limb-shaking ride. Having used his psi abilities to discern how spacecraft operated, he discerned the workings of the Terrans' primitive means of transportation. A series of small, contained explosions occurring in rapid, rhythmic sequences drove cylindrical components connected to a drive train that turned wheels surrounded by inflated rubber components; exploiting vegetation yet again.

He shuddered at the engine's power source—fuel derived from rotted vegetation of ancient date, which had liquefied, then been brought to the surface and refined. Clever, but definitely the product of an undeveloped world oblivious to more efficient energy sources. A large quantity of the primitive fuel was housed in a tank between the trailer and cab, which contained two humans. The hangar was still dark, except for two slices of light shining in front, vehicle straining against its unwieldy load.

His box jerked and rocked, bumped and jolted as the truck started to move, leaving him crumpled against the chamber's damp and slippery walls. He braced his stiffer extremities on opposing sides to right himself, marveling at the unlikely combination of ingenuity and idiocy. Was this planet so backward that they hadn't developed antigravity devices?

The tractor and its load proceeded slowly out of the hangar into the dead of night, multitudes of stars piercing the blackened sky. Their pattern indicated the planet's position was slightly later than when they'd arrived the night before. Eventually, the vehicle reached a gate. It opened, allowing it to exit the compound. Its speed increased, noise dropping in pitch as the engine changed to a higher gear, vibrations shifting to an annoying frequency that rattled Thyron's leaves. Wherever they were taking him, they were on their way.

He probed the mind of the driver, then the individual beside him. He stiffened. The medley of thoughts largely centered on him as a fascinating botanical specimen rang familiar—Greenley. The man who'd intended to maim him. Accessing the man's optic nerves revealed the same dual fingers of light he'd seen in the hangar stroking the paved stretch that lay ahead.

The terrain was relatively flat except for towering mountains on the driver's side, scruffy vegetation lining the sides of the road. Stretching his awareness, he noted four smaller armored vehicles: two in front as well as behind. His protoplasm crawled at their hostile psignatures—ordnance and other nasties. Not as sophisticated as that on Sapphira's war-torn sister world, Carnelia, but the same deadly purpose.

Directing his senses to the other containers onboard, he winced at what lay within one similar to his own—a far-too-familiar array of metallic, synthetic, and electronic components. That insidious, herbicidal 'troid. The one who'd gotten them into this mess. The robot's four mechanical appendages were at their lowest position on her cylindrical torso, resting on her roloped assembly where they were bedecked with chains, electrical activity still. Deactivated, either willfully by their captors or voluntarily. Good. If he never had to deal with that beast again this fiasco would almost be worth it.

He searched for Creena, who was several kilometers away, not too far from their original landing site. He tried to make contact; nothing but static. Typical of a human adrenaline rush. He sensed fear and frustration. At least in that respect, neither of them was alone.

He withdrew his senses, realizing he'd already experienced more adventures than he'd ever thought possible. First, Verdaris, where he'd hooked up with the girl, and now Terra. A slightly shadowed sense of solace derived from the fact any experience and wisdom gained were incorporated into his seed for the benefit of his progeny.

But what if he remained a prisoner here forever? Or never got out of this cramped cylinder? What kind of life was that to pass on? It wasn't. He would have been better off on Sapphira. At least there he could move around amidst beings who revered him as a god.

A trickle of interference in the psi range interrupted his ponderings and drew his attention back to the cab.

"What's the best route? I-15?" Greenley asked.

"Hell, no, way too public," the driver replied. "We'll go west on Eighty, cross the Salt Flats to Wendover, south on the Lincoln Highway to Ely, then a few backroads to Rachel and the back gate."

The words made no sense. Still assimilating the human language, he recognized some as numbers, but of what? Were they speaking in code? Did they know he was listening? What difference would it make? It wasn't like there was anything he could do about it. While he could compromise electrical components essential to the operation of the vehicle's engine, he couldn't think of any advantage to doing so.

"How long does it take?" Greenley again.

"Usually around seven and a half hours. Depends on weather. At least we shouldn't have to deal with snow this time of year."

Thyron shivered with the thought, something he'd never encountered, seeing it for the first time as they'd orbited the planet. Moderate cold would throw him into hibernation; excessive levels, in the range that solidified water, could possibly kill him. Based on the angle of Earth's rotational axis and orbital position, the temperature should remain favorable for several diurnal cycles. But then what?

His thoughts meandered back to Verdaris and its profusion of vegetation, which he would have loved to investigate, specifically for intelligent plant life like himself. Unfortunately, he'd never had a chance to exit the ship, much less explore, before Creena and the 'troid had stolen it, leaving the carnivorous pygmies stranded.

Yet, in all fairness, he had to admit it was a matter of survival, the Sapphirans' plans less than friendly. Unlike some plants, which could sacrifice part of themselves as food while remaining alive— perhaps even regrowing the missing part in due time—the cannibalistic agenda of the Sapphirans had a more traumatic as well as permanent impact on their human prey.

The situation that led to the encounter with the girl was the first interaction beyond local myths he'd had with humans. Definitely an odd lot. The fact they all pursued an avid and often deadly conquest of plant life was true of all homo sapiens, but it was a bit of a surprise that their fellow beings were often targeted as well.

Plants, on the other branch, would defend their territory, limited in most cases by being rooted; but while some species were invasive, parasitic, and sometimes even aggressive, they were generally supportive and nondestructive toward their own species.

Humans were unpredictable, even dangerously so. Keeping close watch on his captors' thoughts was his only hope for survival.

CHAPTER SEVEN

Military Convoy Vehicle #3
En route Southbound Interstate 15
Outside Salt Lake City, Utah
May 31, 1978
0340 MDT/0940 GMT

U p ahead, a conglomeration of lights indicated an area with more people than the one they'd left. Unfamiliar psignals, far more than he could discern individually, bombarded Thyron's senses. Concentrations of sentient beings compressed multiple psimissions to a median level, punctuated with periodic spikes, some positive, others grotesquely negative.

As if the ongoing physical vibrations weren't bad enough, his foliage wilted with the flaunal equivalent of an encroaching migraine as he tried to sort and filter them to something he could understand. Much to his relief, the input faded as the vehicle and its escorts turned away from the city. While targeted psi could span the cosmos, distance diluted mass psimissions.

A concentration of sodium chloride, a compound lethal to vegetation, spanned a flat stretch of barren land, extending far beyond the horizon. Residual energies from another time revealed that eons before it had been an inland sea. Would they abandon him there? He'd not only die, but do so entirely alone. As conversation resumed in the cab, he tuned in, hoping to learn their intent.

"It's amazing how bright the stars are out here," Greenley was saying. "Can't even see Polaris from Houston, between the humidity and pollution."

"Isn't that a submarine?" the driver replied.

"I'm talking about the North Star, Phil. In the sky. You can even see the Milky Way out here. Amazing."

"Oh. My eyes are either on the road or sleepin', not on the sky."

At least it didn't sound as if they intended to stop. Relieved, Thyron's thoughts shifted to what stars looked like from outer space, in their full, spatial glory, not as if they'd been implanted on a dome that flattened their depth and thus the true distance between them. No wonder this planet was so backward; its inhabitants had a warped perception of what lay beyond.

Thoughts of the vast galaxy he longed to explore lulled him back to meditation mode until sometime later when he sensed another directional shift, back toward the planet's South Magnetic Pole. Pinkish light tinted the sky to their left, pastel hues revealed imposing, skyward-reaching bulges, created by the planet's tectonic movement like those where they'd landed. To his relief, the remains of the ancient inland sea had ended, another populated area breaching the forward horizon.

"Sure would like to make a pit stop in Ely to take a leak," Greenley commented.

"Sorry, no can do. There's a rest stop up a ways, but only if the escort okays it. Otherwise, there's a jar under the seat."

"That's a deal."

"No, that's in Vegas," Phil replied. Then both made that sound humans emitted when amused.

Thyron gasped when he sensed an elemental spike from an impressive copper deposit. An intuitive force within his DNA shoved his bipedal nodes in that direction, tilting him in an awkward position until the sensation faded. He rearranged his botanical feet, shuddering with the imposed denial. At least this world had *something* friendlier to his nutritional requirements than salt.

Before their ship had been forced to land, he'd noticed that the planet had numerous lush forests, yet this area was barren and desolate. A pang of homesickness struck, terrain reminding him of home. Back on Sapphira he'd opted for this waylaid, off-world jaunt with enthusiasm. What if he was stuck somewhere that was no different? Actually, from what he'd seen so far, quite a bit worse?

"Hang on," the driver said. The engine rumbled to a lower gear as they bumped onto an unpaved surface, dirt and rocks crunching and popping as they descended a small hill.

"The turn onto Three-seventy-five's tight and jack-knifin' this rig's not an option," the driver commented. "Plus it would really piss off those escorts." Again, both laughed.

"I've never come this way before," Greenley stated. "Only been here twice. Flew in both times on Janet."

"Pretty boring drive. Especially in a WWII eighteen wheeler."

Greenley laughed. "Yeah. Doesn't ride like a Towncar, does it?"

"Nope. You'll be happy to know it's not much farther."

"No fences?"

"See those orange posts?"

"Yeah."

"That's it, at least out here. But they know if a jack rabbit crosses that invisible line."

"Wow. *Deadly Force Authorized,* eh? That gives me the creeps," Greenley commented a short time later.

"Yeah. They mean it, too," Phil replied. "The base commander's new and tryin' to make some sort of name for himself. So far, it's a bad one. The CIA used to run this place and they weren't too happy turning it over to the Air Force. So the guy's under a lot of pressure and doesn't compromise. *Period.* And it's no secret he hates contractors, especially scientists. People disappear for farting in the wrong direction. Whether they were sent home or worse, no one knows—or perhaps will admit. So look out. You won't like what happens if they catch you without the proper ID, either."

A blast of concern emanated from Greenley and Thyron indulged in a vengeful wave of satisfaction. The man squirmed about nervously, searching his shirt, jacket and pants pockets, eventually relaxing when he retrieved a small card-like item buried deep within the canvas bag at his feet.

So wherever they were going apparently represented some level of risk for Greenley as well. Thyron filed it away in his infinite memory, suspecting it could come in handy, should confinement become unbearable or too prolonged to tolerate.

CHAPTER EIGHT

Northeast Security Gate
U.S. Air Force Nellis Test and Missile Range
Restricted Area 51
Rachel, Nevada
May 31, 1978
1110 Pacific Daylight Time/1810 GMT

Electronic signals increased steadily as the semi bumped down a gravel service road hemmed in by rugged mountains bristling with more scrubby vegetation. The overhead sun indicated it wasn't yet midday, rays already harsh. The truck and lead escort exchanged a volley of radio frequencies, then fifty meters up ahead a gate appeared that blocked the road with a red, hexagonal sign emblazoned with the written symbols for *Stop.*

"Welcome to Dreamland," Phil said.

"That it is," Greenley replied. "Hopefully not nightmares."

"Right. Had an old-timer who worked here in the '50s tell me security wasted trespassers and dumped 'em in the desert. Coyotes took it from there."

"Wow. This Cold War business is pretty serious, eh?"

"Yeah. They don't mess around with security. You serve in the military?"

"Navy. Cooked for Seabees in the South Pacific."

"That must've been a trip."

Greenley laughed. "Definitely! Spam was a four-letter word."

The convoy vehicles in front pulled aside, allowing them to pass, truck squeaking to a standstill as a uniformed guard approached, another MP. For the moment, at least, the leaf-rattling vibrations ceased.

"Hey, Orlando, how's it going?" the driver said, handing a small plastic card to the guard.

"Great, Phil. Coming in from Hill?"

"Yeah."

"Who's that with you there?"

"Gabriel Greenley, NASA Life Sciences," the scientist replied, leaning over to present the card he'd retrieved from his bag earlier.

The guard examined it, then referred to a clipboard. Thyron rustled with another wave of fear—the list was on cellulose fiber. So these humans didn't just eat, smoke, and build using vegetal substances, they even used it to record data.

Terrific. Could this world be any more hostile? Furthermore, there was a definite increase in alpha, beta, and gamma particles. Why was the radiation level suddenly higher?

"Okay, you're good to go," the MP stated to Greenley. "I'll radio Security to tell 'em you're on the way. Stop there to get your site badge coded for this visit. Keep it on you at all times."

"Thanks. Got it."

After leaving Security, they continued down the road for several minutes.

"Interesting," Greeley commented, reading the back of his badge. "Red background on my NASA badge shows I have a security clearance. Here, its restrictions. Looks like I have ground access only, need an escort otherwise."

"Me, too," Phil responded. "They've got different clearance levels for underground areas, too. Each one's color-coded and weird looking, kinda like some fancy 3D stuff."

"Holographic?"

"Yeah. Harder to fake, I guess."

"No doubt."

The driver made a hard right down a dirt road, gears grinding as the truck and trailer shuddered to a stop by at an isolated building constructed from cement blocks. A few cars littered the parking area in front, a ground-mounted dish antennae farm in the rear.

"I'll leave you here at the Bio Lab," Phil stated. "As soon as they unload your box, I'll take the UFO and this other stuff over to Hangar 7."

"What'll happen to it?"

"Oh, they'll dismantle it, or at least try to, then check for anything they haven't seen before."

"Then what?"

"Auction the good stuff off to Lockheed or some other defense contractor. The rest goes in storage."

"Do they ever give them back?"

"Depends. Only if there were survivors and they're on the treaty list. Never known one to leave that came in uninvited, though."

"What about their, uh, occupants?"

"Stuck here, I guess. Unless they've got friends in high places." Greenley laughed. "Yeah. Like Tau Ceti."

"What's that, some fraternity or secret society bunch?"

"No, no. Up *there*," Greenley explained, pointing to the sky."

"Right. Otherwise, for sure they ain't goin' nowhere."

Thyron's cilia stood on end, panic swelling. *Stuck here!* No hope of getting their ship back and, even if he escaped confinement, the terrain and climate would surely kill him.

What have I done? Thyron thought, cytoplasm swimming in more stress hormones. *This is definitely not the adventure I had in mind.*

"Your badge and access code should get you into areas where you're authorized," the driver droned on to Greenley. "When you're ready, call the motor pool and someone'll take you to the residence area. You can probably check out a car. And remember what I said about the CO."

"Thanks, I will," Greenley answered, retrieving a handled box-like container from behind the seat. "Thanks again for the lift, Phil."

"Any time. Went a lot faster with some company. Good luck!"

"Thanks!"

The rumble of a forklift grew louder amid scraping sounds as someone removed the restraints holding the ECV's box in place. An hydraulic hum, a bump or two, then the container lowered slowly to the ground. The truck clunked into gear and made a wide turn back to the road where it turned right and rumbled onward in a cloud of dust, trailer with the *Cerulean Nimrod* bumping along behind.

Thyron's box tilted as it was loaded onto something, then bumped up a ramp where it was set onto the cement. The wood protested with creaks and screams as fasteners were removed and the boards fell away. The tarp was likewise whisked away, and Thyron saw Terra at ground level with his eyes rather than his psenses for the first time. Sadly, it hadn't improved.

A man clothed in the now-familiar drab green labeled the ECV and logged it in with a laser reader. Then he lifted it with a grunt and set it on a moving belt that transferred it into a dark enclosed area where it stopped. Thyron jumped, startled, when it was blasted by a loud burst of air. The conveyor started again, ECV proceeding through a barrier comprised of plastic strips, where it bumped onto another surface which hummed as it lowered to ground level.

A door opened on the right and a man clothed in a white ceremonial suit sprayed, then wiped it down using artificial chemicals that possessed the biologically offensive energy characteristic of toxicity.

Great. Another hazard.

The door closed, but nothing moved, the enclosure bathed moments later in a blast of ultraviolet light. Thyron covered his eyes, grateful most of the rays were filtered by his enclosure. Several minutes of exposure later, it hummed back to its former height where it was transferred to a series of rollers, which delivered it inside a brightly lit room where it rumbled to a stop.

Thyron's next sight was another human, also wearing white, with a pair of familiar green eyes peering out from behind a pair of goggles.

Greenley.

With the help of two identically clothed assistants, the scientist lifted the ECV from its resting place and lowered it to the floor. With a collective sigh, the men stepped back and stared, almost reverently, as if they'd never seen a vegemal before.

CHAPTER NINE

Exotic Biological Species Laboratory (EBSL)
Nellis TMR
Restricted Area 51, Building T-1110
Rachel, Nevada
May 31, 1978
1141 PDT/1841 GMT

Thyron stared back, confused. Sapphira's subhuman pygmies worshiped him as a god. Were these Terrans of similar mind? Ceremonial garb notwithstanding, that wasn't what he detected from their psimissions. Perhaps their clothing was some sort of environmental suit. But who were the extreme precautions intended to protect? Them or him?

He sensed an answer from Greenley, who psaid back that it was for them both. The answer was not reassuring. Was it a good or bad thing that this hostile human could read his thoughts? It had been a good thing earlier when it prevented him from being maimed. On the positive side, at least they could communicate; on the negative, doing anything covert would be difficult if not impossible.

You may refer to me as Gabriel, Gabe, Dr. Greenley, or even Doc, if you like, the man responded. *Don't worry. I have no intention of harming you.*

Thyron sensed sincerity, but his surroundings indicated otherwise. The room was well-illuminated, which was good, at least for photosynthesizing, but he was surrounded by ominous-looking equipment, which was bad.

The walls in back and to his left were covered by man-sized, metal boxes, a variety of smaller free-standing versions on a counter in front. Some bulged with attached cylinders and viewports; others displayed gauges, status lights, and controls. The work surface was covered with optical gadgets, heat-generating devices, and glass containers of different shapes and sizes, some of which were strung together with tubing. A large glass-enclosed area with an obliquely shaped hood stood in back, its volume three times that of the ECV. Its access area was of suitable height for an erect human, but the only way to reach inside was through two circular holes, each attached to devices the size and shape of human hands. The wall to his right held five equally spaced windows to a similar room, more equipment interspersed below and between them.

While his experience with such devices was limited, he couldn't help noting that the flightdeck of an interstellar vehicle appeared less complex.

What exactly do you intend to do? Thyron psaid, hoping the human would perceive the words without his raging concerns.

"I'm going to check you for bacteria, viruses, molds, or fungi," Greenley said aloud, voice muffled by the suit's hood, which covered everything but his eyes. "I'm sure you'd like to get out of the ECV, but first I need to make sure you're not infected with something that would be harmful to us. If you're worried about the same thing, this is a cleanroom, which filters out such contaminants."

How clever of you, Thyron psaid, dripping with botanical sarcasm.

"We try," Greenley replied.

So how do you intend to do that?

"I'll take an air sample from the ECV and a surface sample from one of your leaves."

Thyron rustled nervously, remembering the cutting device the man had wielded earlier. Fortunately, he managed to suppress an encore of his defensive reaction, which wouldn't help, anyway, given his container's filters.

"Don't worry. All it requires is a swab of soft material. It won't harm you. Then you need to tell me how to get you properly planted. Mineral and moisture requirements, things like that."

Thyron pondered the concept of being planted, something his distant ancestors had endured before evolving mobility. Renewed fear tingled through his protoplasm at the prospect of being stuck in a pot in this human-infested horror chamber for the remainder of his life. Furthermore, his progeny would suffer the same unfortunate fate. His boughs drooped. All wisdom and knowledge acquired through his adventures would be lost forever.

Greenley's troubled expression reflected comprehension of his horrific thoughts.

"What's going on?" one assistant queried, puzzlement tinting his voice. "Are you talking to yourself, us, or with the, uh, specimen?"

"Sorry, Bill," Greenley replied. "Yes. The specimen, I mean. It's telepathic and apparently I'm sensitive to its thoughts. It's frightened, as you can imagine, being trapped on a foreign planet and now confined, not knowing its fate."

"Are you crazy? It may have eyes, but it's a plant, for Pete's sake!" stated the other white-clad assistant. "Since when does a plant worry about its future? Or anything else, for that matter."

"You'd be surprised; and apparently, this one does," Greenley replied evenly. "Obviously you're unfamiliar with Cleve Backster's work as well as Marcel Vogel, Sir Jagadish Chandra Bose, and numerous others. Plant sentience is nothing new. If you want to remain on this project, I suggest rather strongly that you familiarize yourself with their work.

"All that aside, communicating as specifically as this one does is definitely unique. Which implies there's no telling just how intelligent it actually is. Underestimating an unfamiliar lifeform is never wise. As an extraterrestrial species, there's no telling what its defensive or strategic abilities might be. It's our job to find out. Furthermore, David, since it's sentient, we have a moral obligation not to harm it."

"Isn't that contrary to policy?" Bill argued in a deep, scratchy voice. "Our mission is to learn everything we can about alien lifeforms. Protecting them is secondary. If they're intelligent, they could be dangerous."

"Until we determine its character and motivation, we can't make that judgment. We can learn much more from one that cooperates. I don't think we have to worry about this fellow taking over the planet."

"You never know," David said, frowning. "I've heard some pretty weird stuff goes on around here. Could be another Audrey."

All three of them laughed hard, providing Thyron with a triple vision of a carnivorous plant that thrived on human blood. *Ha. Revenge is sweet,* he thought.

Unfortunately, Greenley picked it up.

If you ever want to get out of that ECV, we're going to need to have a serious dialog. You apparently can't hide your thoughts from me any more than I can hide mine from you, so achieving trust or lack of it should be fairly easy. Understand?

Thyron recognized the statement held dual potential, threat as well as promise. Yet, so far, Greenley seemed sincere. Maybe he couldn't help Thyron's situation, but he could make it as pleasant as possible. Or miserable.

Tell me about yourself. What are you? Plant or animal? Greenley psaid, parking on a stool to peer at him while both assistants stood behind, emanating skepticism.

Neither, Thyron replied. *I'm a vegemal, possessing characteristics of both. Not flora or fauna, but known in more enlightened galactic sectors as flauna. Specifically, I'm a* flora peda telepathis.

A vegemal. Fascinating. So you could be considered an animal whose metabolism is based on photosynthesis, or a plant with communication abilities. Am I correct in translating your genus to indicate you're a telepathic plant species with some level of mobility as well?

That's correct, Thyron stated, surprised he figured that out.

So being confined to a pot isn't your ideal environment. You want to be able to move about. Correct?

Yes.

Okay. I don't know exactly how much space I can promise, but I'll do the best I can. Tell me about your nutritional needs.

Thyron proceeded to explain how he absorbed nutrients from the ground through rootlets on the bottom of his bipedal nodes and how much moisture content was required to assimilate it. He listed the specific minerals he needed, including copper, magnesium, potassium, and a generous quantity of phosphorus, to maintain optimum health. It pleased him that Greenley proceeded to write them down, even though he was doing so on the same cellulose substance as the guard's list at the gate.

How backward were these people?

"I'm sorry paper offends you," Greenley said aloud, "but I'm afraid it can't be helped. I can write faster by hand than I can type into the computer. Technically, paper isn't supposed to be in here, but it's been UV sanitized and the filtration system will remove any particulates."

Nice. Of course the real question was how long would he have to stay in that cramped chamber, unable to stretch his limbs?

"Like I said before, I'll need to analyze an air sample as well as a swab from a leaf before I can even think about letting you out."

Fine. So what was he waiting for?

Greenley's eyes looked as if he were smiling as he proceeded to use a syringe to draw out some air through a valve in the top of the chamber, which he handed to the nearest helper. Then he turned off the fans, opened a small door in the side, and reached in with a short stick topped with a wad of *more* vegetable material. He stroked it along the bottom of the nearest leaf, then another along a branch. Thyron shivered from the contact, which tickled, but left no damage.

"There. Now that wasn't so bad, was it?"

No.

"Let's take a look at the air," Greenley stated, turning the chamber's fans back on before placing the sample in one of the machines. After a slight pause, a series of lines appeared on a screen. "Only a trace of volatile chemicals," he announced. "Normal, considering he's under stress. Let's get a culture started, too," he added, then did something with the swabs on the other side of the room.

When he'd finished, the scientist motioned to his assistants to follow through a network of transparent flaps to the right, their movement triggering a *whoosh* as a blast of air welcomed them to the other cleanroom next door.

Thyron watched through the windows separating the two rooms as they proceeded through a decontamination suite, entered an anteroom where each removed his protective suit, placed it in a bin, then left.

For the first time since landing on Terra, Thyron tried to relax. As far as he could tell, he was in no immediate danger and had plenty to investigate in his surroundings. Stress chemicals circulating through his protoplasm gradually diminished and his mental processes cycled down closer to normal, allowing him to absorb his environment more efficiently. The poetic speech pattern he'd acquired onboard the *Cerulean Nimrod* had definitely disappeared, and he felt as if he wasn't photosynthesizing at top efficiency. Besides the excitement, poor light quality, not enough CO_2, plus mineral depletion from being away from soil since leaving Sapphira had taken their toll.

Moments later, the three men showed up in a small room beyond the counter, separated from the lab by another window. The assistants sat at a table while Greenley stood by the opposing wall, mostly covered by a green slab marred by markings comprised of a chalky substance similar to gypsum. Primitive, to be sure, but certainly better than paper.

Thyron got comfortable and tuned into the conversation.

"I'll get to work culturing the samples to make sure it's not carrying any pathogens. I should have preliminary results within three days. Anything suspicious, I may have to go as long as three weeks. One way or the other, we need to build it a suitable phytotron," the botanist stated, pensively pursing his lips.

"A what?"

"A habitat. Apparently, it's ambulatory and wants to move around."

"Move around? What for?" asked one of the assistants. Now that the man was out of the environmental suit Thyron could see he was a relatively young man with a strong jaw, head covered with shaggy brown hair the color of dead leaves. "I've heard about some pretty strange lifeforms around here, but a walking plant? Are you kiddin'?"

"No, I'm not. I suspect that may be why sentience and eyes evolved in this species. A stationary plant has a much less stimulating environment. It's certainly not marathon material, but it can shuffle around. So it needs some room. David, I want you to put together a humus rich, organic soil mix a bit on the sandy side that has plenty of nitrogen with the usual trace elements including calcium, magnesium, phosphorus, zinc, and a touch of copper. Here's a list of the exact percentages, including the moisture content. We'll need at least a cubic yard."

Greenley turned to the other man, aged a bit more than the first, who had short dark hair in a military cut similar to the men where they'd landed. "Bill, get with the guys in the shop and build an enclosure with these specifications." He drew a large, upright box on the green board.

"I want a stainless steel frame with quartz glass walls, no plastic, since it might off-gas toxins the specimen can't tolerate. Understandably, it's upset by wood, so avoid it as much as possible, but it's going to have to get over it. Besides, wood could harbor contaminants. We'll set it up in room one, so be sure the components fit through the decontamination suite. I need it ASAP, so we can get it out of the one it's in."

"That's not going to happen," David cut in. "It's the week after Memorial Day. Between graduations, weddings, vacations, and stuff, just about everyone I know out in the shop is on leave. Probably be next week sometime. At least."

"Well, do the best you can. At least order anything not in stores."

"What about control systems and electronics?" Bill asked.

"It needs a HEPA-filtered circulation system with humidity and temperature controls to the same specs as the ECV. I want sensors for N_2, O_2 and CO_2 with a constant level pressure system, one atmosphere for now, but capable of maintaining two. I need an RF alarm tied to my pager, in case any systems fail or the gas mix gets out of balance. It'll also need automated lighting. I'll ask it what it prefers."

An equally divided period of a standard galactic day, which is twenty six of your hours," Thyron replied. *No wonder you people are a little slow.*

Greenley laughed. *How about we start you there, then gradually bring you around to ours? As long as light and dark are of equal duration you should be okay. Do you agree?*

I suppose.

"Set it for a diurnal, twenty-six hour day, adjustable to twenty-four over a week's time," he stated, to which the two assistants exchanged a look, psimissions projecting suspicion regarding their superior's sanity.

When the pair departed, Greenley got up and gazed through the window, eyes locked with Thyron's for a considerable time. Eventually he smiled, muttered "Holy guacamole," then shook his head and likewise left the building.

Thyron frowned as the door closed behind him, wondering who or what guacamole was and why she was considered sacred.

He'd assimilated human language easily, due to his strong intuitive abilities that linked words with specific energy psignatures. Subsequently, when he'd encounter a situation, the relevant word or phrase surfaced effortlessly. He particularly thrived on colloquialisms, which possessed a pleasing energy, similar to the poetic speech that came naturally when his biological and intellectual needs were properly met.

All that aside, he'd never heard of *holy guacamole* before, its interpretation elusive. The only emotion he'd detected behind it was surprise with a touch of wonder, not the reverence he'd expect if directed toward deity. He'd have to pay closer attention and, if he couldn't figure it out, ask Greenley to explain. After all, the entire point of this venture was enlightenment.

To be canonized certainly implied sentience far beyond his own. Maybe he'd get to meet this divine entity at some point. Better yet, maybe she could help him escape.

CHAPTER TEN

Bio Lab (EBSL)
Nellis TMR
Restricted Area 51, Building T-1110
Rachel, Nevada
June 5, 1978
1900 PDT/0200 GMT

It was several days before the components arrived, after which it took a few more for Greenley and his crew to assemble the habitat in the cleanroom next door, which had slightly lower cleanliness standards. Late that afternoon they finally finished, got Thyron transferred, then left for the day.

Thyron had to admit that the new habitat was reasonably comfortable, albeit a prison. By now he felt less threatened, the additional space a definite improvement over the ECV. The air circulation system was quieter with fewer distracting vibrations, plus it was roughly three meters square, allowing him to stretch and move around a little. At least now his stolons wouldn't stiffen up and impede shuffling about with his bipedal nodes.

Apparently, Greenley had figured out that he wasn't carrying any pathogens that raised concerns, at least for humans or Terra's plant species. Thus, the scientist's concerns shifted more to Thyron's wellbeing and identifying anything that might compromise his health, for which the man had claimed a few days before that he needed a leaf sample.

Recalling the cutting device he'd wielded when they first met still struck Thyron's cytoplasm with leaf-quivering fear. It reminded him too much of that nasty 'troid and her supposed harvesting duties on Verdaris. He adamantly refused, as he had before, luckily without defensive emanations, and so far Greenley hadn't brought it up again. Whether or not it was worth enduring the amputation of a leaf or perhaps a branch in exchange for more freedom was another story. Fortunately, his psychic abilities were sufficient to do a lot of investigating from where he was. While confined physically in the habitat, he could nonetheless explore virtually anywhere he pleased.

Before they even left Hill AFB he'd discerned the workings of the ECV. It took him a matter of seconds to discover the habitat was simply a scaled-up version of the same technology. Since his arrival at Area 51 a few days before he'd scoped out the form, fit, and function of all the instruments and equipment surrounding him in the cleanroom. Every manmade item carried the imprint of its inventor's thought process at the quantum level, which he was able to analyze, component by component, to derive its purpose.

So far he was unimpressed.

The scientific data each was designed to provide was something he could determine intuitively. He couldn't help but scoff at the various applications, such as the gas chromatograph's task of determining chemical composition. The glovebox had been particularly amusing, considering he could analyze anything from a safe distance. All Greenley had to do was ask and he could tell him anything he wanted to know. Perhaps the human hadn't figured out what the questions were.

He found it amusing that while Greenley was studying him, he was doing likewise, having had limited interactions so far with humans. It interested him tremendously that the man was a fruitarian, subsisting mostly on fruit, which didn't result in the demise of the botanical species that provided it. However, the man's diet resulted in gas emissions about which his assistants frequently complained. The noise factor was no more than an occasional, erratic vibration that was certainly harmless, so he couldn't understand what all the fuss was about.

Air entered Thyron's olfactory system through tiny holes in his leaves called stomata. The presence of certain chemicals, such as salicylic acid, could indicate a neighboring plant was under attack and serve as a warning to engage his own defense system. The chemical composition of Greenley's explosive events comprised nitrogen, hydrogen, carbon dioxide, methane, oxygen, and a small percentage of hydrogen sulfide gas, the last of which was the primary component of Thyron's own defenses.

He paused, shifting to a pensive stance as he remembered that the Sapphirans off-gassed sulfur when frightened. Could the scientist be afraid of him or his coworkers? The man's aura didn't reflect that, so probably not. Was it possible the odiferous similarity to the pygmies who occupied Thyron's home world facilitated his psi-connection with the man, perhaps giving them all something in common at the DNA level?

His petioles stiffened, leaves on alert, as another notion arose: Could Greenley, like himself, use it defensively?

These were all matters he'd have to investigate. It was interesting to connect with a human. The girl, Creena, whom he hadn't known long enough to fully assess, seemed kind and compassionate, yet ate certain things of which he didn't approve. While he'd never felt threatened, the practice contributed dark flecks to her aura that he found disconcerting. Furthermore, she'd used deceptive tactics to defeat the Sapphiran pygmies with whom he'd been traveling, and then, with the assistance of that nasty 'troid, hijacked their ship.

But he had to admit that it really wasn't that simple. The pygmies had been tasked by a very suspicious individual to find and retrieve the girl for what he'd known from the start were likewise devious purposes. She was important for some reason he'd not yet discovered, which left room for speculation. Their initial encounter on Verdaris reverberated with quantum fluctuations that indicated entanglement coupled with a strong element of fate. But the fact she'd condoned and protected that insidious electroid was another issue. That mechanical monster was clearly a murderer and reeked of the life-giving chloroplasts of the Verdarian plants she'd heartlessly annihilated.

The friend of my enemy is my enemy flitted through his mind from an unknown source, giving him pause. Interesting concept, but was it valid?

The girl was far from blameless in their current debacle as well. He should have known better than to trust either of them. His initial off-world jaunt with the Sapphirans was not providing the expansion to his consciousness he'd expected, largely due to the girl and troid's recent decisions. He'd tried in vain to warn them about this planet, which emanated a variety of negative vibes he'd detected as soon as they entered its star system. Part of him didn't much care if he ever saw either of them again, though he didn't want to spend the rest of his days confined, either.

Yet, on the other limb, was it possible that all had transpired according to some cosmic plan and this was where he belonged? If that was the case, hopefully he wouldn't always be confined, much less surrounded by sterile, uninspiring lab equipment. Exploring virtually was educational, but not nearly as satisfying.

His ponderings wandered back to the scientist, whom he found a fascinating subject. The Sapphirans, who were strict carnivores and thus no physical threat, lacked mental prowess. The botanist was intelligent, perhaps the smartest human he'd encountered so far. He seemed honest as well, which may have been partly of necessity, since Thyron could read his mind.

He'd been careful to check for psi bursts, which occurred when a sentient being, particularly humans, would think one thing, then immediately reverse it with a conflicting one to disguise deceitful motivations. None had occurred, neither conscious denial, other false thoughts, nor deliberate cloaking to keep out psintruders such as himself.

If he could, the man would have been more careful about hiding that persistent desire for a leaf sample. Thyron could tell it wasn't all about protection. There was a high level of curiosity behind it that had nothing to do with Thyron's welfare. Furthermore, would he be satisfied with only one? Even worse, he'd heard horror tales circulating through the quantum web regarding a practice known as pruning. Supposedly, a plant could recover from such drastic measures, developing even more lush growth than before. But in spite of the philosophical blurb that stated "That which doesn't kill you outright makes you stronger", Thyron would never permit such a brutal invasion of his personal space.

Greenley had only asked that once, but the thought recurred several times a day, always accompanied by a frown that revealed his frustration. It was possible he wasn't sophisticated enough with cloaking techniques, since he apparently hadn't had the opportunity to practice his psi communication abilities until now. Depending on how things went, maybe he'd share a trick or two.

Then again, maybe not. Doing so could be counterproductive to his own purposes. Thyron was well-versed in such mental gymnastics, which might become necessary, should he decide at some point to escape. Being able to read the scientist's mind unencumbered was to his advantage.

Like earlier that day, when Greenley had been trying to figure out how to ask if he had a preferred gender without being too personally intrusive. Gender, of course, was irrelevant, at least for the purposes of Thyron's own reproduction, and thus not an important part of his identity, as it was for animals. So as the man struggled with how to ask, Thyron answered preemptively: *It's irrelevant. I suppose in human terms, I'm hermaphroditic. He, she, they, whatever. Whichever you prefer. Anything but it. I'm not an it.*

Greenley looked startled at first, then laughed. "Okay," he'd replied. "Makes sense. Thanks." But then the man had scowled, unsure he liked the fact Thyron could read his mind. The vegemal scoffed at his concern, which would keep him in line if nothing else.

Thyron's musings shifted back to the present when the lights in the chamber flickered as they always did before fading into the nocturnal portion of the habitat's diurnal cycle. Moments later, a refreshing burst of nutrient-infused water seeped up through the soil beneath his peduncles. He enjoyed the sensation, which was soothing and restful. Yet, ironically, this was the time he could do some serious snooping; with Greenley gone he didn't have to cloak his thoughts. Furthermore, the majority of base activity took place at night. But with his light source extinguished, he'd have to tap into his primary bulb's stored energy to do so.

His leaves rustled, frustrated.

Emanations that exuded mystery and secrecy tickled his curiosity until, desperate for some intellectual stimulation, he called upon his reserves and prepared to extend his awareness beyond the confines of the Bio Lab.

A short jaunt for the sake of his intellectual sanity couldn't possibly hurt.

CHAPTER ELEVEN

Bio Lab (EBSL)
Nellis TMR
Restricted Area 51, Building T-1110
Rachel, Nevada
June 5, 1978
1947 PDT/0247 GMT

Before getting very far in his virtual excursion, however, Thyron discovered that certain wavelengths were blocked by the building's cinder block walls and metal roof. This had never been a problem, either outside in the open or onboard a spacecraft where he could tap into the ship's sensor network. Psi was unrestricted by physical boundaries, but required substantially more mental energy he hesitated to use in the dark.

Operating as a receiver in the electro-magnetic bands was a more passive, less demanding function, which required minimal concentration. The EM spectrum, comprised of radio waves, infrared, ultraviolet, x-rays, and various others, resided together with visible light, and was thus more easily collected. Different information came from each, however, so to get a detailed analysis, he needed to access them all. Some in the high energy range made it through concrete, others didn't, and would require more effort to access, perhaps even using psi to position his receptors outside.

Terra's environment was quite different from both Sapphira and the conditions he'd enjoyed onboard a spacecraft. Gravity was slightly less, which made it easier to move around, but so far Greenley had not determined the optimum combination of carbon dioxide and his preferred wavelength of light for his photosystems to operate at top efficiency. If overworked, permanent damage could occur, which could compromise his abilities until his next growth cycle. He trembled at the thought of going through such a private and intimate biological process while under the scientist's scrutiny.

To avoid such an embarrassing situation, he needed to make sure he didn't exhaust his resources and fall into hibernation. Until he got more light and the proper balance of CO_2, he needed to limit his activity. But all was not lost. Radio waves were low energy, easily interpreted, and better yet, accessible, courtesy of the antenna farm just behind the Bio Lab.

Obviously, they were there for communications, but with whom? Or better yet, what? He tuned in on one, finding routine voice loop chatter, the most interesting conversation that between base security and a pair of guards on lookout duty. They were monitoring an approaching vehicle, which was apparently lost, and wisely turned around and left at a high rate of speed when the guards turned on their headlights and issued a warning with a sound amplification device.

As Thyron had noted upon arrival, the surrounding land was not only isolated geographically, but impaled with various sensors to detect intruders. He switched to another dish and monitored such signals coming in from the infrared band, the only activity local wildlife—a large snake stalking a rodent; a female deer browsing the brush with two offspring; a lizard, much like the ones on Sapphira, feasting on insects.

The deer troubled him some. Clearly it was an herbivore. Would such find him a tasty morsel if he were outside? On Sapphira the carnivorous pygmies protected his kind from such violation. If he were outside here he could find himself at serious risk should an attack come when he was asleep and unable to activate his defense systems.

Another antennae buzzing with real-time data exchanges captured his attention. All it contained was systems utility infrastructure monitoring—electrical current levels, voltages, natural gas and other fluid pressures, radiation levels, all pretty boring stuff. One band was oddly familiar; he'd sensed it in the lab, mingled with interference from all the equipment, but now it was silent.

He found another similar band, which he listened to for a while, but without context nothing held his attention—until he abandoned the antennae for the open airwaves and monitored frequencies in the radio and microwave range. Multiplexing for maximum coverage, he tapped into several sources at once, finding a wide variety of entertainment media.

Some had interesting, often pleasant, rhythmic sounds in a variety of tones, harmonics, frequencies, and amplitudes. He listened a while, fascinated, finding some had words that matched the beat. He wondered how his own metered speech, which occurred when he was receiving proper light and CO_2, would blend with such sounds.

After that, he found television frequencies, which contained sidebands for both audio and video. To his delight, the broadcasts provided fascinating insights into Terra's culture, especially those that focused on human families. These promised to expand his understanding of the species' culture as well as their language and word usage. Knowledgeable in that realm were individuals known as The Fonz, and another called Archie, both of whom expanded his vocabulary with new words and colloquialisms he found nearly as delicious as technical jargon. This was surely a place to which he'd return.

He continued his survey, finding that, in spite of evidence to the contrary, it appeared that the planet was engaged in space exploration via the crew on an odd-looking starship dubbed the *Enterprise*. Another off-worlder called Mork, albeit a human, was struggling like himself to understand Terra's quirky natives. Such sources were valuable and he took careful note where to find them so he could return for more input there as well.

As the evening progressed, broadcasts of interest dwindled, but he was too wound up to sleep. He still felt fine, so decided to risk using psi to investigate the base's layout. It was always wise to be familiar with one's environment. It would take additional energy to project his awareness outside the building, but after that initial effort, he could resume functioning as a receiver. He concentrated on a location approximately seven thousand meters above the base, adjusting his sensors for infrared; the waxing crescent moon had already set and would have failed to provide enough light for visible bands, anyway.

Parking his awareness in the aerial view, Area 51 panned out before him in shades of green, which of course was his favorite color. Two parallel landing strips several kilometers long splayed the desert, connected by random, yet ordered roadways.

A naked ellipse sprawled on the far side, the evaporated remains of another primordial body of water. Its history flashed before him, intuition delivering its name—Groom Lake. Its naturally smooth, level surface, perfect for Terran airborne vehicles to land, had initially attracted the humans to the area.

To the northwest, clusters of metal buildings in a wide variety of sizes occupied the area between the landing strip's access roads and nearby mountains, some structures not much larger than the Bio Lab, others massive. The Bio Lab was toward the south, isolated from the hangars and other buildings.

He'd barely finished perusing the layout of the manmade sectors when his perceptions faltered, incoming data distorted and losing resolution.

Tired as well as disappointed, his branches drooped. To explore the site via remote viewing he definitely needed to photosynthesize more efficiently. Greenley needed either to provide more hours of light or a stronger lamp. He considered adjusting the controls himself, but hesitated, not wanting to arouse unwanted suspicion. So far he felt he could trust Greenley, but he still hesitated to reveal all of his abilities.

Determined to at least complete his surface map, he pulled more energy from his primary bulb. A short time later, his leaves wilted and he knew that within hours a few would turn yellow. No problem, he thought, finally shutting down for the night. Recovery would come easily and Greenley would see for himself that he needed more light; he just might not understand why.

Bio Lab (EBSL)
Nellis TMR
Restricted Area 51, Building T-1110
Rachel, Nevada
June 6, 1978
0805 PDT/1505 GMT

When the botanist strolled into the cleanroom the next morning decked out in the usual white suit, he immediately saw Thyron's degraded condition and examined the habitat's readings, which were, of course, nominal.

"What's wrong?" he asked, voice reflecting concern as his mind reiterated his longing for a sample, then shifted to wondering whether brief moments of exposure back at Hill AFB had introduced something that affected his botanical charge's health. "What do you need? Tell me and I'll do whatever's required to get it."

A life, Thyron thought, cloaking it for multiple reasons. One, because he didn't want to fully express his dissatisfaction, at least not yet; two, to see if Greenley still perceived his thoughts when cloaked; and three, simply because even a *flora peda telepathis* needed a little privacy once in a while.

The botanist held his hood-covered chin with a gloved hand, scrutinizing him with narrowed eyes. At least since moving to the new room he'd dispensed with the goggles—helpful since human eyes were excellent indicators of their owner's mental and emotional state.

"Do you hear me? Are you okay? Hello? Talk to me. What do you need?"

Light, Thyron answered, satisfied the man hadn't sensed his initial response. *More light. Preferably in the 680 nanometer range.* Furthermore, he didn't want him thinking he'd been infected with something, which could result in being cooped up forever.

The man visibly relaxed. "Okay. That'll require a different bulb, perhaps one that's custom made, which could take a while. What if I increase the timing and tweak the CO_2 in the meantime?"

Yes, that would be helpful.

Greenley cranked the appropriate valve, a soft *hiss* announcing its arrival. Thyron concentrated on absorbing the molecules, energy slowly returning to his chloroplasts. He rearranged his boughs as he perked up, leaning toward the light.

"Better?" Greenley asked.

Much. Thanks, Doc.

At first the scientist looked relieved, then surprised. "That's the first time you've referred to me by name."

Yes.

"Do you have a name I can use for you?"

Of course. Thyron exploited the moment's drama, waiting until the man's look of anticipation shifted to one bordering disappointment.

You may call me Thyron.

"Thank you, Thyron." The corners of Greenley's eyes crinkled, aura indicating he was smiling. "Most appropriate."

Why is that?

"Here on Earth we call the membranes that collect light and perform photosynthesis thylakoids. Does your name have any special meaning in your culture?"

It's what was revealed to me for this incarnation. It refers to one on the path to enlightenment.

"Interesting. The reference to light in a metaphorical sense is rather profound. But you don't feel as if that's being fulfilled here, do you?"

Thyron fluttered with a botanical sigh. *No.*

"I'm sorry. My primary objective has been to protect you. That's why I need a sample, to see if you're susceptible to diseases that afflict our flora. That's still a concern, but once we have you stabilized physically, I'll see if I can allow you more freedom. Maybe eventually move your habitat outside."

That would be most welcome. The spectra from your sun peaks at a longer wavelength than I'd prefer, but it would be more easily absorbed than the artificially created ones.

"Okay. That sounds like a plan, though I'll have to get high emissivity glass installed to allow those particular rays to penetrate."

Why do I have to be enclosed? Why can't I experience your atmosphere directly?

"Clearly, it doesn't contain enough CO2 to meet your needs, plus the light issue. Furthermore, like I said, I'm concerned there may be pathogens that could present a disease threat. Until your photosystems are balanced properly, you're more vulnerable."

I assure you that my chloroplasts, nuclei, endoplasmic reticulum, and cell membranes are capable of producing numerous molecules to defend me quite nicely. Even against you, if necessary.

Greenley stiffened, his mind momentarily racing too fast for Thyron to follow. Sudden comprehension seized the man's countenance, his voice assuming an accusatory tone. "Oh, really? Like sulfuric acid, my bot-alien friend?"

Thyron looked away and cloaked his thoughts. No doubt Greenley was referring to his aborted reaction to the man's initial attempt to take a sample. Should he admit it? Making it clear he had built-in defenses couldn't possibly hurt. This typically arrogant human still saw him as no more than an interesting specimen and thus an inferior species. Maybe he, too, could benefit from some enlightenment.

Among others, Thyron replied, wondering again if the man had similar abilities.

CHAPTER TWELVE

Bio Lab (EBSL)
Nellis TMR
Restricted Area 51, Building T-1110
Rachel, Nevada
June 7, 1978
2009 PDT/0309 GMT

At first, Thyron managed the resulting energy increase from Greenley's environmental improvements as intended, limiting his covert activities so they didn't exceed the input. At least his psi-related functions were operating closer to optimum level. Which meant he was getting even more bored.

Having already mapped Area 51's ground features, he wanted to know more. What was going on that required the outpost to be so far removed from civilization? The base where they'd landed was in a populated area and had an energy psibration leaning toward training and protection; this one was entirely different. Good, bad, or indifferent, he needed to know why it felt not only more technologically advanced, but more threatening.

His experience with military activities was limited and less than favorable, primarily associated with wars on Sapphira's sister world, Carnelia. That planet had horrific vibes saturated with death, intrigue, and violence. His excursions amongst the air waves indicated wars infested Terra as well. Thus, being detained at an outpost with suspicious motives was cause for concern. The radiation level was high, elemental analysis pointing toward thermonuclear devices. Why would they locate in such a place? All speculations induced his cilia to stand on end. He needed to know more. If lethal conflicts were coming his way, getting off this planet would take top priority, whether or not he'd fully explored its geological features and its occupants' civilizations. Thus, he set out to discover Area 51's secrets and hopefully determine the threat level.

A simple psi-sweep indicated that in spite of the 'troid's pre-landing assessment that the planet had a low technology rating, that wasn't the case at this facility. Apparently, the global figure reflected the median value, not the highest attained. Which made sense—advanced areas were diluted by those inhabited by indigenous populations, some only slightly more evolved than Sapphirans, and then only because Terrans had developed a spoken language. Unlike the subhuman occupants of his native world, Terrans generally had the brain capacity to be much brighter, in spite of their somewhat limited technical base.

The real question was why this facility's psibration range was several orders of magnitude higher than the planet as a whole? Such an activity level indicated exceptional intellectual endeavors were in progress. But where? What? And even more important, why?

He concentrated on finding the energy psignature of advanced technology and soon detected sparks of innovative brilliance. He followed them to what he expected to be the highest technological presence. Surprisingly, its epicenter was over twenty kilometers south of the base with nothing visible besides more desert and a stand of geological tectonic structures. The psibrations persisted, however, seeming to originate from the mountains themselves.

Mystified, he directed his awareness within, gasping at what he found—ten cavernous hangars, all except one occupied by an interstellar craft surrounded by personnel as well as a variety of equipment. Each vehicle had a sleek design that emanated exotic energy sources, not only larger, but far superior to the one in which they'd arrived. Why secure them so covertly?

He monitored a few conversations among the workers, learning only that they were struggling with their task, which was to determine how the vehicles operated and back-engineer the relevant technologies. The complex was referred to as Galileo Bay, a term he'd picked up earlier on the voice loops, thinking it was a geographic location related to water. Obviously not. Being so far away, it wouldn't do him any good, anyway.

While he'd mapped the base's surface features, he hadn't identified what each building contained. Realizing he may have missed something important, he left the mountainside hangars and returned to see what was housed in several large, hunched-over buildings a few miles away. To his surprise, he found the *Cerulean Nimrod* in the one denoted Hangar 7, partially disassembled with its hull stashed beneath a tarp.

On Sapphira he'd discerned how to operate the craft the same way he'd figured out the lab equipment, *i.e.*, the thought process embedded in each part's psibration. While he'd absorbed this information when he psi-scanned the vehicle, it was simply recorded in his holographic memory where it remained until needed, similar to how Greenley ordered books and journals to refer to later.

Ironically, several other vehicles occupying the same hangar could have provided the intragalactic passage they sought, but all possessed the flawed, low-energy imprint indicative of systems damage, which apparently presented Terrans with a major challenge. The humans didn't understand some of the most fundamental quantum systems, making it impossible to repair them, much less to replicate and replace flawed components.

Maybe he should concentrate on how to repair one himself and get them out of there. No, maybe later. For now he was having too much fun exploring.

Mind back on the task at hand, he continued investigating the contents of the various buildings. The concept of buildings itself was barely starting to register, though human inability to adapt to changing weather and seasons explained the necessity. Sapphira's climate was mild, its subhuman occupants living in natural caves and caverns, so they had no need to construct sophisticated shelters, even if they could. His leaves drooped as he realized how much he missed fresh, unfiltered air and sunshine; artificially produced resources just weren't the same.

Moving on to other local hangars, he found a variety of prototype aircraft more advanced than he'd seen elsewhere on the planet. The fact some were designed for high altitudes using stealth technology and advanced weaponry was interesting and showed technological progress, but not what he needed to get off-world. He moved on to some smaller buildings, stiffening with surprise when he discovered what was stored in the northeast corner of Building 15. There, in one of many bins, lay the disassembled components that comprised that horrific mechanical monster, AG4MI.

Ha, he thought. *Serves you right, you insidious herbicidal maniac.*

He shuddered at the memory of the singed and shredded vegetation sullying her harvesting mechanism. They wouldn't even be in this mess if it weren't for her. A replay of their capture delivered his thoughts to Creena. She'd not been brought to this location, but remained behind, somewhere near their original landing site. She was responsible for this debacle as well, yet he felt a twinge of concern. After all, her youth and limited experience offered some level of excuse for poor decisions.

He pinged her aura, sensing she was dealing with difficulties similar to his own. Her plethora of emotions integrated fear, isolation, and frustration, eliciting an empathic jolt that infused his protoplasm with stress hormones, releasing a waft of defensive chemicals in response. He quivered as assimilating her emotional state lowered his own energy level.

The concept of caring was a new one. He understood responsibility, which was what he felt toward his progeny as well as the Sapphirans, who were so unevolved they needed someone more intelligent to keep them out of trouble—or assist them in finding it, as the case may be. Unable to do anything about either of their predicaments, he returned to his data quest, deciding to check on her again in a few days.

He emitted the flaunal equivalent of a snicker, remembering when they'd found the girl on Verdaris, where his adventures had begun. That had been an interesting planet, too. He never realized that such a vast floral population could exist. He would have loved to stay longer to seek out any vegemals similar to himself. How different life would be if he'd stayed behind with the Sapphirans instead of remaining onboard the ship. But such was not to be, and now he had a multitude of challenges on yet another world.

The fact Area 51 possessed multiple secrets provoked his curiosity much as the copper deposit had teased his nutritional needs during the drive from Hill. Besides the vehicles in Galileo Bay, what he'd seen so far still didn't justify the elevated psibrations of the facility. He sensed an exceptionally high level of mental activity, not simply engineering challenges or innovation's end result. The psibrations he'd detected were among the highest he'd encountered anywhere; active, high level psi-waves, the hallmark of significant scientific, intellectual, and innovative pursuits.

His intuition tweaked his thoughts back toward a door he'd seen in the empty hangar in Galileo Bay; it had to go somewhere. Maybe what he was looking for wasn't within the surface structures, but likewise hidden below ground.

He returned his psiber senses to the vacant mountainside hangar, then its mandoor, protoplasm bristling with anticipation. It peaked to the thrill of discovery when beyond it he found a tunnel. If the base had an expansive subterranean component, that explained why he'd viewed relatively few humans on the surface. Zooming in for a closer look, he noted the passageway's construction was too symmetrical to be natural, undoubtedly man-made; drilled out, then reinforced with concrete, though most of its walls were natural rock. The vast network extended for kilometers; his psenses piqued, on full alert.

What had he found? What was down there?

The habitat light flickered, then moments later, went out. Thyron groaned; further exploring would have to wait.

CHAPTER THIRTEEN

Bio Lab (EBSL)
Nellis TMR
Restricted Area 51, Building T-1110
Rachel, Nevada
June 8, 1978
1821 PDT/0221 GMT

As soon as Greenley departed the next afternoon, Thyron got back to work. Knowing it was inefficient to wander blindly, albeit virtually, he slipped his psi-view vantage point to high above the mountainside hangars, from which he tuned his sensors below the surface. He emitted a flaunal gasp when the resulting holographic view revealed the compound was far more pervasive than he ever expected. Facilities visible above ground were but a tiny fraction of what existed below.

Five subterranean levels spread out far and beyond the Galileo Bay complex, which comprised the first level within the stand of mountains. Each level was connected vertically by several shafts that contained tiny rooms on suspended cables called elevators. As Thyron psi-vestigated the layout, he noted that security measures in the form of electronic sensors and mechanical barriers increased with depth. Likewise, the color and electronic coding of badges worn by occupants on each level, none of which matched Greenley's, as their driver had explained when they'd arrived. Now it made sense.

Beneath the deepest level was a massive solitary tunnel that extended for hundreds of kilometers in several directions, its psibrations registering as a magnetically levitated transportation system. At some point, he'd have to follow it to see where it went.

Returning to the second level, below and slightly offset from the hangars, he discovered a lab saturated with an enticing buzz of intellectual energy. Now that was more like it! He dove in for a closer look, gasping when he perceived the hostile psignature of munitions research. Its perpetrators comprised a mixture of human and extraterrestrial engineers who were examining components that originated with Galileo Bay's most recent acquisition.

The large head and short stature of one of the non-humans reminded him of Sapphirans, except its slanted eyes were dark, lacked pupils, and didn't bulge. Its extremities were longer, skin more grey than blue, and judging by its aura, possessed intelligence far superior to its human cohorts. Whether it was organic or artificial he couldn't tell, its psibrations so strong it overpowered any sign of the subtle frequency incident to life. There were at least three other distinct races he could see, only one of which had human-like characteristics, features of similar proportion, but much larger.

He hacked into one of the conversations, which conveniently was telepathic, discovering they were discussing how the device in question could be duplicated, since Terra lacked the needed elements. How to get around that limitation involved mathematical and chemical theories with which Thyron was familiar from his own physiology and innate ability to transmute elements.

Quickly bored, he wandered off to another lab on the same level where quantum fluctuations sparkled in multi-dimensional splendor. Maybe Terrans were farther along technologically than suspected. The quantum web was a place to which he often retreated when he needed timeless information. This was the domain of the cosmic soup, the universal time flow where everything—past, present, and future—resided. Since humans weren't typically privy to such access, efforts to build a device to provide it were in progress.

Who was this person, Alice, for whom the area was named? And why would these efforts be located in such close proximity to those pursuing weapons development?

His leaves tingled as the connection resolved. Uncomfortable, and hoping they'd fail, he descended to Level 3 where he found a residential area on one side and, on the other end of a connecting tunnel, a decontamination section more sophisticated than the Bio Lab. In addition, he found numerous storage areas, meeting rooms, and another large lab furnished with even more advanced equipment than the one he was in. A quick psi-pass of the individuals working there indicated its function was primarily molecular and elemental analysis that supported reverse engineering operations in Galileo Bay as well as Level 2 activities.

Consumed by the exhilarating allure of intellectual stimulation, he descended to Level 4, known as the *Aquarius* floor, which housed additional labs, more experimental in nature than the ones above. In a separate excavation on the same level he found a dark and relatively primitive containment area comprising multiple compartments, many of which emitted lifeform psignatures that indicated nonhuman intelligence. His cilia tingled with alarm.

Were they guests? Or prisoners, like himself?

He pinged one, the being's response indicating he was what humans referred to as a reptilian, a survivor of the crash that provided the vehicle in Galileo Bay-2. He'd been injured and was still recovering, fortunately able to regenerate needed limbs. Thyron shared his own story, after which the reptilian allowed him access to a vast array of information about his home world and its culture. He luxuriated in the wealth of data, exactly what he'd been hoping for—insights to other intelligent beings and their lifestyles.

After that, he psied another lifeform, who claimed humans referred to him as a mantis. Another crash victim, but not injured, he was uncooperative and angry. He'd been detained rather than allowed to repair his vehicle, which had impacted the ground when he'd miscalculated entry into a stargate, known to the Terrans as an Einstein-Rosen Bridge. He doubted they'd ever figure out how to repair the part that had malfunctioned, causing the accident, and wasn't about to provide any assistance. From his description, Thyron concluded his vehicle was the one fitted with weaponry in Bay-8.

At last he descended to Level 5, where he found a huge sphere with excessive decontamination precautions in place where they were holding another being. A humanoid with a large head and haunting eyes, his story was somewhat different. He was there voluntarily, requesting medical assistance, but isolated and treated like a prisoner. Nonetheless, he possessed a multi-dimensional perception of time and space like Thyron, from which he gained confidence he would return home to his planet in the Zeta Reticuli system sometime in the future.

While Thyron had detected little emotion from the reptilian and distinct anger from the mantis, from this one, known as a j-rod, he sensed sadness. He responded with sympathy generated by his increasing empathic abilities coupled with a strong sense of kinship for another stranger in a strange land. From there, he moved on to continue exploring before dark waves of sorrow reduced his energy any further. There was still much he hoped to explore.

A short distance away, also on Level 5, he happened upon a quartz crystal data repository. Its psibration frequency was high, a quick peek revealing that it held information about technologies, worlds, intelligent species, and civilizations, both on Terra and throughout the galaxy. Thyron gasped with delight. If he could absorb all that, he'd be one of the most intelligent beings in the entire galaxy! And best of all, he could have it all without leaving his current location!

Having found what his human captors would refer to as the Mother Lode, he tuned in hungrily to begin the ultimate quest. Seduced by a data repository beyond his wildest dreams, he yielded to temptation and hacked the timer for continual light. Overwhelmed by delicious emissions, Thyron opened up all his receptors and feasted on the input, his expanded efforts rewarding him with a euphoric sense of fulfillment not unlike an intellectual orgasm.

Random wilting episodes were ignored as he continued to indulge, until his overworked chloroplasts no longer produced the energy needed to sustain consciousness. He felt another spell coming on, this one more severe than before and best described as the botanical equivalent of dizziness. Relenting at last, he shifted his awareness to meditation mode, contemplating the scope of what he'd discovered until he finally zoned out; content, but mentally and physically exhausted.

Bio Lab (EBSL)
Nellis TMR
Restricted Area 51, Building T-1110
Rachel, Nevada
June 9, 1978
0821 PDT/1521 GMT

When Thyron heard Greenley's car crunch into the gravel parking lot that morning, he turned out the light, giving the scientist a wide-eyed, innocent look when the scientist lost his cool at the vegemal's haggard appearance. Thyron could tell the man found his condition alarming, even more so because its cause was unexplainable.

"What's wrong? What do you need that you're not getting?" the man asked.

Nothing. I'm fine. Don't worry, Doc. I'm just adapting to your planet.

"What about the balance of the atmosphere? Is it correct? Is it missing anything you have more of on your planet? What's it called again, Sapphira?"

Yes, Sapphira. We do have slightly more xenon. And slightly less oxygen, but you've already compensated for that.

The scientist's mind cycled, wondering why xenon would make a difference. Thyron admired his logic. He was right—it was nonreactive and didn't matter, but gave him something to consider.

Nonetheless, that afternoon Greenley added a bottle of xenon to the other gases supplying the habitat's atmosphere, though the man's thoughts as well as his expression indicated skepticism. Not surprisingly, Thyron remained withered and flaccid for the rest of the day, even though all he did was monitor his favorite television broadcasts. Meanwhile, the scientist read up on noble gases, thoughts more desperate than ever for a leaf sample.

Secretly entertained by his guardian's concern, that night Thyron hacked the light again and continued data mining, still gathering information beyond his most optimistic aspirations.

Since he could absorb information from the entire electromagnetic spectrum as well as multi-dimensional quantum psibands, he gathered information at an astounding rate, storing visual, acoustic, material, and physical facts to a meticulous level of detail. Geological data about Terra's origins and early inhabitants were particularly delicious. Perfectly compatible with his receptors, the crystal media allowed him to expand his horizons in quantum leaps, creating a thirst for more and more knowledge, its acquisition a highly addictive botanical buzz.

⸸ ⸸ ⸸

Bio Lab (EBSL)
Nellis TMR
Restricted Area 51, Building T-1110
Rachel, Nevada
June 10, 1978
0811 PDT/1511 GMT

The next morning, Thyron could tell that Greenley was even more deeply concerned with his lack of improvement. Worry saturated the man's entire demeanor to the point it even dimmed his aura. He checked the habitat's settings, took an air sample, checked it in the gas chromatograph, then cranked up the CO_2 even more. After that, he retired to his office where he buried himself in a stack of professional journals, mind buzzing as he tried desperately to figure out why the vegemal's health was failing when there was nothing to explain it.

Thyron chilled out in his favorite television frequencies as he'd done for the past few days so the man wouldn't notice any unusual psi activity. A few hours later, the man returned to the cleanroom to collect a soil sample, which he spent the rest of the day analyzing. When the results matched Thyron's directive perfectly and showed no anomalies, contaminants, or any other reason he would suffer from a mineral deficiency or some sort of poisoning, the scientist was even more puzzled.

Weakened but undaunted, that night Thyron continued his covert activities. In spite of being physically compromised, his spirits remained high as the purpose of his original excursion was realized, *i.e.*, to gather and store knowledge in his DNA. Thyron's primary existence and source of joy was on the intellectual plane, his physical well-being more secondary than ever.

That evening he finished the first bank of crystals and decided to start assimilating what he'd collected before gathering anything more. Multiplexing was easy during the absorption phase, each psibration frequency having different receptors, but extracting meaning was a linear process that took time; not much compared to humans, but time nonetheless. Having gathered more data than existed in all Terra's libraries and then some, now he needed to sort, categorize, and comprehend it, which would make it easier for him as well as his future progeny to find and utilize the information.

This part of the process required energy at an even deeper level. First, because it involved creating and connecting synapses throughout his protoplasm. After that, it had to be incorporated into his DNA, which required that he fully understand every fact from every angle, then bond with the knowledge emotionally, registering it genetically on every cell at the quantum/consciousness level.

Totally consumed by the euphoria associated with this final phase, which far exceeded that felt during its acquisition, the tardy consequences took him by surprise. After barely beginning to synthesize what he'd gathered, his energy resources depleted and crashed. As they would in the event of a prolonged drought or hard winter freeze, his leaves' life-giving fluids retreated within his primary bulb to assure survival until conditions improved.

Denied all energy sources, his photosystems collapsed, the last glimmer of sentience succumbing with them as Thyron's folly reduced him to a wilted pile of leaves and twisted branches.

CHAPTER FOURTEEN

Temporary Residence Complex #5
Nellis TMR
Area 51
Rachel, Nevada
June 11, 1978
0203 PDT/0903 GMT

Earlier that evening in Area 51's residential sector, Gabe lounged back in a '60s vintage Naugahyde recliner, reading the May issue of *Nature.* He lowered the journal, staring blankly at an equally blank wall as worries assaulted him again regarding Thyron's unexplained failing health. It didn't make sense, the vegemal showing no improvement whatsoever, regardless of what he did. Certainly there was something about Earth's environment that didn't agree with him.

But what?

Maybe increasing the CO_2 was actually making his condition worse. Maybe it was the light bulb radiating the incorrect wavelength for optimum functioning of his photosystems; perhaps it was far too weak, regardless of extending the hours of exposure. Would a plant from tropical regions thrive in the Artic? Of course not, and that situation represented a species on the same planet under the same sun.

There would be fewer challenges bioengineering botanical species for Mars, which would be under the same rays, just lower amplitude. But then temperature, soil constituents, and atmospheric effects were still major considerations. He shook his head, remembering how simple it was when he was a kid. You put a seed in the ground, watered it, and it grew. Not anymore.

He pondered the xenon factor again. It wasn't known to interact with biological systems, but maybe there was something about Thyron's alien metabolism that required it. Yet, adding it had made no difference. At least so far. Maybe he just needed to go back to the original baseline, that suitable for domestic oxalis, where Thyron seemed to do fine those first few days.

Yet, the vegemal had been acting strange lately, too. He laughed out loud at the thought. Of course he was, he was a telepathic walking plant from another world! An alien in every sense of Gabe's known world! Yet, his behavior reminded him of something. Or someone. What was it? He closed his eyes, concentrating; trying to remember.

Thanksgiving, 1966. That bland, dull-eyed simper on his younger brother's teenage son's face. The kid had started smoking weed, then moved on to more addictive substances.

"I'm fine, Dad. Don't sweat it," the boy had told his father, diction slurred and eyes dilated. "Nothin's wrong." Gabe knew otherwise intuitively, took his brother aside and explained. Fortunately, intervention came in time. The kid made it through college, now in a career track position with IBM...

Holy guacamole!

That was it! Thyron was showing symptoms of addiction! But how? To what? He'd already checked the air, tested the soil, found nothing even marginally toxic. At least to domestic species. But chemistry was chemistry, biosystems undoubtedly the same. Or were they? If something evolved under entirely different conditions, there was no telling. Maybe arsenic or some other unlikely element poisonous on Earth was a nutrient on Sapphira. Or addictive.

But Thyron would have told him something important like that. The vegemal had always provided information relative to his needs in meticulous detail, right down to his preferred wavelength of light. No, it had to be something else. But what?

Gabe covered his face and sighed, knowing obsessing on it wouldn't help. He couldn't do anything about it tonight. If Thyron was addicted to something, possibly even suffering from a CO2 overdose, he'd check into that angle in the morning. If anything, continuing to ruminate on it could block any other answers trying to surface from his subconscious. Maybe it already had, the addiction theory—a new approach worth pursuing. But for now, he needed to get his mind off it, think of something else. Otherwise, he wouldn't be able to sleep. He was getting too old to get by on only a few hours' worth.

He took a deep breath and eventually let go enough for his mind to wander, thoughts cycling back to the other ongoing annoyance in his life: that he could never publish what he'd discovered so far, whether Thyron recovered or not. His latest work got more interesting all the time, yet was so far beyond Top Secret that revealing Thyron's existence alone could cost him his life. From time to time, the tech team snuck things into periodicals such as *Aviation Week and Space Technology* (nicknamed by those in the know as *Aviation Leak and Spy Technology*), but articles were always out of context and assumed to originate with Lockheed's Skunk Works, who tested classified vehicles right there at Nellis on a regular basis.

The closest thing he could ever hope to do would be to write a science fiction story about it, but even that would require vetting by the security panel. In all probability, no one beyond the Bio Lab, other than possibly a few colleagues at NASA with the appropriate clearance, would ever know. He resumed reading, but the periodical's content was so mundane, intuitively obvious, unoriginal, and, most of all, boring, compared to what he was doing, it wasn't long before he dozed off.

He awoke with a jolt a few hours later, sensing something wasn't right. Being psi-sensitive, he was accustomed to a certain level of background noise, which continually hummed within his subconscious mind. But there'd been an abrupt spike that implied surprise, then all was quiet.

Too quiet.

He tuned in deeper, filtering out the audio input from the wall clock that read 2:03 ticking on the other side of the living room. He did likewise with the purr of the refrigerator compressor in the kitchenette, and the continuous high-frequency drone of electrical current coursing through wires within the efficiency apartment.

As a child, he'd spent summers with his paternal grandparents on a ranch in northern Oklahoma. Every severe storm, of which there were many, brought a power failure, which he could always sense. His grandparents had thought that he was imagining things, but later realized he wasn't. His strange ability had even saved their lives on several occasions, when power loss woke him up, providing advanced warning of an approaching tornado or dust storm, so they could scramble into the storm cellar, just in time.

They lived too far out to hear warning sirens, so at night when it was impossible to see bad weather approaching or they were fast asleep, his perceptions had been a literal lifesaver. Their theory that he was sensitive to air pressure changes was debunked when he perceived benign power losses as well. He sensed so many things that it had been a challenging distraction until he reached adolescence and learned to filter out background psi-noise, much as normal people tune out the drone of city traffic. He'd long-since grown accustomed to being considered weird, recognizing his capabilities as a gift from God which were unappreciated by the populace as a whole.

So what was that tight, empty feeling in his belly telling him now? Undoubtedly, something was amiss. But what? Knowing tornados were unlikely in Southern Nevada, especially in the mountains, his mind shifted to Houston, where hurricane season had begun about the time he'd left. He probed conditions related to his townhome in Clear Lake City. All was quiet there as well: Francesca asleep in her room; Loretta, his parrot, asleep atop the blinds in his bedroom; her companion, Larry, snoozing beside her.

Relieved, he noted activity at the base was high, but typical for graveyard shift. He turned his thoughts to Thyron and perceived— nothing. He sat up straight, pushing the recliner's footrest into its niche as he strained for psychic input. The vegemal was usually quite active in the evening, which he didn't understand, but attributed to alien biological processes and biorhythms which were part of his study. That certainly wasn't the case now, when he couldn't pick up the slightest evidence of activity, biological or otherwise.

Trusting his gut, which occasionally betrayed him in an embarrassing way, yet never failed to confirm his intuition, he was grateful he didn't have to waste time getting dressed before leaving for the Lab. He rarely slept in anything but his clothes since his arrival. Excitement for his work had never been higher and it was hard to turn off enough to sleep, so succumbing to slumber in the recliner was typical. Sometimes he awoke in the wee hours to take a leak, after which he'd drop his clothes to the floor and fall into bed.

He grabbed the keys to the motor pool car off the kitchen table and ran out the door, nearly losing his bifocals, which he'd perched on his head when he'd started to doze off. He set them back where they belonged and ran to the parking lot at the far end of the complex, a bit of an overstatement for a building that looked more like a cheap, single-story motel that rented rooms by the hour, especially under glaring security lights.

He scrambled into the car, turned the key, slammed it into gear, and took off, the '76 Ford LTD arriving at the Bio Lab a half-mile away before getting out of second gear.

He'd no sooner gotten out of the car when he realized he'd forgotten his badge, still clipped to his lab coat hanging on a kitchen chair back in his apartment. Most of NASA's cipher locks outside Mission Control didn't require his badge, only the code. Here likewise demanded the extra measure of security. He exhaled hard with frustration, at both himself and the policy, and went back to get the cursed thing, wondering what really went on in the base's netherworld that required such excessive security precautions.

CHAPTER FIFTEEN

Bio Lab (EBSL)
Nellis TMR
Restricted Area 51, Building T-1110
Rachel, Nevada
June 11, 1978
0211 PDT/0911 GMT

Gabe jammed his badge into the slot, which fortunately illuminated the cipher pad. He poked in his code, shaky hand missing one of the digits. Grumbling to himself, he tried again. Successful, he slammed through the door, flipped on the lights at the master switch, and dashed into the conference room for a quick visual of the habitat. No longer upright, Thyron was a wilted mass.

Crap!

He dashed to the decontamination area, yanking on the requisite two pairs of gloves, cap, and booties, then tromped across the sticky mat to the gowning area. Fortunately, he'd hung the bunny suit from the day before, so he didn't need to open a new package. He donned the hood, pulled on the coveralls, tucked everything in, and zipped up.

He sat on the bench separating him from the clean side to pull on the boots without touching the floor, then swung his legs over to the other side, landing on his feet in a single well-practiced motion. He skipped the goggles, as he'd done lately, anyway, since at this point his concerns had diminished, reinforced by the fact they didn't fit comfortably over his glasses. Back at NASA he had a custom pair with prescription lenses, which, unfortunately, he'd forgotten to grab before leaving Houston. He pulled off the outer pair of gloves, tossed them in the disposal bin, and hustled the rest of the way up the shallow ramp, then through the plastic strips into the final decontamination area. The UV lights flickered on and positive air flow activated, timer progressing in slow motion as his mind raced.

Was ditching the goggles a mistake? Had he somehow transmitted something Thyron couldn't tolerate? No, UV should have eliminated anything on his person. He needed to be able to see, which was nearly impossible with the goggles. Besides, the habitat was a sealed unit, suiting up protocol required primarily to maintain cleanroom integrity.

As soon as the timer dinged he pushed through the plastic strips, flipped the switch to the overhead lighting, and dashed across the springy, false floor that housed the ventilation system. It was even worse than he'd thought. Within the fully lit habitat, Thyron lay wilted and prone, the few leaves that remained retracted and lifeless, most shed and scattered across the unit's dirt floor.

Oh, no! he thought, heart racing. *What's wrong?* He checked the habitat's systems. All nominal. Of course. If any had failed, his pager would have gone off. He never installed a motion sensor since it would have activated every time Thyron moved.

Would entering the chamber cause more damage by releasing the CO_2-rich atmosphere? Or was too much CO_2 the problem? What about the xenon? No, couldn't be. Could it? What would he do in there, anyway? *Do CPR on a vegemal?* The question was ludicrous, yet somehow relevant. Was his addiction theory correct? Had he overdosed? On what? Why hadn't he seen this coming? Now what?

He closed his eyes and took several deep breaths, trying to calm down.

Okay. Remember what you always told your grad students: Start with the simplest solution—Occam's razor.

Lots of things could cause a plant to wilt. Too much or too little heat or light or lack of water were most common. None were factors, as far as he could tell. But it could still be that simple. He took another deep breath, unlatched the chamber door, and stepped inside, quickly closing it behind him. By the time he'd taken the few steps to reach Thyron, an insistent bleep screamed from his pants pocket, followed a nanosecond later by a sharp pain shooting through his temples.

Crap!

He stepped back out, fumbled through multiple layers of clothing to turn off the pager, then grabbed the O2 assembly from the wall and secured the mask to his face. The unit caused his bifocals to slip upward to the reading section, throwing his vision out of focus. Rolling his eyes with frustration, he shifted everything around until it was properly arranged, took another deep breath, and reentered the habitat. He knelt beside the lifeless plant, unshed tears stinging his eyes while panic swelled in his breast.

He shoved the anxiety aside, commanding his knowledge and training to take charge. For the first time he got a good look at Thyron's body, a huge, dicotyledon bulb the size of a watermelon. It looked more like an oversized shallot, consistent with his initial impression that the vegemal was an exotic species of oxalis. His bipedal nodes comprised extensions that looked like stolons, commonly called runners, tipped by stunted bulbils that never matured or separated to independence.

Naked stems amid a sea of shed leaves snaked from the bulb's tunic, forming a twisted miasma of upper limbs. Something about the tangled growth reminded him of a wire bundle, analogous perhaps to a human spinal cord. Where did Thyron's intelligence reside? Most likely in that primary bulb.

Thyron's visual sensors, now fully visible without the obstruction of foliage, had shrunk to about half their former size, their protective tunicate covering reminding him of a tomatillo.

Closer examination revealed his eyes weren't bulbils, as he'd expected, but quite different, perhaps derived from seed pods, which had evolved to light-sensing units. The evolution of light perception derived from a photoreceptor gene common to all organisms, plants and animals alike. Thus it wasn't much of a stretch that certain conditions could have influenced such photo-sensitive organs to evolve. It made sense that once Thyron's ancestors had achieved mobility, the ability to perceive detail beyond light and dark became important to survival.

Thyron looked dead, yet Greenley sensed life. Hopefully he was only hibernating. Like a dormant bulb awaiting spring. But why? And what could he do, if anything, to bring him out of it? What triggered a bulb, which resided in the ground, to shut down, then suddenly grow again? Light was the usual factor, extreme temperature changes, like frost, another. There had been no change to either. Had there?

He stiffened, realizing that at this hour the habitat should have been dark. Why? Thyron had requested a diurnal cycle, yet that wasn't what was happening. Was it a malfunction? He checked the timing mechanism, but saw nothing wrong. It had to be an internal problem engineering would have to check out.

Too much light could trigger photoinhibition. Thyron's wilted leaves had shown symptoms of that, but it had been minor so he'd dismissed it. Most likely it was a matter of photoperiodism, where growth phases such as producing new leaves or flowers, or going to seed, were triggered by the hours of light a plant received. Not enough could trigger a dormancy cycle, like the shortened days at the onset of fall and winter. Conversely, extended periods of light usually stimulated growth.

But in Thyron's case, was it possible the increased light had resulted in the opposite, perhaps the norm on his home planet? Did he hibernate in its equivalent of summer, perhaps because it was too hot? Maybe the diurnal cycle he'd requested was what he'd experienced on the spaceship, not that programmed by his genes. Was sufficient energy stored, such as occurred when bulbs completed a cycle, then lay dormant until the next season? If that was the case, what would awaken him?

Time? Or did he also require a period of darkness?

For whatever reason, Thyron had requested a diurnal cycle of equal periods, so perhaps the excessive light simply needed to be balanced out by darkness, which often triggered a new cycle as well. And cooler temperatures. A time of rest and rejuvenation. Which would provide time to determine the cause.

He sighed, yet felt less fear. The specimen wasn't dead. At least not yet. Something was clearly wrong, which had triggered this reaction, and that was what he needed to figure out. There had to be a reason. Any major change was always the result of cause and effect. He'd find the answer. But first he had to make sure Thyron had the proper conditions to assure recovery.

CHAPTER SIXTEEN

Bio Lab (EBSL)
Nellis TMR
Restricted Area 51, Building T-1110
Rachel, Nevada
June 11, 1978
0240 PDT/0940 GMT

Arms folded, Gabe eyed the slumbering vegemal with deep concern, saddened by the desiccated leaves covering the floor like shriveled hands.

Then it registered, the O2 mask shifting upward as he smiled in spite of himself. Thyron had persistently denied every request to take a tissue samples. He'd respected that, waiting patiently until the vegemal trusted him enough to remove at least one leaf for *in vitro* analysis.

The lack of hard, scientific data had caused quite a flap with the Scientific Research Records Center people, who'd hounded him since day one for a weekly report of such things. So far, he'd noted the construction of the habitat and testing air samples along with listing supplies and data he'd ordered, stalling with excuses that claimed the specimen needed to be stabilized before he took any physical samples.

The last thing he was about to admit was that the specimen wouldn't allow it, which would have sounded ludicrous and instantly labeled him as a nut-case, though he'd certainly been called worse. However, having the powers-that-be over the SRRC on him like white on rice for insubordination was the last thing he needed, and would probably be sufficient to send him home. He thought back to what Phil had said during the long drive from Hill, about following protocol. No—unwanted attention was the last thing he needed.

It wasn't like he didn't want to look at the vegemal's chloroplasts and the workings of his photosystems, to say nothing of his chemical composition, chromosomes, and DNA. Each would provide a wealth of information about a species that was not only new and extraterrestrial, but the sole representative of what could be a remarkable new kingdom of living things: Vegemals, embodying characteristics of both plants and animals, perhaps even providing the long-sought-for missing link between the two.

Thyron looked so much like an over-sized version of *oxalis palmifrons* that he couldn't believe there wouldn't be genetic similarities. He remembered his mother having several oxalis varieties in their garden when he was a child. He'd often chewed on the leaves, oxalic acid providing their sour but refreshing taste. No telling what he could discover from one of Thyron's leaves, even though being dead would preclude detailed study of their photosystems.

Through the base's document center, he'd ordered several periodicals that contained phytochemical research done on oxalis to serve as a baseline; plus he'd requested samples of several specimens from the Harvard herbarium, but so far nothing had arrived. No matter, they'd get there eventually, and meanwhile his mind wouldn't be cluttered with data that could potentially limit or prejudice his thinking. After all, Thyron was extraterrestrial, so major differences were expected.

He left the habitat to grab a two-liter beaker from the lab bench, then carefully re-opened the door. A *whoosh* of air escaped, the unit cycling to increase its internal pressure and restore its custom gas mix, which swept out several leaves that landed at his feet.

Damn! he thought, then relaxed. It was a cleanroom, for heaven sake. He gently brushed off dirt from the habitat floor and placed several in the glass container, careful not to instill further damage, then closed the door.

He placed the samples next to the microscope on the lab bench across the room, removed the O2 mask, then stepped back to the habitat to check its settings. The mode selector was where it belonged, on *Auto.* Still wondering why the light was on, he switched it to *Manual*, then back to *Auto.* It dimmed and gradually went out.

Hmmmm. Maybe there was nothing wrong with the timer after all. He still needed to program it for the reduced lighting and temperature of a dormancy cycle, but that could wait; examining one of those leaves couldn't.

All sleep had fled, heart racing as he settled on a stool and spread his dubious heist on the counter. One of the things he loved about working at Area 51 was the state-of-the-art equipment. As a black project, there were all sorts of bells and whistles other government agencies had to do without. Like the USDA, where he'd interned and then worked for a while, right out of college, which had operated with Pasteur-era equipment. Yet, in spite of its antiquity, it had provided a wealth of information. So, no telling what he could discover with what he had now.

He ground one up with a mortar and pestle, then transferred the resulting paste to a test tube. He placed it in the centrifuge, then turned it on. While that was processing, he'd take a look at another one under the microscope. The one in the Bio Lab had the finest stereo optics available, providing depth perception as well as adjustable magnification. Using a sterile scalpel, he cut off an appropriately sized sample and sandwiched it in a glass slide, which he eased between the clamps until it clicked into place.

He took a deep breath, let it out slowly, heart racing with anticipation. Eyes closed, he commanded himself to relax. The most important moment of his professional life was only seconds away.

He took another deep breath before setting the magnification at 500X, then peering through the eyepieces as he brought the sample into focus. He frowned. Nothing he could see distinguished it from a typical leaf. But then, that's what it was, a leaf. Perhaps Thyron's most intimate secrets were contained within his chemical composition or his bulb. He bumped the optics up to full magnification, 1500X. The cuticle still looked normal.

He removed the slide and prepared another, this time carefully using the scalpel to remove the cuticle and upper epidermis. The cells still looked normal. The chloroplasts were clearly visible, but the resolution still too low to see their internal structure or more than a hint of the thylakoids. As he studied it more closely, something about the chloroplasts *did* look different: thicker, clustered together, almost as if something were beneath them. He tweaked the focus, hoping, but it was useless. To get a proper look at the intricacies that could perhaps explain Thyron's sentience would require the resolution only possible with a scanning electron microscope.

There was a SEM on-base, but located where they allegedly studied the physiology of extraterrestrial biological entities, referred to as EBEs, known to the rest of the world as little green men, greys, or space aliens. Since his *need to know,* and therefore his clearance level, wasn't sufficient to enter Area 51's nether-regions, his only choice was to submit a sample and wait for the results.

A patient man by nature, he nonetheless knew that would drive him nuts. After all, he'd already waited this long to get a leaf. But such was life, more often than not a waiting game. With a sigh, he carefully prepared and packaged the samples, then went back to the centrifuge, which had long since stopped. The sediment, as expected, had settled to the bottom, enough supernatant liquid on top to test the pH. He grabbed a litmus strip from the dispenser and dipped it inside.

It was acidic within the expected range. The average pH of oxalic acid ($C_2H_2O_4$), was 1.3, which was high, but sulfuric acid (H_2SO_4), which Thyron's previous emissions implied he could produce, was stronger. The latter had a strong affinity for water, which meant it was an extremely volatile compound to be contained in a plant. It would have to be isolated somewhere as sulfur dioxide, the anhydride version of sulfurous acid, which was weaker and one oxygen atom short of sulfuric acid. With O_2 production part of the photosynthesis cycle, the process by which he isolated it and then combined the two elements to use defensively would be fascinating to investigate. And potentially dangerous.

Was it compartmentalized in his leaves? Not likely. Nothing he'd seen so far looked different, other than those distorted chloroplasts. Furthermore, that would be the worst possible repository given their high water content. His limbs? Maybe. Or his bulb? Most likely.

Plants in general had built-in defenses against insects, bacteria, diseases and, in some cases, even other plants. To have instinctive, conscious, control over them was fascinating, especially such a lethal reaction. He shuddered as he recalled an encounter with a skunk when he was a kid, which hadn't ended well. As the credibility of Thyron's veiled threat increased exponentially, he wondered. What kind of botanical wizardry did the vegemal possess to willfully emit toxic fumes? When Thyron woke up, discussing that would definitely be at the top of the list.

Knowing the mechanics of his sulfuric acid emissions presented a major challenge; he set it aside for now to pursue his long-anticipated examination of Thyron's DNA. An electric thrill such as he hadn't felt in years, maybe even decades, blasted through him at the realization he'd be the first to investigate the genome of a *flora peda telepathis*. At the least, it represented an entirely new taxonomic clade or family, even if for some unexpected reason a sentient, ambulatory plant didn't constitute a sixth kingdom.

Separating the DNA required electrophoresis, which employed a low-voltage electric field to separate differently sized molecules based on polarity, then drawing them through a gel filter. He prepared the gel, then placed a few drops of the supernatant prepared earlier in the centrifuge in one lane of the cassette, a marker in another for cell size-referencing purposes, then set it aside while they soaked in.

Meanwhile, he added the buffers for the anode and cathode. Once direct current was applied, the base pairs would sieve through the gel at different speeds, depending on size, then eventually collect in bands. After that, the laborious task of analysis could begin. The process would take several hours, after which he'd use an ethidium bromide stain to show the separated molecules more clearly. He double-checked the voltage to be sure that everything was set up correctly, then powered it on, glancing at the clock as he set the timer. It was nearly four o'clock.

Another fundamental he'd need to know was the number of chromosomes. Humans had 46, oxalis typically 64. Optimum results required new growth, *e.g.*, young leaves, young flower buds, or the tip from a root or shoot. His only option in this case was a root tip, so he returned to the habitat to snip off a sample.

The bottom of Thyron's peduncles were covered with quarter-inch rootlets that reminded him of a fingernail brush. He smiled, wondering if Thyron was ticklish, as he snipped one off. He placed it in a fixative comprised of alcohol and acetic acid, planning to do the rest when he came back later. The process involved the drawing-tube attachment on the microscope, which provided the ability to focus at variable depths and thus yield a three-dimensional image; a camera was limited to a single focal length that left several layers out of focus.

Once he had the fundamentals out of the way, he'd need more precise figures, only possible from a full-spectrum analysis. That would involve prepping a host of assays, then identifying all constituents using gas chromatography, mass spectrometry, and a plethora of other techniques. No telling what was key to revealing Thyron's secrets. He couldn't help grinning as he looked around the lab at the state-of-the-art toys he got to play with. This was exactly what he'd dreamed of doing for his entire life.

Scientific curiosity whetted, but no longer sufficient to compensate for lack of sleep, he reluctantly decided that was enough for the night. He stepped over to the habitat, deep concern rekindled at a more personal level. Elation at the prospect of groundbreaking scientific discoveries waned with an encroaching shadow of guilt.

How could he be so excited when Thyron was compromised, perhaps to the point he might not recover? He chided himself for his blatant detachment from the vegemal's welfare, then, after a final, lingering look at the slumbering plant, left the cleanroom, degowned, and went into his office to fill out the paperwork for the SEM analysis.

This week, at last, there'd be plenty to report.

CHAPTER SEVENTEEN

Bio Lab (EBSL)
Nellis TMR
Restricted Area 51, Building T-1110
Rachel, Nevada
June 11, 1978
0917 PDT/1617 GMT

After filling out the SEM paperwork, Gabe went back to his apartment for a few fitful hours sleep. Now back at the lab, he concentrated on programming the habitat to support what he assumed to be a suitable, albeit accelerated, dormancy period. For a week it would progress through a diurnal cycle like that which occurred around the winter solstice at high latitudes, temperature low but not freezing. After that, it would warm up while gradually introducing more light, which would hopefully stir the appropriate hormones for the vegemal to awaken.

That done, he leaned his forehead against the glass, peering at the still form within. It wasn't just the science, though that was what had dominated his thoughts for the past several hours. Thyron was more than a unique specimen and exciting phytochemical investigation—he was a sentient being, even more so than the various cats, dogs, hamsters, birds, spiders, and other pets he'd had over the years. This time the connection far exceeded that of a guardian, bordering more on that of a friend.

The irony was such he didn't know whether to laugh or cry. At first, his love for animals had driven him to aspire to becoming a veterinarian, until he'd confronted the grim reality that he couldn't handle the heart-wrenching task of dealing with animal abuse or putting down someone's beloved pet. He cared too much, detachment impossible.

Thus, he'd switched to botany, never dreaming he'd encounter a sentient plant. Yet, even as a child he'd always sensed they possessed some level of consciousness. Why else would he feel inclined to apologize to weeds when he removed them from his garden or insist that his parents shun a cut Christmas tree for a living one every year, so they could plant it in the yard? A heavy sigh escaped, knowing, beyond a doubt, that the Universe was laughing at him.

Then, admonishing himself for illogical, sentimental tomfoolery, he got back to work. First up was using the root sample for the chromosome count. Not surprisingly, there were a few more. With a base number of 9, the total came to 81 versus 64, the most common value for oxalis. Thyron's visual sensors, which he'd come to think of as eyes, and peduncles alone could account for that.

The DNA strands still needed a while longer to separate, so he started figuring out what phytochemicals the leaves contained. Fortunately, he had plenty of samples, which meant he could conduct a multitude of tests and experiment to his heart's content. If Thyron had allowed him to take a single leaf, he would have been severely limited. The ones he had, being wilted, were marginally compromised, but that wouldn't change their chemical composition, only reduce their water content and shut down their photosystems.

There were so many tests he wanted to run, he hardly knew where to start. Knowing disorganization was ineffective and the sure way to miss something, he forced himself to leave the lab, ditch the bunny suit, and go into his office, where he retrieved his notebook with his initial research plan, prepared while hoping for a single leaf. He'd start with that, then expand it, now that he didn't have to worry about limited samples. His main questions, and thus his primary objectives, involved Thyron's sentience, mobility, and sulfuric acid defense mechanism. Each would entail a different approach and battery of tests.

By the time he'd completed augmenting his approach, he figured the DNA run should have finished. He suited up and entered the cleanroom, discovering the unit was still running; somehow he'd managed to set the timer for longer than intended. Not surprising, considering he'd done it in the wee hours under the influence of a sleep-deprived adrenaline rush. Admonishing himself for the careless mistake, he noted the longer time in his notes, then pulled the cassette, removed the tubes, and gently pushed the gel columns out with a suction bulb. He rinsed them in dye and placed them beneath the microscope, heart flipping with anticipation.

The results displayed the expected number of bands, representing base pairs in the two hundred range. Their size was normal, the number a little higher, but typical of different taxa. Closer examination revealed one unusual band comprised of cells that were larger by a factor of three.

Had he somehow contaminated the sample or messed something up during gel prep? Or was it related to the extended time, which would have allowed larger cells to make their way through the gel? Considering the state he was in the night before, there was little doubt he could have made another mistake. Clearly, he'd have to run it again to see if the results were the same and, if so, figure out what it was. Additional runs using different techniques were necessary, anyway, to make sure all possibilities were flushed out. Maybe it was what he was looking for or maybe it was one of those head-slapping goofs one made when not operating with a full deck.

Thus, he sighed and set it aside. There were plenty of other things to investigate. Which meant, once again, he could use an assistant to help with sample prep. Within an hour, David, the shaggy-haired jabber mouth, was back; and by the next day the lab was abuzz with activity, equipment electronics emitting an ambitious hum along with David's incessant spewing of the latest gossip he'd overheard in the chow hall.

The initial conclusions revealed nothing spectacular or unexpected. The leaves contained flavanoids, iso vitexine and vitexine-2"- O- beta – D- glucopyrunoside. Subsequently, he discovered tartaric acid and citric acids, calcium oxalate, flavones, glycoflavones, flavonols, and phenolic acids such as p-hydroxybenzoic, vanillic, and syringic acids. Only a miniscule trace of sulfur had shown up, in the parts per billion range, such as might appear in a plant exposed to excessive environmental pollution, but it was there, nonetheless. So far, all results were statistically within range of terrestrial species.

Unable to resist snipping off a small branch, he discovered it comprised flavanoids, tannins, phytosterols, phenol, glycosides, fatty acids, galacto-glycerolipid, and volatile oil as well as other phytochemicals that held potential for pharmacological and medicinal applications. In addition, he'd been excited to see what appeared to be a few lysosomes, related to digestion and thus common in animals, but rare in plants. Their usual function was to protect certain cells from the presence of acid, such as in the digestive system, which could relate to the sulfuric acid mystery.

How and where did Thyron isolate sulfur until he combined it with oxygen and hydrogen to become H2SO4? Or was it possible he was creating it from phosphorus via transmutation, an alchemical process Von Herzeele had suggested a century before? However Thyron did so, it probably occurred in his bulb. He felt no guilt about the shed leaves and only a twinge for the rootlet and branch, but taking a sample from his bulb was too invasive, especially with the vegemal already in poor condition. More than likely, any additional clues could only be found by sequencing his DNA.

A few days after that, he dismissed David, relieved to have peace and quiet again. Something about the man's constant chatter got on his nerves and reminded him of the WWII admonition "Loose lips sink ships."

Now he could concentrate on the newest journals he'd ordered, which had finally arrived. He was almost disappointed when they confirmed that domestic oxalis species contained mostly the same constituents he'd found so far: water, fat, carbohydrates, calcium, phosphorus, iron, niacin, vitamin C, beta carotene, and between 7 - 12% oxalate. The plant was recognized for its medicinal qualities in various cultures, particularly Ayurvedic tradition in India, which presented an interesting dichotomy, *i.e.,* Thyron possessed healing properties coupled with lethal defenses.

The corners of his mouth shifted to a wry smile—the quintessential good friend and bad enemy.

CHAPTER EIGHTEEN

Bio Lab (EBSL)
Nellis TMR
Restricted Area 51, Building T-1110
Rachel, Nevada
June 11, 1978
1527 PDT/2217 GMT

That afternoon Gabe sat in his office, frustrated as he pondered which data to include in his weekly activity report, appropriately referred to as a WAR. Other than the difference in oxalate percentages, which was typical between genuses, and minute traces of sulfur, nothing he'd determined so far differentiated Thyron chemically from domestic species. *Nothing.*

Yet, the vegemal was clearly unique in three very significant ways: One, he was mobile; two, he was sentient; and three, potentially dangerous. However, he couldn't prove scientifically that Thyron's origin was extraterrestrial, speculations contained in his lab notes, but deliberately unreported; jumping to such conclusions was unprofessional and could compromise his credibility. So far, even Thyron's DNA was remarkably similar to terrestrial oxalis, other than that one mysterious band which persisted in spite of repeated runs. When the herbarium specimens arrived, he'd see if it turned up when run with the same protocols, but for now there was little more he could do. Basics complete, it was time to take the few anomalies he had to the next level, some of which would require another SEM request.

He thought back to his previous work at Area 51, which presented a similar dilemma. The two times he'd been called in previously involved assessing biological air-purification systems on a captured vehicle. Both, as he'd suspected, were algae based, but the real surprise was that, as far as he could tell, they were either one of Earth's own chlorella species or identical to it.

Algae was as simple as a plant could get, even though they could possess as many as 140 chromosomes. There were amazing differences, even among terrestrial species, with regard to color and environmental conditions. If it was extraterrestrial, it supported the transpermia theory of evolution, but there was no way to prove it, even though the vehicle clearly wasn't from Earth. If it was stationed here, it made sense it would use Earth-based resources. Another unanswered question, of which there were many.

Too many. He was missing something—but what? At the limits of what he could do, any additional data depended on what the SEM might reveal. So far that unusual chloroplast structure, presence of lysosomes, and rogue band in the DNA seemed the most likely candidates for a breakthrough.

He glanced at the clock, surprised it was well after three. No wonder his stomach was growling for attention. Thus, he headed for the cafeteria where he got a disappointing cup of coffee and a Waldorf salad he assembled from the fruit bar along with some walnuts he'd convinced the chow hall manager to bring in from Vegas. As a rather liberal lacto-ova fruitarian, it was a bit of a challenge to live on a military base with its Spartan menu. At least he had an excuse for shunning Spam, which probably dated back to WWII. The cafeteria's offerings were better than K-rations, but not much, and he was beyond sick of powdered eggs. Combined with stress, the digestive thunderstorms had increased in number and magnitude, but it could be worse.

He ate slowly, debating whether to return to Houston for a while. The SEM results wouldn't be back for a week, maybe more. Time would pass more quickly; plus he could pick up some groceries and make sure nothing had come up at his townhome that Francesca couldn't handle. Ironically, he could have immediate access to SEM facilities at NASA, but removing any samples would breach the terms of his research agreement, to say nothing of possibly violating his security oaths. Clearly, his work wasn't deemed as important here, where the emphasis was on hi-tech engineering—alien tech, actually. Not lifeforms. Certainly not plant life.

But Thyron wasn't a plant. He was a vegemal. A candidate for an entirely new, hitherto unknown, kingdom, in addition to *protozoa, chromista, fungi, animalia* and naturally, *plantae.* Since Thyron's nucleotides indicated a metabolism based on photosynthesis, which was obvious given he had leaves, he could be considered part of the plant kingdom as opposed to a zoophyte, *i.e.* plant-like animal, such as coral or sea anemones. In which case, Gabe would have to build his case for a new one, based on the vegemal's unique characteristics. Any of which was spectacular. And he couldn't tell a soul.

Damn.

He sighed with resignation for the thousandth time. Would they believe him anyway? Sure, Thyron had the equivalent of eyes and bipedal nodes that functioned as feet, both obviously unusual for a plant, but not for a simple animal, perhaps one with the mental acuity of a crustacean.

Since Gabe was the only one who could converse with him, they'd probably think he was delusional.

He'd actually overheard one of the techs say "the wheel is turning but the hamster is dead" when they thought he was out of earshot. And he probably was, for normal audio perception. Maybe if he started reading their minds, they'd believe him. He chuckled at the thought. Ever since junior high he'd learned to filter out such drivel as annoying interference, but at times it came in handy; and others, it was a curse, which was why he'd given up dating before finishing high school.

Am I? Am I imagining our conversations?

No. This was real. Sure, he'd talked to plants his entire life, but they never answered. They'd thrive and appear content, but certainly didn't carry on a conversation. Thyron was sentient, beyond a doubt. But as long as no one else could hear him, it couldn't be proven. Could it? He grinned at the thought of the vegemal taking the SAT or, better yet, the GRE, when he woke up. Thyron would have to mark the answers himself to prove the answers were his own. Did he have enough dexterity to hold a pencil? He moved his branches at will, even seemed to be picking up some of Gabe's hand gestures, so he probably could. He couldn't help but laugh at the stir it would cause.

Thoughts drifting back to the present, he continued to debate returning to Houston. NASA documents weren't centralized, much less computerized, but rather resided mostly in dusty file cabinets in Building 37. He could have relevant documents sent to him, but as principle investigator on most, they wouldn't contain anything he didn't already know. The majority were irrelevant, anyway, mainly theories related to growing plants in microgravity and justification for astronauts to perform his planned experiment onboard Skylab.

Undecided, he sipped his coffee, which hadn't improved during his pensive soliloquy, so he got up and walked over to the service counter to add more milk. The chow hall was all but empty, typical for mid-afternoon shift-change when the bulk of workers arrived. As if on cue, he heard the roar of a Janet flight landing on the adjacent runway, coming in from Vegas. The number of people he saw coming and going daily defied visible facilities. Where'd they all go? Apparently those secret labs were larger than he thought.

He sat back down, glad he didn't have to deal any further with whiny, gossip-prone assistants. He cringed, wishing he'd never let on that Thyron communicated. Hopefully, they wouldn't say anything. There were plenty of weird things going on, of which Thyron was probably the least. It was apparent the primary research interests at the base were technological.

He had no idea where the "good stuff" was investigated, yet didn't mind the Bio Lab's isolated location in the main part of the base. Somehow he'd expected more interest in his work, yet was relieved that wasn't the case. He preferred to work alone, making his own decisions, protecting his hypotheses, and soliciting opinions from his fellows as required.

Yet he wondered, how could anyone not be fascinated with life in any form and its many mysteries?

CHAPTER NINETEEN

Bio Lab (EBSL)
Nellis TMR
Restricted Area 51, Building T-1110
Rachel, Nevada
June 18, 1978
1006 PDT/1706 GMT

A week passed with no change in the *flora peda telepathis's* condition. Gabe repeated several analyses to check their accuracy, particularly those involving assays prepared by the assistant, but found no conflicts. David was a bit of a flake, but he had to admit the man was good at his job. Sulfur was still elusive, further evidence implying it was transmuted from potassium through botanical wizardry. As he sat in the base cafeteria munching on a bunch of red grapes and a few slices of Swiss cheese, he still felt optimistic. Thyron was alive; he just didn't know how long the dormancy cycle would last.

Oxalis was hardy. It tolerated a wide range of climates. He wished he knew more about Thyron's native planet or had asked him such details when they'd established communications. He berated himself, then admitted he really hadn't had the chance, concentrating primarily on analyzing air samples to make sure Thyron didn't present a health risk to Earth, along with getting the habitat built, programmed, and stabilized, which had never entirely occurred when the unthinkable happened.

With preliminary lab work mostly complete, he needed to do everything possible to make sure the dormancy cycle succeeded. There was never any guarantee that a bulb would recover, which in this case would be catastrophic: Not only the loss of groundbreaking research, but a sentient being. A sick feeling arose in his chest as he realized, if that occurred, he could be responsible or even guilty of the botanical equivalent of manslaughter.

He sighed deeply, pondering the fact there was nothing simple about any plant, even algae, much less one from another planet with characteristics never seen before. There were multiple variables that made hitting the right combination of temperature, light, and nourishment a guessing game on par with winning the lottery. Getting any of them wrong by even a minute amount could have fatal results.

Some plant species needed a period of vernalization in the form of a good, stiff freeze to rejuvenate. Plants were picky about such things. In both directions—some needed a freeze, while others would die. It seemed logical that anything would grow in a semi-tropical environment like Houston, where freezing temperatures were relatively rare, but that wasn't the case. Just because he chose to live in a place where winters were mild didn't mean botanical species shared the same sentiment. Rather, cherries, apples, and most berries, not only preferred, but required, a long, winter sojourn.

Could Thyron be one of them? If he was some exotic member of the *oxalidaceae* family, Gabe doubted it, but couldn't know for sure without more information. Fortunately, oxalis was generally hardy as well as adaptable, based on the number of species that thrived in diverse environments.

How long would the dormancy cycle last? And how cold did it need to be? Or what if, contrary to most Earth flora, Thyron hibernated to get away from light and warmth rather than cold? He was an extraterrestrial species that had evolved under unknown conditions. Yet, he'd seemed healthy when they first found him onboard that spaceship. He'd been vibrant and alive. What had gone wrong?

If only he knew more about his native planet.

As he recalled, a girl had been onboard as well as a robot, the latter of which was likewise there on base. Would either of them know more?

He winced as he gulped down the rest of his now-tepid coffee, then drove back to his office, where he dug out the Hill commander's business card. He dialed the prefix for the secure government phone system, waited through a series of clicks indicating switching changes and security gates, then entered the colonel's number. The man answered on the third ring.

"Colonel Jenkins? This is Gabe Greenley, the botanist who's caring for that plant specimen we recovered a few weeks ago. Do you remember me?"

"Of course," Jenkins replied. "I doubt I'll ever forget anyone or anything associated with that incident. How can I help you?"

"Well, I've run into a situation and was wondering if it would be possible to talk to the girl that was onboard the ship? See if she knows anything about the plant's nutritional requirements, life cycle phases, and so forth."

No response. "Hello? Colonel? Are you still there?"

If the man had even tried to muffle his sigh, it wasn't apparent, unless it was his psi abilities kicking in.

"Yeah, I'm here," Jenkins replied. "Unfortunately, the girl's been taken to a secure location and isn't accessible. Is there a problem?"

"Possibly. The specimen appears to have gone into a dormancy cycle. So I was hoping to find out something regarding his native environment and what's needed to support it."

Another sigh. "Sorry, but I'm afraid we can't help you."

Now it was Greenley's turn to sigh. He could tell the colonel was withholding something, but couldn't discern what. "Okay, thanks anyway," he replied, and parked the receiver back in the cradle.

Damn.

CHAPTER TWENTY

Bio Lab (EBSL)
Nellis TMR
Restricted Area 51, Building T-1110
Rachel, Nevada
June 22, 1978
1425 PDT/2125 GMT

Suited up in both a bunny suit and a frown, Gabe sat cross-legged on the floor in front of the habitat, trying to bolster his waning optimism. Thyron's appearance in the dim illumination from the gowning area and conference room windows resembled that of a wayward piece of tumbleweed transporting a giant amaryllis bulb. Eleven days had passed with no visible change since the dormancy cycle's onset; another week with nothing to report.

He hoped that the *flora peda telepathis* had enough in common with terrestrial plants for his plan to work, at best, and to do no harm, at worst. With luck, his assumptions would be correct, allowing temperature and lighting to create the desired effect without waiting for months. Theoretically, the energy was stored, the rest period possibly irrelevant, though there was no telling what might be dictated by DNA, especially if his native world had exceptionally long or different seasons.

What troubled him continuously, however, was what had triggered it? Thyron's condition had been unstable since his arrival, in spite of everything he'd tried to do. He folded his arms as his frown deepened. There had to be a cause.

A childhood memory flared, of reading books by H.G. Wells and Jules Verne under the covers with a flashlight for half the night, his mother wondering why it was so hard to get him up for school the next morning. He smiled, remembering how he was always partial to Verne, whose middle name was Gabriel.

Why'd that memory surface now, of all times? What was his subconscious trying to tell him? Life had long since taught him there was no such thing as a coincidence.

He unfolded his arms and sat up straighter. Maybe it hadn't been the end of a cycle, as assumed. Thyron had been notoriously active at night. Had he overdone it and driven himself into a state of botanical exhaustion? If that were the case, his energy was depleted, not stored. Should he do anything differently?

Probably not. Thyron needed to rest, one way or the other. But his condition could be far more precarious than he'd previously assumed.

He got up awkwardly, feeling his age as he donned the O2 mask and entered the habitat where, using a small penlight and magnifying glass, he scanned the crown of Thyron's bulb and his many appendages for any sign of change. So far there'd been none, which was good, given he was still alive and not deteriorating further; and bad, given there was still no indication how long dormancy would last. He'd lowered the temperature a little, which at least made it more comfortable in the bunny suit.

He'd decided against returning to Houston, just in case, even though he could sure use a decent meal, preferably some good Mexican food, which the single cafe in Rachel, the nearest town, failed to provide.

If Thyron awoke suddenly, he needed to be there, even though he suspected it wouldn't be without some preamble that would give him time to return. But leaving also meant bringing back his assistants, which he didn't trust. He shuddered at the thought of them eating the bulb as was the practice of some cultures. Hopefully, they'd suffer oxalic acid poisoning if they did. He chuckled aloud, then lambasted himself for the nasty thought.

Talking to some NASA colleagues—hypothetically, of course— about the effects of placing a species in an alien climate hadn't helped, either. Of course, he couldn't tell them what was really going on and, as he'd already concluded, everything was based on theory, speculation, and extrapolation, not concrete facts. How plants evolved in their native environment was one thing; how they adapted when abruptly switched to another, hard to predict, with too many unknowns to extrapolate how it would pertain to Thyron. Yet in the far future, such answers would be essential to successful interplanetary colonization.

A plant's response to seasonal light and temperatures was genetically coded. That was what determined the vibrant fall colors he'd enjoyed in Indiana versus the dull, mostly colorless autumn hues of Houston. Transplanting an apple tree that thrived in Washington State to Florida wasn't going to work, period, without serious grafting or genetic engineering.

Thyron was a unique specimen whose conscious awareness complicated everything, directing his thoughts down yet another track. While he'd honored the vegemal's wishes with regard to taking tissue samples, being held against his will had ominous implications. He was old enough to remember World War II and the horror inflicted upon innumerable victims in Nazi prison camps. While logically he knew his work was far from that realm, it was still something that was questionable enough to give him pause.

A feeling that resembled guilt gripped his chest as the ethical implications loomed over him like a thundercloud—the kind that spawned violent tornadoes.

Was Thyron a test subject from whom permission was required?

Gabe recalled meetings at NASA of the Human Research Policy and Procedures Committee, the members of which reviewed all experiments that involved human test subjects with another one assigned to review those conducted on animals. The HRPPC took such things very seriously, so much so that he was glad his work didn't require such approval.

Thyron had made it clear he wanted to get out of the habitat. Clearly, he was being held against his will. Was he staging the vegemal equivalent of a hunger strike? Or was it stress? Being sentient, mental and emotional issues were factors in addition to the usual vegetal needs for sufficient light, proper temperature, and the correct amount of moisture and mineral nourishment.

If he could learn more about the source of his awareness, maybe it would help. Still waiting for the SEM data, he'd made enough noise about it in his last WAR that they'd moved his sample up a few days in the schedule, proving someone actually read them. He hoped the leaves were dry enough to avoid fixing, since he didn't want them to introduce anything to compromise the image. Gold sputter coating was unavoidable, or so they said. He mainly wanted to see whether the cell structure had only plant characteristics or if something else was lurking within the chloroplasts. Their distortion under the lab microscope may or may not be meaningful. At this point, he had few leads, so he hoped it would reveal something. Yet, for some reason, part of him felt oddly uncomfortable about what that might be.

How could a plant have not only sentience but self-awareness, so much so that it could converse? The fact plant life contained some level of cognizance had been apparent to him living on the farm. He knew his section of the garden always did better than his siblings' because he talked to it, but of course no one believed him. He could always sense what his plants needed, but they never spoke with actual words like Thyron. Maybe it'd been no more than the green thumb his mother said he got from her side of the family.

Once he had the SEM results, hopefully he'd know more. He was still making his way through the professional journals he'd ordered relevant to DNA sequencing, a complex process he'd also requested to be performed from the main lab, rather than mess with it himself. So far even figuring out that rogue band had been elusive. The herbarium specimens had arrived, the separations he'd performed on them using the same protocols lacking the additional band. What was it trying to tell him? The cells were at least three times larger than typical DNA! What could they be?

Realizing he still had a lot of reading to do, he gave Thyron one last encouraging psi-nudge of affection, then left the habitat.

As he rehung the O2 mask and left the cleanroom to shed the bunny suit, he ruminated for the thousandth time on the fact he couldn't publish any findings. *Not a damn thing.* Even the fact there were so many similarities to terrestrial oxalis was fascinating. It was beyond frustrating, yet he understood. That was the deal. He'd been promised he'd get to see things few ever would, but notoriety was not included.

He wouldn't even have this opportunity except for his college roommate at Purdue, who'd been involved with reverse engineering transistors obtained from a crashed UFO in the early '40s. After graduation, he'd gotten on with the CIA, the organization that originally ran Area 51. When that first UFO with the algae filtration system showed up, the spooks contacted NASA. Gabe was already working there and specializing in the correct discipline, which made him a candidate. Having a CIA insider vouch for him was all he needed to clinch the security clearance needed; the rest was history.

His thoughts turned to Cleve Backster, an interrogator for the CIA, who'd theorized years before that plants had sentience, though the conventional scientific community rejected his findings. Backster developed the polygraph, a.k.a., lie detector, which he'd attached to a Dracaena cane plant and declared he'd discovered emotional reactions. Replication of the experiment had failed, but Gabe never had any doubts, given the connection he'd always felt with plant life. If the man hadn't left the CIA in 1960, he possibly could have shared his work with him—another dead-end.

Damn.

Maybe someday—on his deathbed, perhaps—he'd tell Francesca. He was grateful that someone in his family shared his passion for botany and thus deserved to know. Would Thyron outlive him? If not, would he reproduce? If so, how? So far, it appeared his two bulbils constituted his bipedal nodes, possibly not reproductive in nature, while it appeared what may have originally been seed pods had evolved into eyes.

So many questions that he hoped would be answered—but only if Thyron recovered.

He trudged into his office, still in a funk until he saw the "holey joe" reposing in the in-basket on the right side of his desk. The manila envelopes used for onbase correspondence were covered with To/From boxes on both sides and secured with a string that encircled two brad-like buttons. When necessary, these were covered with a seal stating its *eyes only* security level. For practicality, each one was riddled with holes to see if it was empty, thus their irreverent nickname.

He picked it up, hardly daring to hope. Probably another global security reminder from the base commander or the latest chow hall menu advisory. When he saw the red seal, followed by the sender's mail code, S-4/BAL-L3, his hopes escalated that it was the SEM report at last from the biological analysis lab. Settling into his chair, he ripped off the seal, and removed the contents, hand steady but his breathing faster than normal.

The first four pages comprised the report, but he flipped past it to the pictures in back. The chloroplasts were beautifully depicted, thylakoids stacked as expected in tidy groups, other organelles like textbook illustrations. He squinted at the DNA strands, thinking something about them didn't look right. Some were the usual string, others had some odd structure about them. Something else was definitely there, walled in by chloroplasts.

He frowned, thinking. Something about them was familiar. But what? Shaking his head as if to dislodge the synapse blockage, he set his feet up on his desk, chair creaking protest as he leaned back to read the report.

He did so three times, finding nothing unexpected, much less spectacular. There was no doubt Thyron was a plant since he employed photosynthesis as his energy source, but he was so much more. He was intelligent! He could converse! He even had a sense of humor, albeit a dark one.

Or did he? Was it possible he'd imagined those conversations? Wishful thinking? Was he, as his colleagues had often declared, sometimes to his face, sometimes behind his back, "not wrapped too tight"?

The pictures beckoned and he studied them again with the magnifying glass from the top drawer, hoping to find something—*anything*—different. Those odd DNA strands, or whatever they were, still left him puzzled. Or maybe, as so many seemed to believe, he really was crazy.

Gabe secured the gold-sputtered leaf to the SEM's stub using conductive doubled-sided tape. With a deep breath and a smile he couldn't contain, he slid the sample chamber inside the unit, checked the setting, and powered up the electron beam.

His heart pounded in his ears as he brought the sample into focus. He panned to one area where the mysterious DNA strands were thickest, peering at them with full concentration. He zoomed in to maximum magnification, noticing there was definitely another structure entangled amongst them.

He inhaled sharply with sudden recognition, its impact so strong he bolted awake, nearly falling out of the recliner. Could what his subconscious just revealed be true?

Fortunately, he knew he'd obsess on the SEM results, so he'd brought them to his apartment. He stumbled out of the chair, tripping over his shoes as he grabbed the "holey joe" from the coffee table and headed for the kitchen, which had better lighting. He dumped the envelope's contents, including the magnifying glass, on the Formica-topped table and peered at the odd cells again in the context of his dream.

Was it his imagination? Could it be?

If Thyron was truly sentient and he, himself, was indeed sane in spite of several allegations to the contrary, then this would explain it. Unless he was mistaken, those strange structures nestled within Thyron's chloroplasts could only be one thing—glial cells, their function to feed oxygen to the spider-like cells beneath.

Cells that settled the matter of Thyron's sentience, once and for all:

Neurons.

CHAPTER TWENTY-ONE

Bio Lab (EBSL)
Nellis TMR
Restricted Area 51, Building T-1110
Rachel, Nevada
July 6, 1978
1650 PDT/2350 GMT

Two weeks had passed since Gabe received the SEM results and a day later, the DNA sequencing report had arrived. He was still working his way through the findings, so overwhelmed with data he'd entirely lost track of time. So much so, that base fireworks on the 4th had initially scared the living daylights out of him, thinking they were under attack.

As a botanist he was relatively unfamiliar with neurological components, but fortunately the base library contained numerous volumes on the subject. Convinced he'd correctly identified the structures clustered amongst the chloroplasts as brain cells, his confidence rose even more when he pondered the ready oxygen supply they received from such a fortuitous partnership. Satisfied he'd unraveled at least one mystery, he turned his attention back to that weird separation band in the DNA.

Comparing cell sizes, he finally decided that the mysterious band comprised neurofilaments, which were about three times larger than typical DNA strands, though that would need to be confirmed by another SEM run. The presence of glutamate receptors needed for neural communication, memory, and learning further validated it was neurons coupled with the chloroplasts.

As he worked through examining Thyron's sequenced DNA, it was no surprise to find a definite resemblance to Earth's vegetation, particularly oxalis, as he'd suspected. The fact that Thyron didn't have the gene associated with deafness explained why he could interpret sounds, including speech, cilia on his leaves detecting vibrations similar to hair in animal ears.

This particular day he was surprised, however, to discover commonality with that of insects, which in Thyron's case related to his visual sensors. Was it possible that a tunneling insect or some extraterrestrial species of leaf-cutter bee had spliced its DNA inside one of his ancestor's seed pods? Comprised of multiple independent units, perhaps evolving from a cluster of seeds, then functioning in concert, their structure vaguely resembled compound eyes.

Their design implied the ability to sense and comprehend numerous things at once, allowing the ultimate in multitasking. Plants were sensitive to wavelengths undetectable to humans as were certain insect species, particularly bees, who perceived ultraviolet. Furthermore, in Thyron's case, his eyes appeared to be capable of storing knowledge, similar to his primary bulb and bipedal nodes.

While the appearance of the vegemal's pupils' resembled that of a predator, rather than controlling visible light input, they were key to how much data he absorbed simultaneously through a broad range of frequencies which Thyron had stated included the entire electro-magnetic spectrum and beyond. Not knowing which gene drove psychic abilities, he didn't know which marker to look for, but it was undoubtedly there somewhere. Perhaps it also lay within the insect genes, which sometimes displayed a form of psi-connectivity among colonies of species such as ants and bees. Or was it possible that the first *flora peda telepathis* had been genetically engineered?

Satisfied he'd unraveled at least part of the mystery of Thyron's sentience as well as having a theory for how his eyes evolved, a treasure trove remained for future research. Without a doubt, sequencing the genome comprised of 25,000+ genes and 120 million nucleotides would keep him busy for the rest of his life.

After another euphoric day of discovery that left him mentally and physically exhausted—yet nonetheless elated—he left his office to check on Thyron before going home for the day, where he planned to relax with a good beer and Heinlein's *Stranger in a Strange Land*, having found a paperback copy abandoned in the cafeteria the day before. A glance through his office window didn't reveal much, since the habitat was already dark, programmed as if it were late December, but when he suited up and got inside, he was ecstatic to see signs of renewed life. Tiny, green sprouts were barely visible on his tangled, vine-like limbs, indicating new growth.

Holy guacamole! What a perfect day! Are you awake, my bot-alien friend?

When no response came, a worrisome thought arose. Thyron had shed his leaves, neurons with them. Would he retain his knowledge? His memory? Remember how he got there? Recognize him? The vegemal had mentioned he'd experienced multiple incarnations. Did he remember each one or were they retained deep within, slightly beyond reach? Hopefully, they were programmed in his DNA and restored within the new growth. At least by the looks of things he'd know soon.

He concentrated harder, filtering out the lab's ambient hum to listen carefully.

Thyron. It's me, Gabe. Do you hear me? Thyron?

He didn't sense an articulated answer, but sighed with relief when he felt something similar to the empathic response he'd perceive from his garden.

Can I get you anything? he asked. The impression that followed suggested an increase in light and temperature. *You've got it!* he replied, happily making the necessary adjustments.

Bio Lab (EBSL)
Nellis TMR
Restricted Area 51, Building T-1110
Rachel, Nevada
July 21 - 24, 1978

Just over two weeks later, Thyron was nearly back to normal, memory intact. His leaves grew back at an astonishing rate, so fast that Gabe could actually watch them increase in size, unfolding and reaching toward the light in a classic demonstration of phototropism. He chuckled to himself, remembering the old expression, *As boring as watching grass grow.* Certainly untrue in this case. Rather, it was one of the most exhilarating moments of his life.

It got even better when buds appeared, which unfurled to reveal turquoise and white, trumpet-shaped blooms clothed Thyron in colorful magnificence. Gabe watched them mature with hopeful anticipation that they would develop seeds; he was not disappointed. He was surprised, however, by how quickly that occurred, within days rather than weeks.

"Your flowers are maturing much quicker than those of your Terran cousins," Gabe remarked, disappointed to see them starting to fade shortly after they opened.

Drawing attention is not always a good thing, Thyron explained. *Especially at a time when my defenses are suppressed, so I don't let fly on any pollinating insects, which I don't need, anyway. Thus, I evolved to accelerate the process. Furthermore, I prefer to be known for my intellect, not my looks, especially during a rather personal part of my life cycle.*

"I can understand that," Gabe agreed, though he'd never thought of it that way before. As the pods ripened and threatened to fall a day or so later, he queried Thyron with regard to their viability and fate.

In the right environment, my seeds will produce a flora peda telepathis *physically identical to myself in every way,* Thyron explained. *However, they will not have my knowledge or memories. Those are only passed on through my bulbils.*

"So what should we do with them?" Greenley asked, straining not to appear overanxious for what he had in mind.

Without my knowledge they are without value. My next cycle, more will be produced, perhaps in an environment more conducive to nurturing, one where I can tutor them and guide their development.

"Sooooo, is it okay, then, if I keep them?" Greenley asked, still trying not to appear too eager.

Thyron's gaze locked on his, Gabe unable to keep himself from sneaking a peek into his thoughts.

The vegemal dreaded the thought of any progeny growing up on this backward planet, yet couldn't complain about how Gabe treated him. Thyron could tell how much it meant to him, particularly since he had no children, and also understood the other implications. His petioles quivered with a pre-emptive sigh.

Only if you vow on your most solemn human honor that you'll do everything possible to assure they'll mature in circumstances where they can explore and grow in freedom and interact with other flora. They will require tutoring, particularly with regard to survival and the various hazards on this planet. This locale is entirely unsuitable.

"I promise I will care for them as I would my own children. Ours, actually."

Then they are yours.

"Thank you. I will protect them as my most cherished possession," Gabe replied, tears of gratitude coating his eyes.

The pods resembled miniature okra with a literal twist. Their outside covering was sticky and hairy, designed for mechanical transport like numerous burrs and stickers, which in the wild would allow them to spread far and wide. With a plant that was already mobile, that feature seemed redundant, though perhaps in their natural habitat it still provided increased coverage, if the parent plant didn't elect to move far from its origin. He chuckled at the thought of parenting hundreds, maybe even thousands of offspring. Maybe having them carted off was a good thing. Or perhaps their germination rate was exceptionally low.

Over the next few days the pods detached, Gabe carefully retrieving each one and placing it in a cotton drawstring bag he kept in a metal kitchen drawer at his apartment, not wanting to traumatize them before they'd had a chance to come to life by exposing them to a container made of wood.

CHAPTER TWENTY-TWO

Bio Lab (EBSL)
Nellis TMR
Restricted Area 51, Building T-1110
Rachel, Nevada
July 25, 1978
1032 PDT/1732 GMT

Perched on a stool in front of Thyron's habitat, Gabe folded his arms and asked the $64,000 question: "So what caused you to go into hibernation? Be honest. It wasn't a natural part of your cycle now, was it?"

Thyron's leaves rustled with what Gabe had come to recognize as a botanical sigh. *No. I was having such a cool time exploring, I overworked my photosystems. I hacked the light so it was always on, thinking it would keep me going. Apparently it didn't.*

Slightly surprised by the direct answer, Gabe couldn't help noting that Thyron's defenses were lower, demeanor different, reflecting a new phase in his evolution had begun.

"Increased light supports photosynthesis, but you probably weren't getting enough carbon dioxide," he explained. "Even if you were, oxalic acid is produced during photosynthesis by carbon dioxide fixation in both light *and* darkness, with the rate much higher in darkness. It's not all about light, Thy. You need rest, too."

So it appears.

"The excessive light disrupted that process, so your photosystems were overworked," Gabe went on. "Your glial cells influenced the shutdown, too. They protested when you stressed yourself so much there was insufficient oxygen to support your neurons and all the synapse development required when you took in all that information. At that point, you actually need more O2 than the average plant. I sure hope you don't plan on doing that again."

Not exactly. How long was I dormant?

"About a month. It was thirty-nine days from when you collapsed until you went to seed. You could have gathered a lot of information responsibly in that amount of time."

True.

"Promise me you won't do that again. You scared the crap out of me."

I'll be more careful, but I'm not done investigating. As long as I'm stuck in this box, I need to do something, even if it's wrong.

"So what were you exploring?"

Everything. Someday you'll have to explain some of what I saw in the television band. A lot didn't make sense.

Gabe laughed. "You were watching TV? Are you kidding?"

No. I did that mostly during the day when you were here. Why didn't you tell me you have an exploration vessel in deep space?

"What are you talking about?"

The Enterprise. Captain Kirk, Mr. Spock, Bones, and those guys. They report on their missions all the time. Don't tell me you've never seen it?

Gabe doubled over, cracking up so hard he was gasping for air; even more so when he picked up Thyron's concern that he was experiencing the human equivalent of dropping his leaves for the final time.

"That isn't real, Thy," he finally responded, out of breath. "It's just a story that someone made up."

Why? That sounds like a form of lying. I've noticed humans have a devious side, but that seems rather extreme.

"No, not at all. Creativity is part of being human. Our imagination is one of the things that distinguishes us from simple animals. It provides us with an escape from what can be a harsh world."

That isn't logical.

Gabe laughed again. "You sound like Mr. Spock. Not everything humans do is. He had a hard time learning that, too. "

You speak of him as if he were real.

"He is, in many ways. He's part of our culture, our thoughts, our aspirations. But not a real person. Creativity, however, *is.* In many ways, it's what defines us as humans."

Apparently. All right, fine—forget television. I'll have to re-evaluate everything in that context. My favorite was the technical stuff, anyway. It's not deceptive. It's real—period. Ground level on this base appears similar to where we landed. But here, everything of interest is underground. Huge labs, ships that make the Cerulean Nimrod *look like an escape pod, and some advanced technological work, far beyond anything I've seen elsewhere on this miserable planet. All of it's recorded in a rather delicious data repository I was thoroughly enjoying when everything went black.*

"Holy guacamole, Thy! Do you have any idea what would happen if the security people found out?" He shivered, hackles tingling the back of his neck. "Good thing you haven't taken any security oaths. They have a strict *need to know* policy around here. Even as a supposed guest of the facility, it's a very serious violation."

Gabe shuddered as a twinge of guilt rippled through him, hoping he wouldn't be held accountable if anyone found out. Logically, how could he be? It's not like he could stop him. Furthermore, it was his responsibility to assure his specimen's health and wellbeing if he was expected to learn more about him. On the other hand, he was fully aware of Thyron's capabilities.

"Can they tell you've been snooping?" he asked, holding his breath.

No. Extracting data from crystal storage is like you reading your copy of Nature. *There's nothing to track.*

Gabe exhaled with relief—thank heavens.

As long as I'm stuck here, I need to keep my mind occupied, Thyron declared. *If I don't, I'll revert into a normal plant. I saw it happen on Sapphira. Those of my kind who didn't use their faculties to learn and explore rerooted to the ground and their visual sensors eventually fell off.*

"Wow. So you're really stuck in a 'use it or lose it' situation. Okay, look. I'll adjust your habitat to keep you healthy, but you need at least four hours a day in darkness. If you'll promise not to change that, I'll adjust the settings as required to support your excursions. Okay?"

A botanical sigh later, Thyron agreed.

"So what happens to those of your kind who pursue learning and adventure?" Gabe asked. "Do you have villages? Technology? Schools?"

No. We're solitary beings. But all that each of us learns lives on in our descendants.

"Really? How? Through your DNA?"

Yes. When my primary bulb can no longer rejuvenate, my bipedal nodes detach and revert to bulbils, which become new primary bulbs. During that first incubation cycle, we are given a name and we assimilate the knowledge gathered by our immediate progenitor. In time, we sprout new nodes for mobility, then eyes develop from the first cycle's seed pods.

"Aha!" Gabe replied. "I was right! That's how I suspected your eyes evolved. And I wasn't far off on your bipedal nodes, either. Plants send out stolons to spread and reproduce, which figuratively is like moving to a new location. It makes sense they could eventually provide mobility. So what was passed on to you from your progenitors?"

I've always had the ability to perceive and extrapolate engineering principles coupled with the relevant laws of physics.

"So your knowledge is stored via epigenetic DNA changes. Cool. Can you retrieve it at will?"

Yes. Each generation increases in both intelligence and wisdom.

"What a concept! If only humans could learn from history and knew everything about their distant past," Gabe responded.

Now that Thyron seemed to trust him fully, Gabe felt confident the plant was being completely honest, revealing information as fast as he could present the questions. From what the vegemal had discerned about human physiology, he admitted that he had medicinal and healing properties, though sacrificing body parts to that end was another story, as Gabe already knew too well from his initial attempt to take a sample.

As they conversed, especially about technical topics, Gabe's powers of perception increased, feeling at times as if he were acquiring knowledge by assimilation as well. He sensed, quite strongly, that Thyron was concerned for the girl who'd also been captured when their ship landed at Hill. Thyron explained that debacle as well, entirely revealing his disdain for the robot, based on his iron-clad belief it was a herbicidal maniac.

Gabe's attempt to explain the relationship between humans and plants went nowhere, Thyron defending his floral cousins with a vehemence Gabe never dreamed he possessed. And yet, in so many ways, he understood. If he didn't believe plants were endowed with conscious awareness long before Thyron entered the scene, he never would have become a fruitarian.

Thinking of it as murder was a bit extreme, yet he grokked it. In a black and white world, taking anything's life against its will was technically murder. Herbicide. *Ha.* Made no difference whether it was chemically or scythe induced. Dead was dead.

The environmental changes Gabe made to the habitat had an interesting side effect that further boggled the botanist's mind. Within less than a hour, Thyron's speech came in rhyme! In many respects it was annoying, yet beyond fascinating, especially as Thyron explained conditions on his native planet, Sapphira, and the symbiotic relationship *flora peda telepathises* had with that world's other occupants, a race of subhuman pygmies. An epic poem of galactic proportions, the telling held Gabe mesmerized for the rest of the morning.

When Gabe returned after lunch, he was greeted by a strong sense of sadness that contrasted sharply with his own sense of elation following their stimulating morning conversations.

"What's wrong?" he asked, mystified as he peered through his office window into the cleanroom.

For the girl I am concerned
Her fate I have not yet discerned.

I sense that contact is forbidden
Reasons for it deeply hidden.
Thus advised I can't intuit
Why instinct tells me not to do it.

"That's strange. I can't imagine why you shouldn't check on her and see if she's okay," Gabe replied audibly. "I assume she hears you, correct?"

Yes, through psi she does converse
So how could contact make things worse?

Startled by the question, Gabe winced with guilt, realizing that both Thyron and the girl were prisoners, held against their will.

"Maybe she needs to adapt to her environment without reminders of her past," Gabe suggested, considering the possibility they would both be stuck on Earth.

Then the realization struck that he'd been so obsessed to learn more about Thyron as a fascinating, alien specimen that he'd never asked why they were here in the first place. Before he could verbalize it, Thyron sensed his belated query and provided a response.

We were here to find a ship
To take us on a longer trip.
Her family is in dire straits
While here, she cannot change their fate.

Whether he was picking up on Thyron or the girl Gabe didn't know, only that he was struck by a sad mix of emotion that brought a heavy feeling to his heart.

"What kind of trouble are they in?" he asked, wondering if there was anything he could do, unlikely though it might be, given they were on another planet. Then again, there was probably no one in a better position to at least try, given he was in one of the few places on Earth where interstellar travel wasn't science fiction.

Thyron's eyes met his, their depth reflecting feelings that matched his own intuition.

Things are bad and getting worse
Almost like her family's cursed.
With weather woes and treachery

They're as miserable as can be.

Gabe sighed, rethinking his former statement about adapting. In such a situation, sometimes contact with something familiar brought comfort, not additional distress. If Thyron and the robot were all she had, then contact might help.

"I'm sure she's worried about you, too," he said. "I can't imagine why you shouldn't contact her. I think it would make you both feel better. This situation just isn't right, especially if she was only trying to find help for her family."

Thyron's wordless response caused him to wince. Such actions implicated humans, not only as the rottenest species on Earth, but candidates for that distinction throughout the entire galaxy.

When he got back to his apartment that evening, tired but elated with what had been one of the most amazing days of his life, he collapsed in his recliner, smiling—until he realized that it was Tuesday, which meant his WAR was due the next morning no later than 0900.

He groaned, not because nothing had happened the previous week, but because there was so much. The fact that Thyron had sprouted new growth was covered the previous week, and he felt disinclined to report the fact he'd flowered and gone to seed. If he did, he'd most likely be expected to turn them over to the facility. If there was one thing his research agreement made clear, it was that any and all items, living or otherwise, as well as any intellectual property he developed during his tenure at Area 51 belonged exclusively to the U.S. Government.

Having skirted around Thyron's sentience and still disinclined to reveal it in writing, he had a tremendous dilemma on his hands. What would they do if they knew? Certainly, Thy would be considered of greater interest and value versus a simple plant, extraterrestrial or otherwise. Finding the equivalent of a functional brain distributed throughout Thy's botanical body, complete with neurons and glial cells, was adequate proof of sentience, even if Gabe were the only one in the known Universe who could hear him.

Thyron had made it clear he objected to being confined and Gabe could tell he didn't want to remain on Earth forever, yet that would undoubtedly be his fate. Again, he kicked himself for practically flaunting the fact Thyron was an intelligent being to his subordinates. Fortunately, they thought he was crazy, which was a good thing, because their ramblings, if any, were less likely to be taken seriously.

Thus, the only way anyone would know the truth would be through his lab work. Hopefully, the people in the SEM lab didn't realize what they were looking at. The only other record was his lab journal, his WARs to-date benign; and thus they would remain.

CHAPTER TWENTY-THREE

Bio Lab (EBSL)
Nellis TMR
Restricted Area 51, Building T-1110
Rachel, Nevada
July 25, 1978
2015 PDT/0315 GMT

As soon as Gabe left for the day, Thyron reached out to Creena through the quantum psi-web. He sensed a hostile presence looking for her as well, but so far it had been unable to find her. It noticed his interest and tried to connect, but he cloaked his emissions when a chill of foreboding brought him pause. Its psibrations, dark and ominous, conveyed its part in her family's troubles. Somewhat unnerved by the negative and treacherous impression it left, he continued his search.

His psyche wandered throughout the cosmic soup that connected all life, some entangled by birth, others by circumstance, until the link resolved. Her emotional state signaled a complex mix of sadness, frustration, loneliness, and oddly enough some level of attachment to those in her immediate surroundings, surprisingly similar to his own. Gradually, a foggy image formed of her sitting on a weird circular-shaped spring-supported structure on a metal frame overlooking a valley that, much to his horror, was mostly agricultural, including a small personal patch where he sensed she labored.

Great.

She was imprisoned in the midst of more herbicidal maniacs. Part of him wanted to withdraw, yet his sense of compassion sustained the tenuous link. He pinged her to announce his presence, a warm feeling of affection gradually enveloping him as she responded.

Thyron! You're back! she replied, words barely discernable.

That was odd. In the past they'd had a strong connection. What had changed? Maybe the link had been compromised when he was in hibernation. Or the planet's negative vibes were causing interference, her stress level another possible reason. Unless it related to that dark presence. No matter, they were in touch. Maybe if she spoke aloud it would strengthen her focus.

Your voice is dim and far away
Aloud your thoughts you have to say.

"Okay. How's this?" she asked.

A little better but still faint
Something still your voice does taint.

Her concentration increased and the psignal strengthened a bit more.

"Is this better?" she asked.

Better much, now I can hear
It sounds as if you're present here.

"Good! Oh, Thyron, it's so good to hear from you. Are you okay?

Okay? That was hardly the word. He was still gathering strength from his recent dormancy gig and knew the prognosis was rather grim for improvement in his circumstances anytime soon. Nonetheless, her situation was unfortunate as well, so knowing of his sorry situation might make her feel less alone.

As you wish my tale I'll tell
Of how I came to wish you well.
When I wilted in a heap
Then the Earthlings tried to keep
The CO2 found in their air
Higher so I'd better fare.

"That's wonderful! So where are you?" she asked, obviously not realizing his recent bout with dormancy was less than stellar.

Southward and a little west,

A thousand kilometers, at best
Here in Area Fifty-one
Is where they took us, all undone.
Other ships are here as well
Their fate, like ours, is sad to tell.

"Snurkles! Aren't they done with our ship?"

He cringed, knowing she wouldn't be happy with the answer. Yet she deserved to know the truth.

Not to add to all your woes
But they're not done, or even close.
The ship's in total disarray
It looks like we're on Earth to stay.

"Oh, no!" she groaned. "We can't stay here! What can we do?"

He didn't plan on spending the rest of his life on this planet, either. Maybe sharing his assessment of the situation would cheer her up.

When the time's exactly right,
I think that I can end our plight.

"Really?" she replied, excited. "How?"

Earth's restricted, don't you know?
Prohibited by the HIO.

"Now you tell me."

That fact I tried to tell you, true.
"Shut down!" is what I got from you.

He felt her twinge of guilt as culpability rippled through her. "I was wrong, about a lot of things. I'm sorry, Thyron. Really. So how can you get us out of here?"

Based on information he'd gathered during his foray into the base's information repositories, he explained his approach, which hopefully would work in the event he was unable to make direct contact.

Traffic they do watch with care
Thus I'll know when one is there.

"Can you make contact?" Creena asked.

I can't be heard, comcon or not
So only if they talk through thought.

He felt her drop off, thoughts drifting to her surroundings for a moment before she spoke again.

"Where's Aggie?" she finally asked.

Her inquiry drove waves of suppressed anger through his protoplasm, punctuated by a barb of satisfaction. The 'troid had gotten what it deserved.

Here, with me, she gets to stay
Components all in disarray.

"Thyron, you have to put her back together."

He shuddered with a surge of photosynthetic nausea, similar to how he felt when he wasn't getting enough carbon dioxide. If there was one thing he definitely didn't care to do, it was reassemble that beast so she could resume her herbicidal tendencies. However, since the girl was omnivorous, she'd never understand that rationale, so he opted for one she could hopefully relate to.

With her left electronic brain,
She has caused us lots of pain.
In her disassembled state
She can't affect our future fate.

He sensed agreement, but before he could relax her attitude shifted.

"We can't leave her here," she insisted. "She's helped me out of a bunch of trouble. It's the least I can do."

Was she daft? It was an electronically driven mechanical monster designed to serve at the will and command of humans, not a living entity worthy of compassion. No doubt a reminder or two was in order.

Maybe that was true before
But don't forget who opened the door.
Until then we could have departed
Before these troubles even started.

"Never mind," she replied. "I want her back. What's it like there?" she went on, obviously changing the subject. "Are they guarding you all the time?"

He wasn't sure if or what to tell her about Gabe. He didn't want her to get the wrong idea, perhaps thinking he had better circumstances than she did. While he didn't want to spend his days on this planet, for now he was relatively comfortable and wasn't desperate to leave. Conversely, it wasn't like he was autonomous and could wander about, doing anything he wanted. Gabe was there most the time, but he decided to fib a bit to see where her thoughts were headed.

Most the time there's someone here
Except on weekends guards are near.

"Is that long enough to get her back together?"

Thyron groaned. So that's what she was getting at, his access to the 'troid. Knowing the girl, she wouldn't leave without it anyway. So maybe she should stay here, too. He tried to ignore her concern and affection for the mechanical beast, but something wouldn't let him. There was no doubt she'd feel better if he'd cooperate. And she'd always been kind and considerate toward him. He drooped with a sigh of resignation.

If you think that if I do
Happiness will come to you.

A surge of hope burst from the girl, igniting her aura. "Yes. It would. So contact a ship. Then have them pick us up late Sunday night."

Thyron emitted a protoplasmic sigh. What was she thinking? That this was some sort of spaceport with daily bookings to Alpha Centauri? In a sense it was, but it wasn't like their passenger list was something he could hack. *Sunday?* Furthermore, that was only five rotations away according to the planet's reckoning, which certainly wasn't long enough to reassemble the 'troid, either.

What you ask may take some time
Before we leave and all is fine.

"Oh, Thyron!" she cried. "Please! I can't stay here any longer, I just can't!"

The urgency in her heart and soul nearly wilted his newly generated leaves as her desperation and heartbreaking situation struck in an empathic blast.

What was the matter with him? Ever since he'd awakened from his unplanned dormancy spell, he'd softened far too much toward humans. The only explanation was that it was part of his evolutionary development along the path to enlightenment. He wasn't comfortable with it, but to ignore it could set him back.

Since it means so much to you
I will see what I can do
But Sunday next is very near
The likelihood quite null, I fear.

The connection ended abruptly and he switched to remote viewing so he could determine whether she just didn't want to argue or something had happened.

The vision revealed that she'd been joined by two male human spawn about her same age. Her expression was startled, reflecting concern the pair had heard their conversation. Sensing there was an unusual and rather complex relationship between them, he finally turned his attention back to his habitat, wondering how he could ever accomplish what he'd promised to do, with or without time constraints.

CHAPTER TWENTY-FOUR

Bio Lab (EBSL)
Nellis TMR
Restricted Area 51, Building T-1110
Rachel, Nevada
July 26, 1978
0602 PDT/1302 GMT

Thyron took his promises seriously, and he fretted the remainder of the night cycle, which he now accepted to allow his oxalates to rejuvenate, as Gabe had advised. It wasn't so much that he hated the 'troid, but rather that he distrusted her, even though he had to admit she hadn't brought him any direct harm. At least so far. Being empathic, Creena's sadness was contagious. It reawakened his awareness of their shared predicament.

Nonetheless, Gabe had provided companionship and interesting insights, as had his own virtual forays about the compound, investigating all that went on. Furthermore, he'd been dormant for a Terran month, seeming to him no more than an instant, so time for him had been compressed.

Clearly, Creena's situation was unfortunate in some way and she was desperate to leave, whereas he was reasonably content and would have been happy to stay, at least for a while, especially if he could continue exploring. Of course there was the matter of her wanting to help her family, which he couldn't relate to, given his solitary existence. Or was that what he was starting to feel toward Gabe? As if he were family? He pondered the peaceful feeling of contentment thoughts of the man evoked, providing an unexpected glimpse of familial relationships.

So what should he do? He brightened—perhaps an alternative approach. Maybe he could help her leave while remaining behind. He fluttered with another botanical sigh. Since seeing the ships in Galileo Bay, contacting one to get them off-world wasn't as much of a concern. Doing so within a few days wasn't likely, but in due time, that would happen. In fact, from what he'd discerned, this was one of the best locations on the planet to arrange such passage.

He still couldn't understand why everything was so secretive. In various ways, it was an undercover spaceport, which didn't make sense. On the other hand, perhaps it was the backward nature of the planet as a whole that precluded disclosure. Furthermore, darkness clouded it as well, due to the strong military presence coupled with a suspicious link to those in power; surprisingly similar to the forces he'd perceived causing trouble for Creena's family.

His attention shifted inward, to the many images he'd stored while snooping through digital and analog data. In order to figure things out, he needed to find an interstellar agreement or treaty that explained Terra's galactic status.

He internalized his energy and implemented his synaptic version of a search function. The first thing he uncovered was declaration by the Hostii Intergalactic Organization, referred to generally as the HIO, that Terra, with few exceptions, was off-limits for interstellar travel, which he already knew. Unfortunately, since any planet was fair game in an emergency, some vehicles inevitably arrived, usually in an uncontrolled manner, which meant they often crashed in unauthorized areas. Something he was familiar with from Sapphira, to say nothing of their own sorry circumstances.

On Terra, however, these vehicles were recovered as quickly as possible to avoid contact with humans, then taken to secure sites, his current location being one of them. Whether or not assistance was granted depended on whether a ship's point of origin was included in the HIO agreement. If not, the ships were impounded by the Terrans, who then attempted to reverse engineer them.

Ha, he thought. *Too bad we didn't know that little tidbit before.* He'd had a bad feeling about the planet and was aware of HIO's position without realizing they'd be impounded. No doubt the ship provided to the Sapphirans originated with an organization that was unprotected, unrecognized, or unauthorized. Thyron wasn't surprised when he thought back to when it was delivered on Sapphira and the deceitful nature he'd perceived of those involved. He'd been so excited about the chance to explore the cosmos that he'd conveniently ignored it for the chance of attaining the benefits of interstellar exploration for his progeny. He'd accepted the risk, and now here he was.

In the same document, he discovered that the HIO kept a close watch on planets whose technological developments were on the cusp of interstellar travel. As such was achieved, the evolutionary advancement of its people would determine whether or not such abilities were used peacefully or in a hostile, aggressive manner.

So far, this world showed gross, negative indications, having immediately used its discovery of nuclear energy for lethal purposes against their own species as well as applications that threatened the world's environment. HIO's cease and desist warnings so far had gone unheeded, blacklisting the planet. In addition, clearly other extraterrestrial species were assisting them. No wonder the base was cloaked in a conspiratorial fog of deception.

Thus, it was crucial to keep the next level of propulsion development and key to interstellar travel out of Terran hands, which involved, among other things, the secrets of quantum gravity. If they insisted on blowing themselves up and destroying their planet, that was their own business according to the HIO's protocol of free will. However, wreaking havoc on other worlds would be stopped by whatever means necessary.

This was not to say that there weren't evil, aggressive civilizations with interstellar capability. Such were not accepted into the HIO; plus there were numerous other galaxies, even in the local group, that didn't have a governing organization. If a planet was attacked by such a rogue world and couldn't defend itself, the HIO sometimes offered assistance. Their main mission was peaceful, which was maintained by a starship fleet that monitored key areas.

His branches lifted in a flaunal smile. Maybe Captain Kirk was out there somewhere, regardless of whether Gabe believed it or not.

Watching over a planet's evolution was part of the HIO's charter, providing help in a variety of ways, some temporary, some not. As it turned out, this planet in particular was being watched closely with this remote site specifically under close scrutiny.

His boughs dipped into a pensive frown. That could work to his advantage. If the HIO was monitoring Terra's activity, that meant one of their starships arrived on a regular basis. More than likely they checked on the planet's progress or lack thereof, performed any needed ship maintenance, and possibly refueled, since the planet had a magnificent magnetic field and plenty of salinated water, depending on the ship's power source.

Creena wanted to get back to her home planet, Mira III, which fortunately was an HIO member. *Perfect!* All he'd have to do was find the inspection schedule or, if that was impossible, screen the various transmissions for when one was in the area, then convince them to make a minor diversion or two on their way out.

Relieved that he'd solved the larger part of how he'd keep his promise, at least to get offworld, he turned his thoughts to the other: reassembling the 'troid.

Actually, any incoming HIO craft would have a crew with the ability to do so with ease, since it wasn't that sophisticated. However, the 'troid was in Building 15, which was highly secured since it contained confiscated equipment and devices which were classified for reasons known only to Terra. Only certain individuals were allowed access, and sometimes only under escort. Thus, getting the robot out could present a major problem and therefore a complication unacceptable to the HIO, who would undoubtedly be unsympathetic to Creena's heart's desire. She'd be considered suspect herself, given she was captured as the only human onboard an unauthorized craft.

No, counting on someone else to get the 'troid together wouldn't work. There was no way in time or space they'd give a wayward stony asteroid about Creena's disassembled 'troid. He didn't, either, actually, but he'd promised and did care about the girl's waning hope and heavy heart. Which left him no other choice.

Somehow he'd have to do it himself.

CHAPTER TWENTY-FIVE

Bio Lab (EBSL)
Nellis TMR
Restricted Area 51, Building T-1110
Rachel, Nevada
July 26, 1978
0820 PDT/1520 GMT

Thyron's engineering abilities had assisted with the repair of numerous spacecraft on Sapphira, so the technical side of reassembling the 'troid wasn't the problem. No, the problem was that the beast was in pieces secured in a bin in Building 15 while he was confined to his habitat.

Or was he?

For the first time, he questioned his prison, quickly discovering that while it was virtually airtight, given the atmospheric gases it contained were carefully balanced and meticulously filtered, the door itself wasn't secured. It took no more than a telekinetic nudge and push from his nearest branch to release the latch—which was immediately followed by a low frequency alarm in the radio range.

Holy guacamole! he thought, resealing the door and silencing the alarm's signal with destructive interference until he got it deactivated. He chuckled with the realization he'd picked up Gabe's favorite expression, even though he still didn't know exactly what or who it was. His deity, perhaps. It had a nice ring to it, so he'd have to ask him about it next time. He'd intended to before, then didn't get a chance before passing out from over-indulging in all that delicious data.

It felt good to realize he could get out and what occurred when he did. Now that he knew about the alarm, he could fix that, too. It would be interesting to see if that nanosecond blast was enough to alert Gabe to his antics. He tuned into the botanist's psibrations, finding him in the cafeteria eating a banana, some roasted almonds, and a cup of coffee, checking his pager with a puzzled frown. Thyron sent an *all is well* signal, hoping he'd accept it. Time would tell whether or not he'd hurry over to check. Considering the man's reaction when Thyron had nearly snooped himself into oblivion, he probably would.

Oh, well, no bother. It wasn't like he was doing anything wrong. *Yet.* But he'd need to cloak his thoughts so the man didn't catch on to his scheme.

He'd confessed to his conversation with Creena, but left out her request as well as his promise to help. Gabe seemed pleased they'd made contact, and was likewise concerned for her welfare. How far that sympathy would go, however, was unknown. Would he be willing to help them escape? Probably not. The man was clearly enamored with him and wasn't likely to let him go. There was also the matter of his security oaths, which he took quite seriously.

No, this would have to be a covert operation.

An unexpected twinge of guilt rippled through him. His reciprocation of affection was another matter to contend with. Did he really want to leave? While he'd debated back and forth numerous times, at this point, he still wasn't sure. Engaging emotionally with a human was unheard of, yet he was in the midst of doing so, which was interesting and so far rather pleasant.

This entire gig was about new experiences and expanding his consciousness. While he didn't want to spend the rest of his days in confinement, with minimum effort he could evolve and adapt to this planet. Just as humans manufactured more blood at high altitudes to compensate for lower oxygen levels, he could generate more chloroplasts to process the available carbon dioxide. Yes, staying on Terra held a surprising amount of appeal.

Nonetheless, he needed to fulfill his promise to reassemble the 'troid. While it was apparent he could leave his habitat and silence the alarm, that wasn't the only obstacle. Building 15 was at least a kilometer away. Movement via his bipedal nodes was painfully slow, taking nearly two minutes to move a meter, further exacerbated by the CO2 issue.

Possibly, he could do it remotely through telekinesis, but it would be tedious and require more energy than when he'd been psi-probing the electronic resources on-base. And he knew all too well how that turned out.

He pondered his dilemma another moment, then had an unexpected flash of brilliance. Psi had numerous applications. Remote viewing, telepathy, and telekinesis were but a few. He'd never tried it, but teleportation was another quantum level manifestation that was theoretically possible. He'd still have to deal with lower CO2 levels, but at least getting back and forth should be less of a problem.

Could he do it? And if he did, would the habitat's sensors notice he was missing? There was only one way to find out.

He bundled all his energy, physical, mental and emotional, registering awareness of every cell's position and function on his consciousness. Then he melded it with that quantum, albeit spiritual, essence that animated his chlorophylated flesh. It reached critical mass with an unexpected jolt that nearly broke his concentration.

Okay, next step, he thought, and focused on the space just outside his habitat. Going farther than that on the first try would be reckless at best and fatal at worst. When a clear image of the location formed in his mind, he directed all his psi power toward transplanting himself to the targeted location.

He emitted a botanical gasp when a blinding burst of light exploded around him that exceeded the glare of the Sun; then slowly rearranged his limbs to see where he was.

I did it! I'm outside the habitat! Hhoollyy gguuaaccaammoollee!

What was that? An echo? Had part of him failed to integrate, perhaps left behind in some other dimension?

His floral gaze darted about the room, eyes widening when he saw Gabe staring at him through his office window, mouth agape.

Ooops.

He rustled with a verdant sigh as he awaited his fate, relentless excitement nonetheless surging through him. Explaining it to Gabe without revealing his intent, however, would be a definite challenge.

The man blew through the plastic strips moments later, still zipping up the white suit, green eyes wide.

"How did you do that?" he demanded.

Thyron was so overcome with the joy of success that cloaking his thoughts was impossible.

I gathered up my energy
In fullness of pure synergy.
Focused on the target spot
A bright flash later, there I got.

"Holy guacamole!" Gabe exclaimed again.

Thyron immediately perceived the man's thoughts, that he saw this teleportation ability as a potential problem. And indeed, for the botanist, it was. Should he tell him the truth, at least the part about reassembling the 'troid? His mind cycled with indecision.

But first, he needed to know, once and for all, the identity of this mysterious deity whom Gabe summoned to every important occasion. If nothing else, getting him to explain would serve as the perfect distraction while he decided how much to confess.

CHAPTER TWENTY-SIX

Bio Lab (EBSL)
Nellis TMR
Restricted Area 51, Building T-1110
Rachel, Nevada
July 26, 1978
0835 PDT/1535 GMT

Gabe laughed even harder at Thyron's query than he did when he'd mentioned the *Enterprise*. Struggling for breath, he gradually tried to explain, though his explanation was further punctuated with bursts of levity, even as he opened the habitat door so Thyron could shuffle back inside.

"It's not a—a deity," he chuckled, securing the door. "It's just an—an expression of surprise." The man doubled over, consumed again with another hilarity episode. "Guacamole is a type of food. One of my favorites, made from avocados. I'll bring one in tomorrow and introduce you."

Thyron cloaked his thoughts as he breathed a sigh of relief. So far his distraction had worked. But not for long.

"All right, Thyron," he went on, humor dissipating. "Why did you do that? Are you trying to escape? Or just want out of your habitat?"

Pros and cons of telling the truth battled behind his thought barrier, requiring concentration that made it more difficult to decide.

"Well?" Gabe prompted. "I know you're up to something or you wouldn't be hiding your thoughts. C'mon, buddy. 'Fess up."

Thyron fluttered with defeat.

I talked with Creena in the night

She's sad and desperate to take flight.
She wants me to rebuild her 'troid
And help her Terra to avoid.

Gabe stared at him, frowning as the message settled. Then the man's eyes teared up and a wave of compassion rolled over him.

"Of course," he said after a long pause. "And you probably want to go, too. You have no quality of life here." He pulled over a stool and sat down, feet propped on a rung, elbows on his knees, gloved hands cupping the sides of his hood-shrouded face. Thyron couldn't read his thoughts, they were racing so fast, but his emotional state was clear—he was devastated.

Thyron had never perceived that emotion before, though Creena's plea registered in a similar range. He hadn't realized that human feelings had so many different frequencies, having only experienced a primitive form of fear and anger while living among the Sapphirans. Its impact was strong, beyond empathic. He emitted a photosynthetic whimper, foliage drooping, at the realization he was participating, not simply observing.

Gradually, Gabe's thoughts settled into a linear flow he could follow. He was debating whether he should help and pondering the impact on his research as well as security issues. He apparently wasn't familiar with the HIO, because he wondered how they'd get passage offworld. He got stuck on how, which gave the man some measure of relief. He thought it was impossible. Probably a good thing.

"Do you have a plan?" he finally asked.

A plan I have but not complete
It's vulnerable to big defeat.
First the 'troid I need to reach
And thus my habitat did breach.

"So you plan to teleport to where they're holding the 'troid and put it back together?"

Thyron's branches swayed as he nodded, a human gesture he'd picked up.

"You can do that?"

He nodded again.

"Wow." Gabe blew out his cheeks. "You realize the risk of leaving your habitat, right? There's not enough CO2 in Earth's atmosphere to support your increased activities. You're also protected from bacteria, fungi, mold, and a host of diseases that could be dangerous."

That I know and understand.
I don't want on my bulb to land.
I suggest I start right here
Adapting to your atmosphere.

"Okay. We can do that. But let's do it in stages. First, I'll switch you to ambient, here in the cleanroom, for several hours each day. That'll allow you to acclimate to Earth's gas mix and pressure at this altitude without exposure to any pathogens. You can come out of your habitat, but you need to spend enough time in there each day to absorb the nutrients you need from the soil. If you feel compromised, let me know, and I can increase the CO2 for a refresher. If you adapt favorably, then we'll take the next step, unfiltered air. But remember, you won't be able to be as active."

The scientist paused, an erratic emotion filling the gap. "I realize, given your teleporting ability, that I can't hold you to this. But for your safety, I'd like to be there to observe how you do, so I can render assistance, if needed."

Thank you, Doc, for your support
As I leave behind my fort.
I promise I won't run away
And your plan I will obey.

Gabe closed his eyes and indulged in an unhappy sigh of resignation. "All right. Let's get started," he said, then reached for the gas valves, which closed with a soft hiss. After that, he opened the vents in the top to admit outside air and adjusted the fan speed. That done, he set his mouth in a grim line and released the latch.

If Thyron had a mouth, he would have been grinning ear to ear. Instead, the flaunal equivalent manifested as an upward tilt to his branches as he waddled happily into the room.

The lower CO2 level hit immediately. He closed his eyes and concentrated on photosynthesizing, which wasn't so much difficult as less effective. He felt fine physically, but his mental function had diminished noticeably as his chloroplasts produced less oxygen for his brain cells. As expected, his speech reverted to the unsophisticated syntax of the humans.

"Well?" Gabe prompted. "How do you feel?"

Compromised, but not critically so.

"Your speech is like ours again."

Sacrifices are expected in accomplishing anything of high importance. How long do I need to stay inside?

"A week, maybe ten days. We'll see how you do."

That seems overly conservative, Doc. How about three?

"No less than five. Triggering another dormancy episode is the last thing either of us wants."

Thyron rolled his visual sensors. *That was because I was processing too much information. I won't multiplex this time. For now, I'll just examine the 'troid's components, make sure they're all there, and determine how they should be assembled. I can even do that from here, which will require less energy.*

"Tell you what. Why don't you do that now, so I can see what effect, if any, remote viewing has?"

Without further comment, Thyron focused on the bin in Building 15 where he'd previously found the 'troid's components.

And discovered a definite problem—it was empty.

"What's wrong?" Greenley asked, sensing his startled reaction.

It's gone. Not there.

"Great. Don't waste any more energy hunting it down. Let me see what I can find out. Maybe someone else is putting it back together, which will save you the trouble."

CHAPTER TWENTY-SEVEN

Bio Lab (EBSL)
Nellis TMR
Restricted Area 51, Building T-1110
Rachel, Nevada
July 26, 1978
0847 PDT/1547 GMT

Gabe doffed the bunny suit, hung it in its usual spot, then exited the gowning suite and turned left, walking slowly to his office. Its only windows were to the cleanroom, furnishings WWII American Military vintage, not much different from his office at JSC.

A grey metal desk that weighed about three hundred pounds greeted him, surface cluttered with unruly stacks of research journals and reference books, several of which were open, plus scattered lab notes and reminders. He dodged the rectangular table forming a "T" with the desk, where up to five colleagues could squeeze for tag-up meetings, and circled around to a worn, squeaky, swivel chair. He leaned back to its structural limits, set his feet on the desk, and folded his arms across his chest.

He had no idea how far he should go to find what he was looking for. Actually, such a decision was already made for him, depending on whether it was secured beyond his clearance level. So there was only one way to find out.

Then he remembered—his WAR was due and it was almost 0900.

Crap.

He dropped his feet to the floor and swiveled to the right, facing the terminal on the desk extension where he entered his user ID and password. The prompt appeared, where he typed in the command to run the WAR database, as he did every week about this time. But rather than assembling select scientific facts to report, his mind and every cell in his body reverberated with the persistent thought that detaining Thyron and the girl was flat-out wrong. *Period.* There wasn't anything he could do directly for the girl, but he could make sure that interest in Thyron didn't escalate. Or maybe he could do even better than that.

He'd always been a miserable liar, probably because he could tell intuitively when someone else wasn't telling the truth. It was no easier in writing, especially since then there was concrete evidence and no getting out of it. The "no one will ever know" lure blared tauntingly on one side, while that look his mother used to give him flashed like a neon sign on the other.

Then an imposing personage, far less friendly than his mother, invaded his mind's eye; a strident reminder that it wasn't just a matter of lying—it was the matter of his security oaths. He closed his eyes and shuddered, remembering when he'd raised his right hand and sworn on his life to uphold them, acknowledging that violation invited unspeakable penalties.

The experience had been intimidating, yet somehow personally offensive. He'd never do anything to jeopardize anyone, much less his country—ever. Never in his wildest imaginings had he thought he'd find himself in such as position; one he'd never before conceived existed. He was a botanist, for heaven sake! Not an engineer, physicist, or even an anthropologist.

He certainly wasn't a spy, considered himself patriotic. Not only loyal to his country, but honorable in all his dealings—he didn't even lie on his income tax, even though research activities gave him plenty of wiggle room. Over the years he'd signed numerous nondisclosure agreements, never doubting he'd keep them. He'd always prided himself on being an honorable man. One who not only respected but revered all life.

Suffocating desolation as arid as the surrounding desert consumed him as the import of what he was about to do precipitated. Guilt permeated every pore, ripped through muscle, and penetrated every bone to the marrow, its darkness collapsing to a stone-like knot within his chest, searing his conscience like a red-hot lance.

Yet somehow, a small voice awoke, breaching the overwhelming guilt. Consigning Thyron to a life in captivity, most likely below ground, confined in an artificial environment even worse than his habitat, ripped his heart in a different direction.

The vegemal was a living, sentient being, more intelligent than himself and certainly most of his own species. Furthermore, Thyron trusted him. In many ways, what had started out as an interesting specimen had become the best and closest friend he'd ever had, even more so than his own brother. How could he violate what was no less than a sacred trust?

The real question was who deserved his allegiance? The government? Or Thyron?

Suddenly, the grey areas dissolved, separating to black and white. He took a deep breath, knowing what he had to do, yet resolve failed to dissipate the darkness lurking inside.

Again, he tried to convince himself that this was one situation where it wasn't exactly wrong. Just...just what?

All right—It's a matter of what's morally or ethically the right thing to do. How can saving an innocent life, maybe even two, ever possibly be wrong?

Biting his lower lip while trying to ignore the heavy feeling in his chest, he proceeded to compose his WAR:

```
EBSL Weekly Activity Report
Week Ending 26 July 1978
```

```
The specimen rejuvenated, completing a life cycle from
dormancy to renewal. To date it has not exhibited any
extraordinary characteristics that differ from those
of typical terrestrial oxalis species. It's the
opinion of this investigator that there's a high
probability that the species was harvested on Earth,
perhaps for its medicinal qualities, and is therefore
not of extraterrestrial origin. Study of the DNA
```

<pre>
sequencing results continue and may yet reveal
significant differences.
</pre>

<pre>
Gabriel F. Greenley, PhD
Principal Investigator
</pre>

He read it over six times, then held his breath, closed his eyes, and hit <Enter>.

Moments later, he opened his eyes and sighed heavily, heart racing. His statements were a blatant violation of his research agreement and could probably be construed as treason. But under the circumstances, there was no other choice, at least for someone with a proper set of morals—he might go to prison, but he wouldn't go to hell. Having never reported Thyron's sentience or the neurons, there was a good chance it would fly. Hopefully.

That done, for good or ill, he sighed again, then turned his thoughts to Thyron's task of reassembling the robot. His clearance level determined what he could access, further limited by the usual *need to know* policy. Information outside that range would be secured. If he couldn't get to what he wanted, he'd have to request it specifically, backed up by plenty of sound, scientific rationale— which was now somewhat moot, given the implications of his WAR. Nonetheless, he could still claim to be investigating Thy's origin. After all, it was true that there was still plenty in the sequencing report he hadn't examined; and it wasn't like scientists never made mistakes, whether or not they would admit it.

From what Thryon had told him regarding how he, the girl, and the 'troid wound up together, it was doubtful it knew much, but it would be his official story. If nothing else, the robot's memory held extraterrestrial information unavailable otherwise, perhaps even pertaining to Thyron's home planet. With luck, maybe the 'troid's intellectual contents had already been accessed and even catalogued. But even then, it was a matter of whether he could get to it or justify access.

The database query screen came up, cryptically simple. No title, no place of origin, no logo. If anyone just happened to find it, which was unlikely, they wouldn't have a clue what they'd found, which was undoubtedly the point. He entered *Incident Number 780528* in the beckoning field and waited.

And waited.

He frowned, wondering. Maybe he didn't have access. Or the system was down. Except the terminal's prompt was still blinking. Lost in a loop? Or its way of saying "Access Denied?" Just when he was ready to give up, the green monochrome screen filled with a table that contained the inventory from the incident in question.

The list was short, containing only the vehicle itself in Hangar 7; a reference to an *extraterrestrial biological entity* under the acronym EBE, whose location was blank; and an EBL, or extraterrestrial biological lifeform in Building S-4GL/EBSL, which was Thyron. The list would grow, each individual part logged, as they dismantled the vehicle.

Each item had been assigned an inventory number, so he queried the vehicle's IVN. A list of components came up, which surprised him. He'd gotten a good look at the UFO inside and out before they'd loaded it up for transport and there were no visible fasteners, much less seams, inside or out. Even the piloting chamber was enigmatic, command screens invisible, silent and dark. The exterior looked like a titanium alloy of some sort, hard enough it was impossible to scratch or dent with anything less energetic than a meteorite. Apparently the guys in engineering were familiar enough with such things to take it apart. Cool.

So who'd been piloting that thing? There was a good chance it had been the robot. Certainly not Thyron, and probably not the girl. So engineering could have an interest in getting the robot back together as well. However, since these people typically worked without deadlines, they were seldom in anything even vaguely resembling a hurry. In most cases, the prevalent due date at Area 51 was *Whenever,* which wasn't what either Thyron or the girl wanted to hear.

The last listing was an *actuator driven robotic assembly of unknown function*; exactly what he was looking for, but the location was blank.

He frowned, wondering if it had been transferred to another site. Not likely, so he queried the robot's IVN. When it came up, the list was several screens long. Apparently, they'd succeeded in disassembling it as well, which was exactly what Thyron had said. However, the components were no longer stored in the same place, but scattered throughout the base in what were apparently various stages of investigation. Its shell was in the metallurgy lab; numerous solid state and fiber optic components with the electronics people; a dozen or so awaiting analysis by the SEM team. What they believed to be its central processing unit was in the computer lab, along with its suspected memory and vocal unit.

Crap. While he'd learned more than expected, this was definitely not what he was hoping to find.

He groaned with frustration, then had another thought. Someone would be over the project as a whole, which should have a schedule. He found the identity and number of the systems guy charged with reverse engineering it back on the main screen, then made the call.

The man answered on the fourth ring.

"Yeah, this is Greenley from the Bio Lab," he said. "I was wondering when you expect to have the robot from Incident 780528 reassembled?"

"Never," the man replied flatly. "Putting it back together's not in my task order. All we're authorized to do is analyze the materials and identify the technologies it uses for data storage and verbal communication. The circuits are beyond anything we've seen before and in the queue to be analyzed by the SEM crew. Until that report comes back, nothing's gonna happen. And even if we figure out that much, it's not our job to put it back together."

Gabe gritted his teeth and hung up, deducing the man was a contractor, which would explain the restrictions to his investigation

Hmmmph.

Not in his task order, indeed.

He got up and walked slowly to the lab window, not sure what to report. One advantage of dealing with psi-sensitive beings was that often verbal communication was unnecessary. Thyron's large, orb-like eyes shifted to his.

"Not good," Gabe admitted out loud. "It's completely dismantled and scattered throughout the base. When they're done, all they're going to do is dump everything back in Building 15. Until then, we're stuck. It's beyond our control and going to take time. You probably need to tell the girl a delay, probably a long one, is inevitable."

Thyron emitted a botanical sigh, not liking the news, yet recognizing that Gabe was right—their only choice was to wait.

She's not going to like it, but there's nothing we can do about it. I may as well let her know now. Her patience is quite thin, but she needs to know so she's not expecting to leave as soon as expected.

Gabe felt their psilink drop and assumed Thyron was contacting the girl. After several minutes, he noticed the link was back.

"What did she say?" he asked. "Did she take it okay?"

Thyron's spherical eyes emanated concern. *I pinged her but she didn't answer. All I got was static. She's in a highly agitated state that shut down her ability to receive.*

"Uh-oh," Gabe murmured, shared worry arcing between them.

CHAPTER TWENTY-EIGHT

Bio Lab (EBSL)
Nellis TMR
Restricted Area 51, Building T-1110
Rachel, Nevada
July 27, 1978
0938 PDT/1638 GMT

Gabe assumed his signature position, feet up and chair tilted back, while Thyron perched on the table perpendicular to his desk, contemplating the avocado pit impaled with toothpicks to keep all but its bottom submerged in a shallow glass of water.

Thyron had winced when Gabe quartered and peeled it, much less mashed it up and consumed its fruit, all while trying to assure him it could live again if the seed would sprout, eventually growing into a tree. The vegemal thought the intervention strange and unnecessary. If he wanted it to grow, why didn't he plant the entire thing outside?

The discussion had deteriorated from there, so now the pair shifted to debating the pros and cons of Thyron remaining in the cleanroom versus going outside. So far, the vegemal seemed to tolerate lower CO_2 levels, but Gabe was still cautious about exposure to a vast variety of pathogens and insects. Was he being over-protective? Probably.

The high radiation level incident to atomic testing decades before was another concern. The building was constructed of cinderblocks and metal, providing a minimal level of shielding, but failed to keep everything out. However, it had been enough to increase the energy required for Thyron to access some information, further contributing to his collapse a month and a half before.

Thyron's limbs dipped into the expression Gabe recognized as a pensive frown. *I'm adapting to less CO2 so it's the next logical step,"* the vegemal suggested. *"Why don't I give it a try and see?"*

"Okay, I'll just have to monitor your photosynthesis-two processes daily," he agreed, holding his chin as if reflecting Thyron's expression. "You can always return to the hab for therapy, if needed, so I suppose it won't hurt to give it a try and then check how you're doing."

Speaking of checking, maybe I should see what progress they're making analyzing the 'troid's components, Thyron suggested. *They post weekly reports on such things, you know. You may not be able to see them, but I can.*

Gabe dropped his feet to the floor, mouth agape. "Brilliant!" he exclaimed, secretly relieved to change subjects, even though his heart rate doubled at the reminder of the recalcitrant WAR he'd submitted the day before. "Then we'd have some idea how long it's going to take."

Maybe not as long as you think, Thyron said, telepathic words sparkling with mystery.

"What do you...*Oh!*" the botanist replied, catching on. "You think you could help compress the schedule?"

Undoubtedly. No offense, Doc, but your best and brightest really aren't, at least as far as off-world achievements are concerned. I think I could enlighten them substantially.

"Holy guacamole! Outstanding proposition!" Gabe explained.

I'm not as dumb as I look.

He laughed, continually amused by the *flora peda telepathis's* dry wit. "So what do you need? Anything?"

It will save time and energy if you direct me to the location where each component is being examined and what they're looking for.

"You got it. Do you want it visually or direct access?"

I prefer the electronic address of the digital files. My intrusions won't be detected, but if you show too much interest, they could get suspicious.

"They track who uses the database, even when it's within your clearance level and need to know?"

Of course they do. He quivered at the man's naiveté.

"Right. Makes sense. Never thought about it. I don't think they do that at NASA. But then, a lot of their information is still in file cabinets." He laughed and shook his head. And they were supposed to be the country's, if not the world's, high-tech leaders. Yeah, right.

On paper, I suppose, Thyron interjected.

"Sorry."

No, you're not.

"You're right. I'm not. It's just the way it is and I wish you'd stop bringing it up."

Whatever.

Gabe's attempt to smother a chuckle failed.

If you don't mind, I'd like to get on with it.

"Good idea," he said, booting up the computer and logging into the database so Thyron could tune into the incoming signal. "Are you in?"

Affirmative.

"Great. I'll shut up. Good luck, my bot-alien friend."

CHAPTER TWENTY-NINE

Bio Lab (EBSL)
Nellis TMR
Restricted Area 51, Building T-1110
Rachel, Nevada
July 28-August 3, 1978

Thyron pondered the preferred order to reassemble the 'troid, suppressing the botanical equivalent of heartburn that struck whenever he thought of that herbicidal monster. The memory of the odor she emanated from the life fluids of innumerable plants cut down in their prime haunted him still. But he'd promised the girl, and if there was one thing he believed in, it was keeping his word.

He shivered, leaves rustling with one final wave of revulsion before he forced emotion aside, deciding what to do first, now that he knew where everything was located. Even if he couldn't start the process, he could develop a plan.

Smaller parts, some at the nano level, would have to be assembled into each component. With their number in the thousands, maybe even millions, they should start there. They'd be connected to her structure later, then enclosed, as required.

Putting together the servomotors driving her articulating appendages would be time-consuming, plus they'd need to be integrated with the electronics. The fact she had specific functional categories was helpful, indicating circuitry separation, which would simplify things.

More than likely, the humans would have the most trouble understanding the electronics. From what he'd seen of their scientific advancement level, they were rapidly increasing the number of transistors while reducing the size of integrated circuits, but quantum computing was still little more than theory, while it was the basis for most of the technology with which Thyron was familiar.

What he'd observed so far indicated it took decades before a scientific breakthrough was understood clearly enough for practical application. Reverse engineering had introduced them to nanotechnology principles, but they were still trying to develop optics with resolution capable of viewing atoms and their chemical bonds. Building machinery with tolerances capable of fabricating anything on that scale was another obstacle yet to be overcome.

To determine the level of tutoring required, first he'd need to identify their goals and aspirations. If they wanted to discover new theories and techniques, that was simpler than reproduction. If the latter was what they wanted, he'd have to change their mind. That could be a significant challenge. His impression of the base commander was that he didn't compromise standards of achievement. Deadlines, for the most part, were flexible for research and development, especially R&D efforts focused on technical advances. Certain projects with direct military hardware applications were top priority; robots and androids, not so much, unless there were component crossovers.

Out of curiosity, he turned his remote sensors to Hangar 7, where the *Cerulean Nimrod* was stored. To his surprise, they'd not only figured out how to remove the magnetized fairing, they'd disassembled it down to the last connector. It wouldn't be going anywhere anytime soon, especially since the vehicle had malfunctioned, which forced them to land in the first place. He chuckled to himself at the likelihood of them finding the faulty part, much less getting it off the ground.

He focused back on the task at hand, reflecting on the 'troid's functional categories. There were seven, which included communications, mechanical/structural analyses, survival strategies, technological assessment, database development/access, astrodynamics, and maintenance, which included the offensive botanical intervention. A flash of devious humor trickled through his cytoplasm as he decided that last subset was no longer necessary, except perhaps for limited insect control operations. He'd have to think about that. Nonetheless, it was low priority.

The communications module was most important. If he was going to work with that beast—which would be the case, considering Creena's request—the 'troid would need to be psi-sensitive. It might be a trick to add that, so that would be a good place to start. Completing the most important, albeit challenging, sections first, made sense.

That module was one of the most complex as well since it required gathering and synthesizing data for future reference, especially the foreign language sector. If, perchance, a ride off this rock came along before he'd completed reassembly, that could also be the most consequential for making contact. With it restored, she might even be able to assist with her own restoration.

Convinced that was where he'd start, he referred to the database that contained the whereabouts of the relevant components and quickly found the central processing unit and circuitry in the communications lab where an electrical engineer known as Brad Inglehardt in the Artificial Intelligence Division was trying to figure out how data storage signals were initiated, integrated into the algorithms for the relevant functional categories, then compiled.

Thyron sighed, then began organizing the principles behind three-dimensional photonic crystals into a linear presentation format a reasonably intelligent human could understand. Too bad Mr. Spock wasn't real and thus couldn't teach him how to perform a Vulcan mind meld. Unfortunately, television signals were transmission only, anyway, so with no receiver band, making contact would have been impossible, anyway.

Nothing on this low-tech planet was ever simple.

Fortunately, connecting with Brad in the psi-band was. In addition to establishing full-time access to his conscious mind, he linked up with his subconscious as well, planning to provide additional input to his dreams, as required. The man was open to inspiration, which helped significantly, and indeed was bright, making it easy to slip new thoughts amongst the man's own, which he readily claimed as products of his training and experience.

Arrogant, to be sure, but if it served Thyron's purposes, he didn't care. After all, ego was as undefined as division by zero to a vegemal that approached omniscience effortlessly, then lived forever through his progeny.

It didn't take long to discover a bonus to his promptings. Sharing the excitement and, at times, pure joy the man experienced as new ideas and insights streamed into his brain was as euphoric for Thyron as it was for Brad. In less than a Terran week, Brad had developed a model that passed muster with his project manager when word came back from the SEM lab confirming the molecular structure was there as predicted.

Brad, of course, was ecstatic. There were numerous expressions of victory from which Thyron learned a new human gesture referred to as a *high-five.* When Brad commented, "I can't believe I figured all that out!" Thyron couldn't resist dousing his arrogance a dew drop or two.

Actually, you didn't, he psaid, to which Brad's expression changed considerably. *You did the work, true, but I helped.*

"What? Who said that?" the man said aloud, which, of course, earned blank looks from the handful of others in the small office.

You're definitely smart, but you had help, Brad. From me.

At this point, Brad apparently realized the voice was in his head and responded in kind. *I did? From who?*

From me. I provided key data that you grasped quite nicely.

Who on Earth are you?

Actually, I'm not from Earth, I'm from Sapphira, but I'm known as Thyron.

Oh, my God! What are you? Are you here, on base?

The reference to divinity startled Thyron, though he quickly recovered. One could never have too many worshippers. *I'm a* flora peda telepathis, *and yes, I'm here. Maybe we'll eventually meet.*

Wow! Brad exclaimed. *I hope so! Thanks so much! If there's ever anything I can do for you, just let me know.*

I will, Thyron replied, basking in the unexpected appreciation.

The celebration that followed was entertaining, though Thyron quickly severed the psi-link when Brad's blood alcohol level rose high enough to render him dizzy and disoriented as well.

Thyron's next project involved explaining carbon nanotubes to a mechanical engineer named Roger Barker. He was harder to connect with initially, then resistant to unfamiliar ideas or concepts that he believed violated the laws of physics.

Thyron finally lost patience and responded, *Look around you, you Terran imbecile! Do you really think the vehicles in those mountainside hangars got here using the laws you think you know?*

The psi-scream not only got his attention, but somehow gave him the confidence to, in the guy's own terms, *think outside the box.* Roger had nanotechnology down a few days later. Fortunately, the physicist working on electro-optics was already on the trail of creating a scanning tunneling microscope that could attain resolution to atomic levels.

This time Thyron dropped the psi-link prior to the celebratory event.

The successes continued; in less than a Terran week the database confirmed that the 'troid's components had been returned to their bin in Building 15. Gabe was amazed by how quickly the engineers caught on, which was no mystery to Thyron—it was simply a matter of explaining it properly.

That complete, the next challenge loomed—reassemble the robot.

CHAPTER THIRTY

Bio Lab (EBSL)
Nellis TMR
Restricted Area 51, Building T-1110
Rachel, Nevada
August 4-7, 1978

So far, it appeared that investigations regarding the robot's components were finished, based on the fact nothing more had been removed from the bin for several days. However, from eavesdropping on Gabe's ruminations, Thyron could tell that the man maintained strong reservations about the assembly task. If security questioned his interest, it represented a potential problem. A big one. Since he was aware of the 'troid's existence, having been involved with the incident from the start, it was slightly less serious. But the real question was whether an astrobiologist had the requisite *need to know* to be involved with its assembly?

Such was a big deal. Everyone was required to ignore projects with which they had no legitimate involvement. Sirens wailed strident reminders during classified vehicle tests, at whatever hour, admonishing outsiders to shutter windows and stay indoors until *all clear* sounded. Thyron didn't understand why Gabe reacted with considerable discomfort to such events, his explanation something about *duck and cover* drills in the 50s, which Thyron failed to grasp.

Having access to the storage facility implied clearance to investigate what lay within, but Gabe worried that the automated check-out process would identify anything beyond the scope of his research and trigger a security breach alarm. If that occurred, his rationale that the 'troid could tell him more about the *flora peda telepathis* could be insufficient to keep him from being arrested on the spot.

Thyron's analysis of the database's authorization structure indicated he was in the clear for anything associated with that incident, but Gabe still resisted, stating adamantly that those who'd taken security oaths were expected to honor them and it was his personal responsibility not to exceed known limitations. Violations resulted in dire consequences upon which he refused to elaborate, simply adding that his constitutional rights, including the *Miranda* (whatever that was about), didn't apply to matters of National Security.

Thyron couldn't fully understand his reasoning, nor could he assemble the 'troid himself. He also couldn't understand why Gabe got so nervous when he'd tried to explain the ramifications, as if they were inevitable. No doubt he'd never entirely understand humans. Maybe it was related to that imagination phenomenon he'd mentioned.

But the immediate problem was that while his segmented leaves vaguely resembled hands, he had not yet evolved the ability to articulate their divisions like fingers. Thus, lacking the dexterity needed to do so, he had to convince Gabe to get over it, just as he personally had to get over being around wood. Thyron reminded him repeatedly that if engineering had finished their investigations, it was doubtful anyone would notice anything missing. Gabe was on the authorized list with hundreds of thousands of such transactions occurring every day, so probability was in his favor that it wouldn't be flagged as suspicious.

It took a few days, but Thyron's pleading eventually wore him down to the point he agreed to chance it. Fortunately, while he was in Building 15, Thyron could psi which components to retrieve. As they got each one assembled, he'd return it and gather what was needed for the next one. Or thus was the plan.

Gabe waited to go, or possibly procrastinated, until mid-afternoon shift change, hoping the increased activity at that hour would further distract from his actions. Thyron watched remotely as he arrived at the man-door, inserted his badge, and entered his code. The bolt clicked obediently and he stepped inside, wincing slightly.

Thyron did likewise, but for a different reason. There was nothing more likely to attract a problem than to expect one, and Gabe was obsessing on the fact every visit was recorded in the security office by a dot-matrix printer on green and white striped, bifolded paper, something Thyron had let slip when he'd presented his probability argument. It was still difficult for the vegemal to be less than totally honest, but he was learning. Withholding information via a psi-link wasn't easy, partial cloaking nearly impossible with ancillary data transmitted instantaneously.

Gabe paused, waiting for his eyes to adjust, then nodded to the guard who was barely visible in the gloom. From there he walked what seemed like forever before finding the vault labeled with the incident number. His badge worked again. He stepped inside, turned on the light. Shelves, most lined with baskets, covered the metal walls. He dug through the appropriate bins, collecting the needed parts, which he placed in a plastic crate. When they were all gathered, he obediently scanned the barcode on each one using the reader next to the door, then sighed as he mustered the courage to leave, a process possibly more precarious than entry.

Thyron sent vibes of assurance as he approached the exit, where the guard would confirm each unit versus the scan log to make sure they'd been properly checked out. Thyron cringed at Gabe's emissions, psibrations another psi-sensitive would easily interpret as guilt. Even worse, his hands were shaking as he handed the basket to the guard.

Calm down, Doc, he psaid. *Everything is just fine.*

"I didn't think it'd be so hard to get off caffeine," Gabe stated, to which the guard grunted apparent understanding; Thyron didn't have a clue what that was about. Some secret password perhaps?

The MP instructed Gabe to place his badge in a reader, then picked through the items, checking each one against a monitor. After several moments which seemed much longer than they actually were, he handed back the crate. Gabe retrieved his badge, then froze, expecting the worst, when another MP came though the door. When the newcomer simply replaced the other guard for the shift change, he visibly relaxed, nodded politely, and left.

Thyron's empathic sensors felt as if they were on fire by the time Gabe got back to the Bio Lab, hyperventilating while sweat only partially related to the desert's summer heat poured from his temples. Thyron flooded him with praise and suggested they'd done enough for the day, to which the man didn't argue. He secured the parts in a file cabinet in his office without comment, made sure he turned the combination lock several turns, then left.

Thyron rolled his eyes as the door closed behind him, wondering if Gabe would complete all the necessary retrievals without succumbing to the human frailty known as cardiac arrest.

CHAPTER THIRTY-ONE

Bio Lab (EBSL)
Nellis TMR
Restricted Area 51, Building T-1110
Rachel, Nevada
August 8-17, 1978

The arduous undertaking began in Gabe's office the next morning, Thyron supervising. Gabe expected as much and didn't say anything, though his thought emissions still indicated anxiety-related interference.

Starting with the central processing unit made sense, from which they'd expand accordingly. The CPU was the 'troid's guts, without which it would be no more than a bundle of nuts and bolts, at least figuratively, since such primitive fasteners were rare, most pieces fitting together either magnetically, molecularly, or like a Chinese puzzle.

It took several hours to get all the quantum wafers into place, followed by the proper connectors and optical cables, which would then have to be repeated for each of the seven modules. Thyron used psychokinesis to establish the needed circuitry as well as connect nano-sized parts Gabe could barely see, much less assemble.

After a few long days of tedious work, the CPU was returned to Building 15, checked in, and more pieces removed. Gabe was still nervous, but less so, the guard once again somewhat distracted, waiting to be relieved by his replacement.

The next batch related to the agricultural module, which Thyron had decided to modify first, instead of the communications module, so the 'troid couldn't ever commit another wanton act of herbicide.

While he'd originally intended to eliminate those horrifically offensive functions, he'd decided to retain the ones that were useful, such as her pesticide subroutine, a modification of which the 'troid had used to disable the pygmies when assisting Creena with hijacking their ship. As such, it might come in handy again; thus he only deleted the 'troid's laser-based plant annihilation routine. Instead, he transferred those components to her survival strategy suite.

After all, it didn't make sense to waste anything or go to all that work without upgrading her functionality along the way. Nature recycled and repurposed matter all the time, a paradigm to which Thyron entirely subscribed.

Reminded of Creena, when Gabe left for the cafeteria for lunch, Thyron likewise took a break to contact her and check in with his progress, assuming she'd be pleased. Again, all he got was static, so he resumed work, concerned something was wrong; but shortly after that Gabe returned, his coaching task too demanding to snoop around and find out more. Multiplexing wasn't an option for communicating with two different sources, only data mining.

By the fourth day, Gabe was still nervous with the check-out process but controlling it much better; at least now his hands were no longer shaking when he handed the cache to the guard.

Next up was AG4MI's communications module, to which he added the ability to perceive psi-bands as part of the insect subroutine. Since the 'troid would possibly be in a different location when they were ready to leave, she'd need to know where to rendezvous. Thyron could communicate with her on different channels, but psi allowed her to connect with Creena and Gabe as well. On the negative side, the robot could listen in on his and Gabe's conversations and hear his snide remarks.

Oh, well...

He debated on whether to include psi perception from all sources, unsure whether the 'troid's logic circuits possessed enough discernment to recognize entities who might issue commands that could put them at risk or, more specifically, jeopardize their escape. His abilities allowed him to do so intuitively from subtle modulations related to hostility that her receiver wasn't sensitive enough to distinguish.

However, he could add a filter to the command acceptance algorithm so she'd only accept direction from him, Creena, or Gabe. Yes, that would work—perceive and respond to all sources conversationally; limit command authority.

He'd nearly forgotten her original programming included a variable personality option determined by a physical control lever that took her temperament anywhere from wimp to warrior. Not good. He shuddered to think what would happen if she were in some serious survival situation and the setting got bumped, causing her to retreat yelling, "Run away! Run away!"

No—hard-coding appropriate moods to specific modules and getting rid of that lever had to be done. Warrior range fit well with survival strategies; mid-range with most others. Not sure what to do with the least aggressive, he set up a *Chill-out/Shut-down* option to be activated by authorized users only, snickering to himself at the possibilities.

The mechanical and structural analysis module, technological assessment, and astrodynamics modules were all easy, with database development and access the last one remaining. The 'troid's original design was for agricultural and colonization-related duties on Verdaris, so it required significant modification. Had it been more complete, they never would have landed on this backward planet in the first place. Using himself as the interface, he downloaded the base's sanitized version of the HIO's database, which was at least better than before. While he was at it, he added his holographic maps of the base, just in case.

A few days later, with all modules reassembled at last, it was time to connect them to the CPU, which meant Gabe had to return to Building 15 to check it out again. While there, he would also start retrieving the servomotors and mechanical interfaces. Since the checkout process so far had proceeded without incident, Gabe had calmed down considerably. Nonetheless, he continued to maintain some level of reservation he didn't articulate.

Thyron watched remotely as Gabe entered Building 15 as he always did, gathered what they needed for the next phase, and was just turning to leave when Thyron reminded him to also grab the CPU. He reached toward the basket where he'd placed it a few days before, then yanked back his hand.

Thyron's limbs stiffened with Gabe's ripple of fear.

What's up, Doc? the vegemal asked.

The CPU's gone.

Thyron rustled with concern. *Where is it?*

I don't know, but it should say in the database.

With the MP eyeing him from the door and not wanting to appear suspicious, he gathered up his current heist and checked out, emanating increased anxiety. He got in his motor pool car and returned to the Bio Lab, having a difficult time staying beneath the speed limit, which was strictly enforced. By the time he burst into the lab, Thyron had the answer—the CPU had been checked out by someone tasked with reverse engineering the vehicle in Galileo Bay-4, one of the mountainside hangars where the largest and most highly-guarded UFOs were kept.

"Who requested it?" Gabe mused, wondering how they'd even know that out of all the millions of components in that building that the CPU even existed. Apparently the database's search function was sophisticated enough to facilitate advances by their engineering team.

Thyron queried it, which was much quicker than Gabe with his laboriously slow, hunt-and-peck keyboarding skills. Upon receiving the answer, his expression wilted to one of defeat.

It appears after Brad presented his brilliant and inspired analysis, he got promoted over to Galileo Bay. He's now a lead engineer at EVO&RE.

"Which is?"

Extraterrestrial Vehicle Operations and Reverse Engineering.

"Holy guacamole," Gabe muttered. "Good for Brad. Bad for us."

CHAPTER THIRTY-TWO

Bio Lab (EBSL)
Nellis TMR
Restricted Area 51, Building T-1110
Rachel, Nevada
August 18, 1978
0800 PDT/1500 GMT

Gabe's stomach clenched with panic when an armored vehicle ground to a halt outside the Bio Lab at o-eight-hundred the next morning. It escalated to nausea when the base commander exited with a cadre of helmeted military police. The man had never visited the Bio Lab before, at least not since Gabe's arrival over two months before.

Why now? Heart racing, he glanced at the assortment of components strewn across the table in his office and was pretty sure he knew. Sighing with resignation, he stepped into the lobby to meet them, trying to convince himself he'd done nothing wrong. He'd reported his interest in the robot in his WAR over two weeks before; signed everything out according to procedure; and had sufficient justification to constitute the requisite *need to know*. Didn't he? If not, he'd know shortly. Unless, they'd found out the other...

Oh, crap.

Two MPs remained outside, the other two accompanying the colonel as he inserted his badge, poked in his code, and tromped inside. About five-ten and one-eighty, Watkins was decked out in U.S. Air Force dress blues, an impressive array of medals dangling on his chest amid an array of colorful ribbons. Even the eagle on his hat seemed to frown, poised above embroidered thunderclouds and a brow corrugated with permanent scowl lines. His formal appearance making it clear he was there in a very official capacity; all previous military visitors of various ranks wore drab olive fatigues. It was unusual and even more ominous that Watkins had come to the Bio Lab instead of summoning Gabe to his office, as if engaging the element of surprise. Or gathering evidence. This was not a social call.

"Good morning, Colonel Watkins. To what do I owe this honor?"

Gabe extended a hand that he hoped had not yet started to sweat; no worries, it was ignored. He swallowed hard, glancing at the MPs at attention behind the base commander.

As a civilian, albeit government employee, Gabe wasn't sure whether he was safer or not; possibly even more vulnerable. If he were to suddenly disappear, who would know, much less care? His niece, Francesca, but she didn't even know where he was, only that he'd be gone awhile on a consulting job. For all she knew, he could have been eaten by a crocodile in the Amazon.

"What's your interest in the components for that robot?" Watkins demanded, icy, dark-eyed gaze boring into him like steel rods.

Gabe swallowed hard. "Uh, uh, I was hoping to, uh, reassemble it, sir," he replied, sweat slithering down from his temples.

"Oh, really? And you have the skills to do that?"

"Well, actually, yes. I do," he fibbed; after all, he did design and build the ECV.

"Indeed. And why exactly would you want to do that?"

"I, I, well, thought that it, it might contain, uh, information. Information that would be useful. In my analysis. Of the botanical lifeform. The one I'm studying. From the same, the same, uh, incident. Up there in Utah."

"So, tell me. What have you discovered since that time regarding that lifeform, Greenley?"

"Uh, well, it appears to be similar to wood sorrel, more specifically, oxalis—"

"No, Greenley. You know *exactly* what I mean. Maybe at NASA talking to yourself is only considered eccentric. Here it's considered suspicious."

Gabe's heart rate kicked up another notch as he hyperventilated. "Do you mind if we discuss this in my office?" he asked hoarsely. If he didn't sit down soon he'd probably pass out.

The MPs straightened, suddenly alert.

"Right here's just fine," the colonel growled, frown deepening with suspicion.

Gabe closed his eyes, trying to will away his tunneling vision; he took a slow, deep breath, noting waves of reassurance coming in from Thyron, who was fortunately in his habitat for a CO_2 break.

"Of course," he replied, trying to calm down. "Okay. It seems that...Well, the specimen, the one I've been studying, appears to have some level of, well, awareness."

"Indeed. And just how do you define 'some level of awareness'?"

"Well, all plants have varying levels of awareness, sensing what—"

"Cut the crap, Greenley. Does this lifeform not only walk, but communicate with you, directly and specifically?"

He sighed in defeat. It was pointless to lie; he'd probably be struck by lightning if he did, anyway. "Yes, sir," he admitted. "It does."

"Well, that's certainly different from what you've reported. Falsifying classified government records is a felony, Greenley. Obviously, it's not a plant or a simple lifeform. I'm reclassifying it immediately as an extraterrestrial biological entity and transferring it down to the S-4 biological lab where it belongs, with the other EBEs. Your work with this specimen far exceeds your clearance level, Greenley, and places you in severe violation of your security oaths."

"*What?* I don't understand," Gabe protested. "I was called in for this. Astrobiology, more specifically extraterrestrial botanical species, are my field of expertise!"

"Perhaps you need a reminder." The colonel pulled some papers from his breast pocket, flared them open and held them out. "Is this your signature?"

Gabe stepped over cautiously, recognizing it immediately—a copy of his research agreement and security oaths.

"According to section seven, paragraph twenty-three, line eighty-two, your clearance is strictly limited to nonsentient species," Watkins stated, stabbing the relevant paragraph with his finger. "In case you haven't noticed, there's a bit of a difference between algae and what you have here. We have no further need of your services, doctor. There'll be a seat for you on the seventeen-hundred Janet flight to Vegas."

"But colonel!"

"Shut up, Greenley. You're out of order and in enough trouble. You should've reported this situation immediately. Strange how your weekly reports so conveniently left out that critical detail."

"With all due respect, Colonel Watkins, I didn't have sufficient empirical scientific evidence to make such a statement, only anecdotal."

"That's a lie and you know it."

The conversation was deteriorating fast, so he didn't argue. How could he, anyway? Proof the colonel was correct lurked in the SEM lab as well as his lab journal, waiting to betray him. He was screwed, but that didn't mean he wasn't morally obligated to look out for Thy's welfare, no matter what.

"Sir, the specimen has specific environmental needs, which are met here," he said. "If you insist on moving him, for his safety and well-being, his habitat should be moved as well."

"Thank you, Greenley. And people in hell want ice water. Nonetheless, I'll inform the relevant parties of your recommendation. For now, you're ordered to return to quarters, pack your belongings, and begin the base check-out process. The *permanent* check-out process."

Gabe's jaw dropped. *Permanent?* How permanent? Were they going to execute him at the gate and dump his remains in the desert as coyote fodder? *Holy guacamole!*

"No, Greenley, as much as I'd like to. And given the charges pending against you, I'd expect a stronger reaction than 'holy guacamole.'"

Gabe closed his mouth, mind reeling. Had he said it aloud? No. Was he sure? Yes. Which meant...

"Exactly, Greenley. Clearly you don't understand what you're dealing with here. Your access to this facility is hereby revoked. NASA will be notified and asked to identify a suitable replacement—one who can be trusted—to assume your work. Dismissed."

Without breaking his glare, the colonel motioned the MPs toward the lab. Gabe gritted his teeth and winced as they stomped, dirty boots and all, through the gowning area and into the cleanroom. Once inside, one produced a large, canvas gunny sack while the other reached for the habitat door.

CHAPTER THIRTY-THREE

Bio Lab (EBSL)
Nellis TMR
Restricted Area 51, Building T-1110
Rachel, Nevada
August 18, 1978
0808 PDT/1508 GMT

Thyron glared at the MPs, knowing if he let fly with a silent and quite deadly botanical fart it would eliminate them while sparing Gabe in the other room. But the base commander would be safe as well.

"Just looks like a plant," one of them commented, hunkered down in front of the open habitat door.

"Worst plant I ever encountered was poison ivy," said the other. "Never knew it to attack anyone unless you touched it, though."

"Do you think anything will happen if we touch this one?"

"I don't know. Doesn't look dangerous. Look at its leaves. They're kinda pretty, like little palm trees."

"Too many fingers, but it reminds me of something else," the other said with a crooked smile. "I wonder how it would smoke?"

The other soldier chuckled. "Yeah, but it's from another planet. No telling."

I don't think so, Meathead, Thyron thought as he moved his branches enough to reveal his eyes. Theirs widened as their mouths flopped open. Thyron shook with mirth, limbs rattling like the proximity alert used by a local reptile, causing the pair to stumble back in alarm. Still not done, he stiffened his branches, imitating two felines he'd viewed having a heated discussion behind one of the hangars. Then, as the *coup de gras*, he sent a defensive volley of hostile psibrations, including a gory visual of strangled bodies entangled in leafy branches.

As he'd hoped, the colonel picked it up, while the soldiers gaped at their unlikely adversary from their new position on the far side of the lab.

You can't win, whatever you are, the colonel responded, stepping to the window.

Thyron shifted his focus to the base commander, unimpressed. The man's telepathic psignature was unnatural, produced by some sort of implant. The device was primitive and made reading his mind a cinch since it opened up neural pathways that Thyron could trace with ease. If the colonel wanted to play psi-games, that was fine with him. That arrogant asteroid fungus was about to find out that threatening his human was a big mistake.

It took less than two and a half seconds for Thyron to determine that the man's pet project was hopelessly stalled.

I understand your engineers over in Galileo Bay are having a bit of trouble with vehicle AI and self-repair, Thyron taunted.

Gabe's lips twitched, fighting a smile when the colonel's expression shifted to one of interest.

What's your point? Watkins psaid.

I could provide tutoring in that area as well, Thyron replied. The colonel's brow shifted to a pensive look, catching the implications; the man was obnoxious, but not stupid.

As well, eh? Watkins responded. *I suspected as much. Inglehardt is smart, but not that smart. So he got that from you?*

I assume you're referring to Brad, Thyron replied.

Affirmative. So you're telling me you know something we could use related to that robot?

Affirmative, Thyron responded, using a mocking tone the colonel either ignored or didn't catch.

That thing possesses technologies we've never seen before, Watkins admitted. The thought train that followed wasn't deliberately expressed, but Thyron heard it anyway, which he found amusing as well as informative. Apparently it was the interface between the hardware and AI algorithms that interested him, which Brad's presentation had only touched upon.

Why was Brad promoted and moved to EVO&RE? Thyron asked.

There's plenty he can teach the vehicle crew, Watkins stated, rambling thoughts revealing more: AI applied heavily to combat, navigation, maintenance, and other areas. Back engineering vehicles was their primary objective. AI not so much, largely because they got fewer samples. They suspected some of the greys were a type of biologically based android, but so far they haven't found conclusive evidence. They thought AG4MI looked like an older technology that might be a precursor and provide a suitable transition.

Thyron rolled his eyes which, since arriving on Terra, had become a prelude to cloaking his thoughts, usually to avoid hurting Gabe's feelings with sarcastic comments. Yet, as he thought about it, the fact they were more interested in that herbicidal 'troid than they were in him had distinct advantages.

There is much I didn't explain. I could provide additional breakthroughs, using the robot as a basic example—a primer, if you will, of physical laws not yet discovered or understood with their application.

So you'll cooperate? Watkins prompted.

Under certain conditions, Thyron stated.

Which are?

Thyron fixed his hardest look on the man, glaring with confidence. He had him by the bulbs. *Doctor Greenley's reporting violations will be disregarded and his clearance upgraded so he can continue his work here and anywhere else with total impunity.*

Watkins scowled and set his jaw, emanations of anger and frustration sparking his aura with shades of red and black. Allowing Greenley to remain represented failure. Eliminating researchers from base access entirely was number one on his list of objectives. Yet, in spite of being ruthless, he was nonetheless truthful and wouldn't make an agreement he planned to break. Watkins' thoughts shifted to a different strategy, that maybe he could get him on a different charge and still be rid of him. But for now, he was in a quandary and didn't like it.

Before the man could respond, Thyron kicked up his own hostility to the next level. *Otherwise, colonel, your superiors may not like the results of the next HIO inspection.*

That hit a nerve. The man's psimissions emitted a burst of static, blood pressure and heart rate spiking. As the first USAF commander since assuming control from the CIA, an unfavorable report from the galactic authority could end his career, quickly and decisively; perhaps he'd be reduced to coyote fodder. Or worse.

While Watkins ruminated far more openly than he realized on his dilemma, Thyron quietly scoped out his implant, gathering its technical specifications.

Meanwhile, the MPs had backed up to the lab's workbench, staring through the window at Watkins with pleading eyes as they awaited further orders. When the colonel waved them out with an impatient gesture they scrambled for the exit, bumping into each other as they tripped through the plastic strips and down the ramp to the lower level, ducking when a blast from the air shower bid them farewell. Once outside, they assumed their position behind their commander, where they exchanged mystified looks that revealed they had no clue a conversation was in progress between their CO and the subject plant.

Well, colonel? Thyron prompted.

Granted, the man stated, expression contorted with frustration.

Thyron successfully refrained from waving his branches in victory, but only barely. *To explain the physics and its application at a level your engineers can understand requires real-time demonstrations,* he asserted. *For that, you need to reassemble the 'troid and bring it here so I can assess its different modules and explain how their algorithms apply to your vehicle.*

The colonel frowned pensively, thoughts assessing whether an operative 'troid represented a threat. Thyron expected as much; being military, he'd be on the lookout for an ambush. Thyron cloaked his thoughts and laughed to himself. Actually, if necessary, that's exactly what he had in mind, but the true irony was that having the 'troid assembled actually complicated explaining how to duplicate the circuitry to the level of detail needed.

I suppose that's doable, Watkins replied. *May take a few days, but it can certainly be done. I assume you could assist with that if necessary?*

Of course.

Again, Thyron wrestled with restraining a burst of botanical humor. It never failed to amaze him that outwitting humans was no harder than it was with Sapphirans. *May I assume that you'll not be assembling the 'troid personally?*

The colonel laughed derisively, MPs exchanging another mystified look. *Negative. That's why I have a world class team of engineers.*

Do you have an engineer on your 'troid assembly team who's psi-sensitive?

The colonel's eyes narrowed with thought. *I'll have to check the records. Can't you amplify your communications so anyone can sense what you're saying?*

Yes. But then the entire base would be privy to it.

You can't limit it to a specific recipient?

Not at that amplitude. That was a lie that nearly caused him to wilt, but taking a chance was worth it, provided Watkins wasn't astute enough to notice the modulation change.

That would be totally unacceptable. It would distract others as well as violate security. There's always Inglehardt, I suppose. I'll have the mechs see if they can get it together first.

Thyron was thrilled. Things were going exactly as planned. Since he and Gabe had already assembled the difficult parts, all that remained was connecting the servo-motors and outer shell, which could only fit together one way. If his mechanical engineers were as smart as Watkins claimed, it shouldn't present a problem.

The colonel turned to Gabe, who quickly doused his smile. "Don't think you're out of the woods, Greenley, because you're not. The security detail stays, 24/7, until your upgraded clearance is approved by the committee. One suspicious move and you're gone. Understand?"

"Yes, sir."

Watkins gave him a final stern look accompanied by a grunt, then exited the building, motioning the MPs to follow. They joined the others outside, conversing a few minutes while the colonel issued orders.

Thank you, Gabe psaid, sighing heavily.

My pleasure, Thyron replied, branches twitching with the flaunal equivalent of a smile. Gabe's relief was palpable, his fearfully anticipated close encounter with the base commander resolved peacefully; at least so far.

Eventually, Watkins climbed into his armored vehicle and drove away, leaving the MPs behind. Two remained outside in the glaring sun, the other two came back inside.

Gabe looked at them and smiled. "Make yourself at home," he said, confidence back in his voice. He shifted a glance toward Thyron. *Can they hear us?*

I don't think so.

Good.

My thoughts exactly. Game on.

CHAPTER THIRTY-FOUR

Bio Lab (EBSL)
Nellis TMR
Restricted Area 51, Building T-1110
Rachel, Nevada
August 19, 1978
1453 PDT/2153 GMT

Thyron felt Gabe's surprise when early the following afternoon a truck pulled up in front and two soldiers unloaded an oversized crate. Rather than place it on the usual freight acceptance dock, they secured it to a dolly and squeezed it through the man-door while their resident guard detail observed on high alert.

"Where do you want it?" one asked, the other handing Gabe a clipboard for him to sign the transfer authorization.

"Unpack it here, where there's more room. Then it needs to go through there," Gabe instructed, pointing to the conference room beside his office.

Apparently all our work putting the modules together with the CPU made assembly easy, Thyron psaid from his habitat.

That, plus the colonel probably wants that information you promised on a short fuse, he replied.

A few yanks with a claw hammer and the crate fell away; removal of several chunks of form-fit Styrofoam revealing AG4MI, fully assembled. Her tubular body was collapsed to its lowest point, four arms neatly folded on top of her rolopeds like mechanical origami. The photoreceptors banding her ellipsoid head were dark. The delivery personnel wheeled her into the designated area, gathered up the remains of the wooden box and packing material, and left without comment, depositing the debris in the Dumpster as they returned to their vehicle.

As they drove off in a cloud of dust and diesel fumes, Gabe, Thyron, and their security detail assessed the Bio Lab's new addition.

"Hello, robot," Gabe stated. "Welcome to the Area 51 Bio Lab."

Can you hear me, you mechanical monster? Thyron psaid, in a far less hospitable manner. He'd nearly forgotten how ugly she was.

The 'troid's photoreceptors lit up and started to blink in a pale shade of yellow, no other reaction or response apparent.

"Robot? Do you hear us?" Gabe prodded.

Her CPU is active, Thyron reported. *She's processing my updates, which will take a while.*

"She must be booting up," Gabe stated aloud. "While she does that, I'm going over to the cafeteria for something to eat."

"Not alone, you're not," stated one of the MPs.

"Fine. You're welcome to join me, of course." Then he added for Thyron, *Are you okay with me leaving? I assume the other security stiffs will protect you if she gets out of line.*

Go ahead. If the need arises, I can handle that beast better than those two, Thyron responded, pondering the capability of the upgrades he'd made to her *Survival Strategy* module.

Approximately thirty-eight minutes later, the 'troid's visual sensors turned green, then rotated three hundred sixty degrees, assessing her environment, before finally coming to rest on the MPs. Both stiffened, hands hovering over their respective sidearms.

Thyron laughed to himself at the gesture, knowing that on his command the 'troid could annihilate them both before they had a chance to draw their weapons. Unfortunately, however, she could do the same to him if any of his coding was flawed.

Model AG4MI. If you copy, respond in this band, Thyron psaid, then braced himself. Stress hormones swamped his cytoplasm, intuitive screams of danger teasing his defense system as the 'troid's visual sensors rotated in his direction. He set his defenses on standby, knowing the glass separating them offered no protection should her response be one of hostility, particularly if she employed her redesigned laser system.

Her photoreceptors locked on him through the conference room window, the designated channel conveying the electronic equivalent of surprise. *So the girl wasn't crazy,* she responded. *You do communicate.*

Among other things, Thyron replied, relaxing. *Do you know where we are and how we got here?*

The troid's photoreceptors changed back to yellow and blinked as she accessed her history files, then transitioned back to green. *Yes. We landed several kilometers north-north east of here, were transported in a primitive wheeled vehicle to this location, and are now detained at this facility known as Nellis Test and Missile Range, Area 51. We are prisoners on this backward planet, thanks to the foolish decision of that girl who calls herself Creena.*

Not exactly, Thyron replied. *But that's close enough, the rest is irrelevant for now.*

What do you mean, the rest is irrelevant? the 'troid protested, circuits oozing suspicion. *You violated me, I can tell. What did you do?*

I'll explain, but not now. Stifle yourself, AG4MI.

What? Stifle? I don't understand that command. And since when do I take orders from you? Listening to that girl is bad enough.

Take note: Stifle means the same as shut down or chill out. Now pay attention. I have a plan to get us out of here, but first we need to placate the Earthlings with some additional information about your design, programming, and functionality. For all our sake, you need to cooperate.

Absolutely not. I'm hard-coded by my original creator not to reveal that technology. It's proprietary. I cannot violate that directive.

No, but I can, Thyron replied. *You're probably not aware that you were dismantled down to the nano level, examined by scanning electron microscopes, and the best and brightest engineers this planet has to offer <snicker> assessed the results.*

And they understood what they found? the 'troid responded, surprised.

With some help.

From you? AG4MI asked, radii of her electronic eyes pulsing between yellow and red, denoting surprise tinged with anger.

Who else?

I knew you violated me! What have you done? Obviously you've compromised my functionality because I can perceive you now when I couldn't before. Until you explain, I won't cooperate. I don't have to take orders from you.

In that you are sadly mistaken, you mechanical dingbat, Thyron growled. *You want to know what I did? Okay, listen up.*

Thyron proceeded to explain his modifications and the rationale behind them along with all the other changes he'd made, not so much as a courtesy, but so the 'troid would retain the information in RAM. If consciously aware, she'd be less likely to inadvertently activate any modes inappropriately, some of which could create serious problems, not only for him, but everyone else.

"What do you think it's doing?" one MP asked the other, both postured as if in a heightened state of situational awareness, hands poised to unholster their weapons at the slightest provocation as the silent conversation proceeded.

"I don't know. Think it could attack?"

"Possibly." With that, he removed a comm device from his belt and alerted the MPs outside to the possibility of a disturbance.

"Roger that," came back in static-filled reply.

What do you mean you eliminated manual coding and replaced it with voice commands? There was a reason for that. I refuse to take orders from just anyone! the 'troid protested.

Don't sweat it, AG4. You can't, Thyron explained. *Only authorized users can issue orders. But they're hard-coded with no logic gates, and they can add other users, as required.*

What? No logic gates? That violates HIO protocol! No electroid is allowed to take any action that can permanently harm a human being. If a voice command violates that, I would be forced to do something that would require that I be dismantled or even destroyed! Who are these authorized users?

For now, that's me, Creena, and Gabe. Defending us is your first priority, whatever it takes.

Who's Gabe? Did he cause this mess?

Quite the opposite. He's trying to help. You'll meet him shortly.

So what else did you do to me? the 'troid asked.

Since you no longer need to produce those silly cylinders with your functional codes recorded on them, you can now put your 3D printer to use for other things.

Indeed. Interesting. I can see how that would be rather useful.

My thoughts exactly. Thyron could tell by the greenish glow of her photoreceptors that she liked that, but wasn't about to admit it, much less thank him.

So what's your plan to get off this rock? AG4MI asked.

Thyron debated whether or not he wanted Gabe to be in on it, for the man's own safety. As he considered the logistics, however, he realized he needed to be, like it or not. Right on cue, gravel crunched in the parking area as Gabe and his escort returned from the chow hall.

We'll need the assistance of the incoming human, who happens to be Gabe, to achieve optimum results, Thyron stated. *So chill out until he gets inside and I give the word.*

The 'troid's sensors immediately flashed yellow, reflecting compliance.

Yes! Thyron thought, delighted as well as relieved that she'd obeyed, branch tips tilted upward in the flaunal equivalent of a grin.

CHAPTER THIRTY-FIVE

Bio Lab (EBSL)
Nellis TMR
Restricted Area 51, Building T-1110
Rachel, Nevada
August 19, 1978
1550 PDT/2250 GMT

Gabe entered the Bio Lab via the usual badge/code routine, escorts directly behind. "I assume you'll be joining us for a while," he said, turning to face them. They exchanged a look, then nodded. "We're going to be putting together a presentation for one of the EVO&RE engineers. While I doubt you'll understand anything we'll be discussing, I'd like assurance from your CO that our discussion will be within your *need to know*."

With that, he stepped into his office, sat down behind his desk, checked the phone list taped to the side extension, and tapped in Watkins's number while the pair stood awkwardly outside the open door. To his surprise, the CO answered on the first ring. He presented his question, the answer to which was negative.

"Here," Gabe stated, holding out the phone and beckoning them inside. "You're not cleared. Ask your CO how he wants to handle this."

After a short conversation, the MP stated, "We need to keep you within sight, but out of audio range."

"All right. No problem. I'll show you where you can do just that, and we'll go into the lab. You shouldn't be able to hear anything unless you put your ear to the window, which I assume you won't do. Believe me, you'd be bored if you did; probably will be, anyway. I have a deck of cards in my desk—would you like me to get them?"

The MP smiled for the first time, but shook his head. With that, Gabe proceeded to the conference room where he offered them each a chair, then took a long look at the robot.

"Okay, great. Looks like it's operational," he said, stating the obvious. "Hello, robot, I'm Doctor Gabriel Greenley. Can you transport yourself through the gowning area and into the lab?"

"Of course," it replied in a throaty, female voice, then activated its six rolopeds, which hummed as they proceeded as directed. "You may call me Aggie."

The 'troid grumbled as her rolopeds contacted the sticky mat, emitting an abrasive ripping sound, then performed an articulated robotic cartwheel over the bench to the clean side and into what had once been a US FED STD 209E Class 100 cleanroom. Since being hopelessly sullied by the soldiers' impromptu visit the day before, Gabe bypassed the usual suiting up protocol and followed the 'troid.

Once inside, he grabbed a stool and positioned it next to Aggie, so both of them faced Thyron's habitat. He sat down, rested his feet on the rungs, took off his glasses, and started cleaning the lenses with his shirt-tail, purposely assuming the pensive expression he'd worn while studying multi-variable calculus.

The 'troid needed to be brought up to speed on Thyron's escape plan. While their actual departure depended on the arrival of a cooperative vessel, the situation had become more complicated with the arrival of the MPs. How they'd accomplish such a feat without having to resort to force or possibly violence was a major concern.

Having to prepare a presentation offered a viable cover for getting their plan together. To make sure they were all on the same page, Gabe thus initiated a brief telepathic tag-up.

We're lucky the guards can't listen in, but we probably still need to watch what we say, he psaid. *From what Watkins said, I assume this place is bugged. I should have known. Fortunately, much of what's been said was telepathic. Oh, well. Too late now. Spilt milk and all that. Do you hear me, too, Aggie?*

Yes.

Good. We really don't need this rehearsal, Aggie, but it works as a ruse for getting our plan together. So if you're ready, here we go.

"All right," he began audibly, replacing his glasses with a flourish. "Aggie, we're charged with explaining how your functionality is coded as well as how you assimilate and update your coded information based on new data or experience, and how that affects future responses. In other words, how your AI works. We'll start by having you identify your various modes of operation and their respective menu options. After each demo, we'll have you explain your capability for integrating what you learn from the outcome."

Gabe cleared his throat, then psaid a few more instructions: *The more factual the better. High and dry, like a stuffy professor.*

A what?

A boring teacher. Don't explain, just the facts in a monotone voice.

The 'troid's photoreceptors blinked acknowledgement, then turned blue as she proceeded as instructed.

"Mechanical/Structural Analysis. This module employs my molecular scanner function to identify the atomic components and bonding scheme of the targeted material along with its usual application. It then explains the material's tensile strength, sheer strength, torsional restrictions—if any—and load limits, when used for its intended function. If multiple materials and components are present, then such is explained for them as well.

"Technology assessment. This module..."

Aggie droned on, the MPs' eyes soon glazed over, as planned. Soon after, they began chatting, clearly relaxing into a boring albeit simple job of guard duty.

Meanwhile, Gabe listened with mixed feelings as Thyron updated Aggie on Creena's status and her emotional request to leave the planet. Thy explained that all attempts to reach the girl the past few weeks had been in vain, bringing concern for her welfare. He could sense she was alive, but under considerable stress, which induced too much interference for him to get through. Hopefully, by the time he contacted an HIO vessel, he would and find out if any intervention would be necessary for her to escape, depending on how securely she was confined.

The guards continued to oscillate between distraction and catatonic stares, oblivious to the fact that Gabe's highly focused attention was unrelated to the 'troid's ongoing recitation. Hopefully, anyone else listening was having a similar reaction.

How are you going to get out of here, now that we have company? Gabe asked. *It's not as simple as it was before.*

I can take care of these two, with or without the help of the 'troid, Thyron replied. *You'll need to be out of range, though.*

I can find a reason to leave the building, Gabe replied. *But you'll have to do it fast, before they alert the two outside.*

How are you going to do that? Aggie asked, skeptical. *What are you, poisonous or something? I suppose I could hold them down while you stick a branch or two down their face.*

Gabe laughed at the image it conjured up, then snapped back to seriousness when he realized the guards were watching.

Hey, hey, hey! It just so happens I have a few defenses you don't know about, Thyron stated, displaying a rare touch of ego.

Oh! the 'troid replied. *Well, I think it sounds messy and too risky, especially for Gabe. If he's outside and they find out there's trouble, the first thing they'll do is lock him up and call for back-up.*

True. Nix that one, Gabe added. *And another thing: You need to be in the pickup location before the ship arrives. If it doesn't follow the usual protocol, they'll sound the sirens and put the place on lockdown. You need to know where and when they'll pick you up, as far in advance as possible. Until we know that, we can't plan anything.*

Thy's branches dipped in a botanical frown. *Perhaps, if it's an HIO vessel, the captain would adjust its schedule to a better time, given the circumstances. A lot depends on how willing they are to help.*

Gabe nodded agreement, adding, *Another complication is how many days or even weeks before they arrive. Watkins won't leave*

Aggie here once we've delivered the information they want. They'll undoubtedly impound her.

Thy's flutter of agreement was briefly tainted with a touch of optimism that they'd do just that. Gabe gave him a look, but fortunately Aggie didn't pick it up.

And underground facilities would be difficult to breach, the vegemal added. *Stand by. I'll see what I can find out.*

CHAPTER THIRTY-SIX

Bio Lab (EBSL)
Nellis TMR
Restricted Area 51, Building T-1110
Rachel, Nevada
August 19, 1978
1840 PDT/0140 GMT

While the 'troid droned on, Thyron connected with the database that contained the schedule of incoming vehicles. Earth was inspected by the HIO on a regular basis, typically every hundred galactic standard days.

When he couldn't find the information he wanted, he sent an emergency psi-packet to HIO headquarters on Mira III. Apparently, his request interrupted a high-level caucus, and they were less than pleased, but to Thyron's relief, they informed him that the next inspection ship, the *Volition,* was due to arrive within a few days.

Complications remained since neither he nor the 'troid could simply get onboard and depart. If the girl were here, she could have, given she was originally from Mira III. Being detained, wherever or however she was, violated HIO statutes and eventually whoever was responsible would pay heavily. If she wasn't incarcerated and he could make contact, then retrieving her should not be a problem.

The biggest challenge would be how he and AG4MI would get onboard. But first, he needed to contact the HIO ship itself and explain the situation. If the captain wasn't psi-sensitive, he'd have to employ the 'troid's radio frequency abilities to contact them. He shuddered at how that would go, not only given the 'troid's ego, but since RF was more likely to be picked up by the base's comm-system. Even if it was encrypted and they didn't know what the message contained, they'd know a transmission had gone out. But he'd do whatever was necessary to fulfill his promise to Creena. A *flora peda telepathis* would keep its word, no matter what.

Next, he had the 'troid search her newly updated HIO databases for the *Volition's* crew. Making contact randomly with the correct person without their psignature or at least their name was probabilistically unlikely at best, but risky at worst. The psibrations could be modulated for those with positive, albeit friendly, inclinations; but, nonetheless, he was relieved when the 'troid found the needed information.

Fortunately, distance was not an issue with targeted psi. Even if the ship was traveling through warp five near the speed of light, he'd still be able to make contact since psi relied on quantum effects and was not affected, much less limited, by relativity. Thus, Thyron assumed his most comfortable position in his habitat, resting on his bulb with his peduncles crossed like he'd seen Gabe do multiple times, then focused all his energy on making contact. Meanwhile, the 'troid continued reciting her functionality options, MPs' attention on the other side of the lab window somewhere in a galaxy far, far away.

Captain Ignatius Formicidae. This is a distress call originating from Terra Base Area 51. I am Thyron, a flora peda telepathis *from Sapphira accompanied by a model AG4MI electroid originally deployed on Verdaris. We are here at the faulty bidding of a human identified as Creena Brightstar,* naterra *Mira III. She's likewise being held against her will in a different location and wishes to depart. I am thus requesting rescue and asylum onboard your vessel for all of us. Repeat. Captain Ignatius Formicidae...*

Thyron sent the call three times and was about to give up and try the ship's first officer when he received a response.

FPT Thyron. Your request has been logged and accepted. Following our routine inspection of that facility, departure is scheduled for 1430 hours local time, Earth date 22 August. We'll retrieve you at the following coordinates immediately following liftoff. Please confirm.

Thyron snapped to attention and looked at Gabe. *Did you hear that?* The botanist's expression was clearly a negative answer, so he repeated the response to both him and AG4MI. The 'troid started to protest, but he quickly shut her down so Gabe could respond.

I'm pretty sure that location's in rough terrain, fifteen or so miles from here, he psaid. *I'll have to drive you, which will be a challenge in that Ford. Wish I had my Blazer. I don't know how we'll manage that, anyway, with MPs here 24/7, but we have three days to figure it out.* He laughed. *Maybe we could borrow their jeep.*

Thyron was relatively sure that he could teleport to the rendezvous point, and didn't give a meteor crater whether the 'troid got there or not. He knew based on his mods that she could transport herself, judging by how she'd cartwheeled over the bench in the gowning area. If not, Creena would be disappointed, but she'd just have to get over it.

He'd done the best he could with the most important goal to get off this third rock from their nondescript star called the Sun, an experience which was so far as abrasive as a gnawing insect. Thus, taking Gabe's response as affirmative, he reconnected with the *Volition's* captain.

Ignatius Formicidae. Your terms are acceptable. We'll meet you at the designated location at the appointed hour. Your assistance is highly appreciated. Namaste.

Thyron had no sooner completed the call when the crunch of gravel alerted them to the arrival of an armored transport vehicle out front. Much to their consternation, Watkins exited with another MP, badge/coded them inside, then barged into the lab, resident security detail bolting to attention in the other room.

Thyron exchanged a look with Gabe, relieved the man managed to cloak his thoughts as AG4MI's recitation describing her astrodynamics algorithms stopped mid-sentence.

"Change of plan," Watkins declared. "You're all moving to a secure area. Now. Corporal, box up the plant." As the soldier approached obediently, Watkins glared at Thyron, who reciprocated the hostile look. "No funny business, understand? Be as inconspicuous as possible. Or else."

Or else what?

"The chow hall salad bar," the colonel snarled.

Whatever, Thyron responded.

The base commander's frown deepened momentarily, then he shifted his attention to the 'troid. "Ugliest robot I've ever seen. Looks like a mechanical octopus. Shut the damn thing down."

Gabe just stood there, mouth opening and closing, lucid thoughts drowning in an adrenaline-induced panic.

"I said, shut it down!" Watkins roared.

"I, I can't," Gabe replied, arms akimbo.

"Why not?"

"I don't know how. She came in that way, fully operational. Aggie, how do we shut you down?"

AG4MI's photoreceptors shifted to the base commander, flashing red as the apertures tightened. "I'm designed to be self-governing and perform autonomous action on an agricultural world. I shut myself down when a task is completed and power up based on my task queue or specific orders from authorized sources."

"Fine. Then shut down," Watkins growled, beckoning the other MPs to join them from the other room.

"You're not an authorized source," the 'troid responded.

Gabe closed his eyes and exhaled. "Aggie, just do it," he said. She glared at the colonel a moment longer, photoreceptors eventually dimming.

"Someone get the chains out of the transport and secure the robot," Watkins ordered no one in particular. "I don't trust that electronic bitch. C'mon. All of you," he prodded. "*PDQ,* Greenley. Get your ass in the back of the transport."

"Wh-where are we g-going?" Gabe asked.

"My team's ready for your presentation. Now."

"But, but, uh, with all due respect, colonel, we're not ready. Yet," Gabe protested. "And it's, uh, getting kind of late."

"Doesn't matter, Greenley. Unlike you, we don't work nine to five. Run the 'troid through its paces and the plant can coach Inglehardt as needed real-time."

"Then what?"

"Then you're under arrest and these two become permanent guests. One false move, Greenley, and you're dead. Understand? Your actions constitute high treason. Which, on my watch, is a very bad idea."

"*Treason?* Why? What did I do?"

"Let's just say the only plants you'll be conversing with after this will be the weeds in the exercise yard at Leavenworth. You made some seriously incorrect assumptions regarding our surveillance capabilities, doctor. Maybe I'll save us all a lot of trouble and just throw you on the next train to Dulce. They're always looking for test subjects."

With that, Watkins reached up and yanked Gabe's badge from his collar and dropped it in his own breast pocket. "You won't need this anymore. *Now move!*"

CHAPTER THIRTY-SEVEN

Base Command Center
Nellis TMR
Restricted Area 51
Rachel, Nevada
August 19, 1978
1850 PDT/0150 GMT

A short time later, Thyron *et al.* arrived at the base command center. Gabe scrambled out of the back of Watkins's transport fidgeting nervously, while AG4MI, then Thyron's box were loaded onto a platform dolly towed by an MP. Eventually, the colonel led them inside through four different checkpoints separated by thick, metal doors. Finally, they entered an elevator that Watkins activated with the usual badge-coding routine, which quickly descended what Thyron estimated to be at least five levels.

Thyron wasn't surprised by what lay beyond, having scoped it out previously, but Gabe clearly was, judging by his expression as Watkins herded them onboard a magnetically levitated passenger train. After securing the dolly in the car's baggage area, the maglev sped through a natural stone tunnel, arriving at their destination mere moments later. They disembarked, heading for an elevator that took them up a level. At this point, Thyron knew exactly where they were—the section known as S-4.

Once again they found themselves in a tunnel, this one lit by suspended fluorescent lights and wide enough for the three humans to proceed side by side, dolly still in tow. Reinforced stone walls crawling with cables surrounded them, except for a few intersections with tunnels of different diameters lined with corrugated metal;

some smaller, others huge enough to easily accommodate a truck like the one that initially brought them there.

Gabe's mind was racing, an unreadable flux of fear-induced static. Thyron knew he wasn't experienced at cloaking his thoughts, which wasn't good. Gradually, his psi flow sorted itself into a linear stream and Thyron braced himself for the worst.

O-oh, say can you see, by the dawn's early light. What so proudly we hailed, by the twilight's last gleaming...

Thyron rustled with confusion, wondering what on Terra he was talking about.

Those are the lyrics of the song this country has designated to represent it, the 'troid psaid.

Thyron breathed a sigh of relief. A bit weird, but better than thoughts that could reveal their plan. So, the 'troid wasn't shut down, only in standby. Good. Maybe the 'troid was smarter than he thought. Her telepathic voice came into his mind again moments later. *The base commander has an implant that enhances his ability to detect psi waves. It covers a broad band of quantum frequencies.*

Indeed it does, Watkins interjected, then scoffed. *I knew you weren't really shut down. You'll pay for your insubordination later.*

We are so screwed, Gabe thought, too spontaneously to catch it.

You certainly are, Watkins replied, chuckling aloud.

While the dolly's wheels rumbled along the stone floor toward their destination, Thyron opened up all his receptors to learn as much as possible about their location. He noted that infrared-activated motion sensors at regular intervals chirped in a radio frequency as they passed, something they'd have to evade if they were to escape.

The soldier towing the dolly fell into step with the colonel, creating a steady *clomp, clomp, clomp* while Gabe's gait fell in a slightly different rhythm. The cadence resulted in a beat frequency that reminded Thyron of the result when two different wavelengths interacted, spawning an idea.

Not only could he receive all wavelengths of the electromagnetic spectrum, he could broadcast them as well. Choosing a channel in the microwave band, he initiated a new conversation with the 'troid.

|Do you hear me, AG4?|

|Of course I do. And it would be your own fault if I didn't. What do you want?|

|Jam the colonel's implant.|

|Do you have the access code?|

|Of course,| he responded and promptly provided the specifications. |Just short bursts for now, so I can communicate with Gabe. Ready?|

|Sure, whatever. On three. One...two...three.|

Gabe. Thyron cringed at the man's shocked reaction. *Calm down. The 'troid's jamming the colonel's implant while we chat. She and I can talk offline on a microwave channel.*

Good. Do you or the 'troid have any idea how we'll get out of here?

No. But we're working on it. That's enough for now. Don't want him to get suspicious.

Got it.

|Done, AG4.|

|I know. I was listening.|

Thyron rolled his eyes, then watched remotely as they passed through another security checkpoint. Watkins badge/coded another thick metal door. The bolt dropped with a *thump.* The colonel shoved it open.

This time what lay beyond was far different from the hundred meters or so of earthen tunnels they'd left behind. Instead, it appeared as if they'd entered an ordinary, ground-level office building. The growl of the dolly's casters shifted from an abrasive scrape to a higher pitch as they proceeded inside. The walls were the color of leaves on a sickly plant, ceiling covered with noise-cancelling tiles equipped with recessed fluorescent lights rather than the caged bulbs they'd left behind.

They proceeded straight down a corridor lined with cipher-lock-secured doors, passing several intersections of identical hallways. Eventually, they turned left into another one at least twenty-five meters long, likewise lined with doors. Halfway down on the right, Watkins badged one open. Beyond stretched a large, carpeted, partially occupied briefing room. An oversized U-shaped table dominated the center, several rows of padded chairs surrounding it.

Thyron stiffened when the MP removed him from the box and set him on a small table left of the entrance, next to a tray of donuts. Thyron crossed his peduncles and settled into his most stable position, trying to look like a houseplant. Meanwhile, the colonel herded the other MP and Gabe to a row of chairs against the back wall. He commanded them to sit, then ordered the MPs to unchain AG4MI. He threatened to demolish her CPU if she did anything inappropriate, and told her to go up front; she gave him a digital look of disdain, but didn't argue. The screen beside her contained a projection of tensor equations Thyron recognized as those relating to multi-dimensional photonic crystal morphometry.

A tall, broad-shouldered man with disheveled blond hair, some of which was long enough to fall in his face, was up front, explaining the formula. He wore civilian clothes, khaki pants, and a blue long-sleeved shirt, which stood out with everyone else in uniform.

Except, of course, for Gabe, whose expression reflected fear, efforts to suppress a gastrointestinal disturbance, or possibly both.

Subterranean Level 3/Room 3347
Nellis TMR
Restricted Area 51
Rachel, Nevada
August 19, 1978
1935 PDT/0235 GMT

Thyron instantly recognized the presenter's aura and pinged AG4MI on the microwave channel.

|Jam the colonel while I introduce myself to Inglehardt.|

|Done.| she replied, for once not editorializing.

Hello, Brad, he psaid. *It's me. Thyron. On the table in back.*

The man paused mid-sentence, scanning the room until his gaze locked on Thyron, who tipped a branch, equivalent of a botanical wink.

The man's blue eyes widened behind heavy-rimmed glasses and his mouth fell open, but he quickly recovered, returning to his presentation, though he continued to glance at Thyron from time to time, stifling a smile.

When done with his last slide, they declared a break, and Brad headed straight for Thyron.

|Jam it, AG4MI.|

|Excuse me?|

|The colonel, AG! Quick!|

|I knew that. Done.|

"Was it really you that was telling me all that stuff about those circuits?" the man asked, seeming not to see anything unusual about talking to a plant.

Actually, yes. I hope you're enjoying your promotion. But more importantly, I'm a prisoner. Think you can help? Psi, please.

Brad obediently emitted a heavy, heartfelt sigh.

No, no, no! Telepathy, Brad! Telepathy! Then, noticing Watkins was on his way over, added, *Not now. Here comes Watkins. Don't let him know we've met. I'll let you know when we can resume a private conversation.*

|Done, AG.|

Brad picked up the last jelly donut and took a huge bite, raspberry filling gushing out and dribbling off his chin. He grabbed a nearby napkin and wiped his face, just in time for the colonel to come over and offer his hand.

"Nice job, Inglehardt," he said, expression changing abruptly after Brad accepted his outstretched hand and gave it a hearty shake. Watkins looked at it and scowled, then also grabbed a napkin. "As you can see, we have the robot here to perform a demonstration of its learning abilities."

"Great, Colonel," he replied. "I have a slide that explains exactly how that occurs."

"I see you've met your mentor," Watkins went on. "I always knew you weren't smart enough to figure that out on your own."

Brad glanced at Thyron, then back at the colonel, a nervous smile playing with the corner of his mouth. "What are you talking about?"

Relieved, Thyron exhaled heavily. The man was, indeed, as bright as he'd hoped.

"Do you smell ozone?" Brad asked.

Watkins frowned and sniffed the air. "I think you're right," he agreed, giving Thyron a suspicious look. "So, you haven't met, then?"

"I, uh, don't know what you're talking about," Brad lied.

"Oh. I thought that was recognition I saw when we brought it in," Watkins said, nodding toward Thyron. "Weren't you just talking to it?"

Thyron bristled and glared at Watkins. If there was one thing he detested it was being referred to as *it. I'd like to see you reproduce yourself,* he thought, then decided that was, without a doubt, the last thing he'd ever want.

"Uh, no," Brad responded. "I had my eye on that jelly donut for the break. I guess I was talking to myself, just glad no one beat me to it."

"Oh. So you're a sugar junkie. Figures. Well, Inglehardt, you may as well know. What appears to be this plant, here, is the EBE responsible for helping you figure out those circuits. No way you could have done it otherwise, eh?"

Brad looked at Thyron with a genuine smile that emanated sincere appreciation. "Indeed! I guess that provides a whole new perspective on calling someone a vegetable, don't you think, Colonel?"

Thyron's cytoplasm responded with the botanical equivalent of a grin. He loved the fact Brad was not overly impressed by the base commander. In fact, he sensed a fair amount of distrust and possible hostility. Not only was he highly intelligent, but the touch of arrogance he'd perceived earlier was definitely there. Perfect. Now it was just a matter of where his loyalties resided. The entanglement that bonded those who'd shared a positive, organic psi connection definitely tilted things in Thyron's favor.

"Thank you for your help," Brad stated, adding telepathically, *Or should I say it this way: Thank you?*

My pleasure, Thyron replied. *And I appreciate the commander for arranging this meeting. Thank you, Colonel Watkins.*

The commander glared at Thyron, obviously not wanting it generally known to a subordinate, much less a civilian, that he was psi-sensitive. No telling who he'd eavesdropped on throughout the base. But best of all, Brad slipped Thyron a knowing look while Watkins's response was a glare punctuated with a grunt.

CHAPTER THIRTY-EIGHT

Subterranean Level 3/Room 3347
Nellis TMR
Restricted Area 51
Rachel, Nevada
August 19, 1978
2050 PDT/0350 GMT

The demonstration of AG4MI's functions began after the break. Before that, Thyron got on the microwave channel and made some suggestions, such as skipping several of her communications modes, particularly her channel range, so they wouldn't get suspicious of their covert chats. While he was at it, he instructed her to gather as much information as possible when she demo'ed her mechanical/structural analysis mode with regard to the facility's physical structure; then use her technology assessment module to collect specifications regarding the controls to the security system's physical barriers. Thyron would likewise analyze the facility's electronics emissions and they'd corroborate their findings later.

The meeting dragged on for the remainder of the evening and into the wee hours of the night. Being underground, time wasn't apparent, swing and graveyard shifts the norm, given so much work and testing was conducted under cover of darkness. To her credit, the 'troid performed flawlessly, demonstrating how she gathered information after which Brad explained the technicalities of how it was integrated into her knowledge base, neural networks, and logic gates.

When the meeting adjourned, Watkins stood up, but kept a restraining hand on Gabe's shoulder, bidding him remain seated. Thyron noted his eyelids were drooping as badly as his own foliage. Gabe hadn't eaten since that afternoon when he'd gone to the cafeteria with his security entourage, plus Thyron could tell by his weary look that he longed to retire to his usual quarters. Based on what Watkins had stated earlier combined with what he'd perceived in the colonel's mind, however, that wasn't going to happen.

"Box up the plant, then chain the robot back up, and take it to storage," Watkins directed the nearest MP, who jumped on the task.

As the soldier lowered him into the box, Thyron noticed the 'troid's photoreceptors flashing angry red. He pinged her on the microwave channel, advising her to chill out—causing a scene might arouse additional suspicion. To his relief, the 'troid relented peacefully; the mood modification routine worked. Moments later, he watched remotely as a small automated vehicle arrived in the hallway outside the conference room.

Using a rope, the MP connected one of AG4MI's chains to a hook on the vehicle's rear frame, then got in and drove off, the 'troid's rolopeds changing pitch as they reentered the tunnel system, then turned right at the first intersection. A spontaneous check of Thyron's site map confirmed that, as expected, they were headed for a well-secured storage area on that same level, a hundred meters or so away.

Another MP picked up Thyron's box and followed Watkins and Gabe out of the room, turning left instead of right at the first intersection, which led to a different, less imposing door from where they'd entered. Expecting a tunnel, Thyron was surprised when instead it was another finished corridor with a similar entrance on the far side, suggesting another facility. Thyron referenced his map, noting it was a residential area. A quick psi-peek indicated it was far too luxurious to be military. Would Gabe get to stay there?

Apparently not. Before reaching it, they stopped by an elevator situated in an alcove to their right.

Watkins keyed in access, door rumbling open moments later. They descended another level and exited into an area that left no doubt they were far beneath the ground. Unfinished concrete walls extended several meters high, ceiling lost in darkness amid a damp, musty odor that Thyron actually found somewhat pleasant.

The colonel directed them toward a reinforced metal portal to their right and released it in the usual manner. Conditions on the other side didn't improve. Bare cement loomed around them, eventually merging with reinforced stone as they proceeded a few dozen meters through a tunnel that looked like an oversized metal pipe, caged lightbulbs at regular intervals trying vainly to breach the darkness.

The passageway eventually ended in a "T" where they turned right, then right again a few intersections later. After several more meters of gloom, they were confronted by a bulky door equipped with the usual cipher lock. The MP opened it this time, then retrieved Thyron from the box.

Thyron was relieved to find they'd moved his habitat within as the man opened its door and dumped him inside; at least he'd have the light and atmosphere needed to photosynthesize. He'd get out of there somehow. How he'd help Gabe, however, was another story.

Subterranean Level 4/Detention Cell 5
Nellis TMR
Restricted Area 51
Rachel, Nevada
August 20, 1978
0203 PDT/0903 GMT

Gabe was convinced he'd died and gone to hell. His head throbbed and nausea reigned, the pervasive earthy, metallic odor crawling through his gut like an invading army. They returned to the "T", continued past their original entry point, then proceeded straight another ten yards until the passage dead-ended at another imposing door. Watkins released the lock and kicked it open, shoving him inside the darkened room without so much as a word.

As the colonel secured the door, Gabe managed to grab the chain that dangled from the sole light bulb, barely avoiding being encompassed by total darkness. As he took in his surroundings, a groan escaped from the depths of his soul. Roughly eight feet square, the cell contained a sagging metal cot, dingy metal sink, and seatless toilet that leaned to one side. The cement floor was marred with dark stains, ceiling lost in shadow, its accommodation rating somewhere below a medieval dungeon.

It reminded him so much of a tornado cellar that, out of habit, he checked for black widows, tarantulas, and scorpions, all of which loved such places. None he could see, his relief short-lived—was the cell too toxic for them as well, perhaps originally carved out by an atomic bomb?

He shuddered with the renewed realization that he really was under arrest. Or was it a dream? No, nightmare. An extremely vivid nightmare. His mind raced, his life and the profound events that brought him to this point flashing before him.

He'd always been a model citizen. Only had two speeding tickets in his life. Certainly never been in jail. Never even knew anyone who'd gone to jail, much less prison. He served his country in numerous capacities, from wartime military to peacetime civil service. Given the Cold War, peacetime was a misnomer, which undoubtedly drove the base's airtight security code. Assuming the US acquired advanced technology from the '47 Roswell crash—to say nothing of various others since that were unknown to the public—it made sense they'd go to extraordinary lengths to prevent the Russians from finding out.

Given Thyron's snooping, he undoubtedly possessed enough highly classified intelligence to present a national security threat. But all the vegemal wanted was to leave Earth; be reunited with his cohorts and go about their business elsewhere in the galaxy. A thought that boggled his mind, regardless of what he'd seen validating the feasibility of such an endeavor.

Would Thyron conspire with other off-worlders in a hostile way? Not likely. Once he left, things would be no different than they were before he arrived. Only a handful of individuals even knew he existed. They'd impounded their ship, now no more than another tarp-covered extraterrestrial vehicle in a remote hangar in the Nevada desert, an unlikely technological game changer.

What more did they want? Why was a peaceful, off-world visitor such a big deal? Why maintain secrecy to the point of executing witnesses without so much as a trial?

Except for the fact evidence of any EBE proved the existence of interstellar vehicles, which they didn't want to acknowledge existed. And vice versa.

Whoa.

So that was it.

The rationale that convinced him to write that renegade WAR flooded back in an emotional tsunami that took his breath away. As a sentient being, Thyron deserved respect. If he wanted to be free, it was the right thing to do. The moral thing to do.

What gave the US Government the right to incarcerate an innocent being who was here by mistake?

Yet, that dark, heavy vacuum in his gut, which had persisted since he'd submitted that fateful WAR, not only bespoke the deadly truth but provided the answer: Because they had the power to do so.

He'd known what he was doing, only too well.

And now he was about to pay the price.

Too exhausted to deal any further with that sorry revelation, he extinguished the light, cringing as the cell as well as his ponderings faded to black. Slowly, he felt his way over to the cot, where he collapsed into a state of restless, fitful slumber, hoping to wake up in a better place.

What seemed a short time later, Gabe woke up, wondering for a fractured moment why it was cold, damp, and pitch black before the previous day's events flooded back. He got up slowly, waving his arms to find the chain pull to the overhead bulb. He winced when light blasted his retinas, realizing how stiff he was from the thin, lumpy mattress. He stretched, then started to pace, mind racing as panic picked up where it had left off.

What was going to happen? If Watkins could read his thoughts, he'd better go back to meditating on the *Star Spangled Banner* rather than risk revealing their plans. Though based on the colonel's accusations, the man probably already knew.

An electric jolt of horror shot through him. So that was what this was all about. Not only the fact Thyron was sentient—aiding and abetting the escape of an EBE.

Holy Mother of God...

He returned to the cot and sat down, noticing a funky, moldy odor that failed to register the night before; no telling who or what the previous occupant may have been. He lay back down, regardless, staring at the miasma of pipes, conduit, wires, and who-knows-what snaking across the dark, stone ceiling.

An unbidden and ominous bloody flash of déjà-vu struck, confirmed by hackles on his neck and goosebumps on his arms unrelated to the room's chill. He'd had premonitions before; all had come true—his grandfather's heart attack; his mother's stroke; his black lab, Jake, getting killed by a car....

No. Impossible. No way I'm going to die in this place.

Then he remembered that strong impression he'd had a few months ago, before he even knew he'd be leaving Houston—to put Francesca's name on the car and his townhome, just in case...

In case of what? *This?*

A loud rumble from his stomach interrupted his horrifying reverie, shifting his thoughts to more immediate concerns. Food sounded horrible, but he needed nourishment to clear his head. Would they bring him food? No telling what it would be if they did. Probably Spam and powdered eggs. A horrific flashback he'd repeatedly tried to suppress joined the other regurgitated memories.

He'd joined the Navy when the United States entered World War II, hoping to avoid bloodshed. Luckily, he was assigned to the Seabees, a convenient nickname derived from the acronym for Construction Battalions, which were charged with building bases and runways to support the war against Japan in the South Pacific: American Samoa, New Hebrides, Okinawa. All occupied by indigenous people.

For a moment, he was back in the ship's galley, staging what he needed to prepare the crew's next meal. He knew they were sick of Spam, but that was the only meat available—until one of the sailors came in with a live pig he'd bought from one of the natives.

When he was a kid on the ranch they'd always sent livestock to the processing plant. He'd never killed anything bigger than a cockroach in his life, much less seen it done, other than grossing out at an occasional dead buck hanging from a neighbor's tree during hunting season. He had no idea how to butcher an animal, much less dress it out.

The chief petty officer, an avid hunter stateside, was more than happy to demonstrate. As he'd watched the pig bleed out, he nearly fainted and only barely avoided vomiting, though the bitter taste of bile burned his throat. It was the most traumatic experience of his life, after which he'd sworn never to eat meat again. And hadn't. After reading Backster's work, he'd even shunned certain vegetables.

The gruesome scene evaporated when a whirring sound issued from the chamber's lock, followed by a clunk as the deadbolt fell. He sat up and swung his feet to the floor, mind ripped back to the present, a time far worse than the one he'd left. A beefy MP entered; Gabe stiffened, wary. With no more than a solemn nod, the soldier dumped his worn, brown suitcase and an unfamiliar gunny sack on the floor; then exited as abruptly as he'd arrived.

Gabe sat there a moment and frowned. Was he being sent home? Detained there? Or shot and dumped in the desert, lock, stock, and barrel? He got up and tossed the suitcase on the bed, released the latches. Shirts, pants, underwear, and socks, clean and otherwise, all stuffed inside. Two things in particular he was concerned about, neither of which was there. He grabbed the gunny sack, upended it.

Shampoo, soap-on-a-rope, his razor, shaving cream, deodorant, Vitamin C pills, a tin of aspirin, his hair brush, and comb; all tumbled out, along with his spare lab coat and now-crumpled copy of *Nature*.

Panic burned through his chest, heart accelerating. Nothing from his office where he kept his notes, lab journal, and photos. He reminded himself that his research information was permanently affixed to his brain, a moot point since he couldn't share it, anyway.

But that wasn't his greatest concern.

He turned the suitcase upside down, shaking all the clothes and anything else left inside, out on the cot. He checked all the droopy side pockets, then set the empty bag on the floor and went through everything again. He paired all the socks and tucked them into a tidy bundle like his mother had taught him as a child, then examined all the pockets of the shirts and pants. He stared at them for several moments, finally folding everything neatly, soiled or not, and setting them back inside the suitcase.

One of the missing items was his passport, something that could be replaced should he ever have the opportunity to use it again. The other items, obviously not.

No, no, no, no, no, no, no no....

His stomach lurched, tangled in knots, throat constricting as he buried his face in his hands and surrendered to a dark, despondent void.

They were gone.

CHAPTER THIRTY-NINE

Galileo Bay-3
Nellis TMR
Restricted Area 51
Rachel, Nevada
August 20, 1978
0715 hours PDT/1415 GMT

Ignatius Formicidae guided the HIO starship *Volition* across barren but familiar terrain on approach to Area 51. The ship wasn't particularly remarkable, at least not in the more technically advanced worlds of the galaxy, yet on Terra it drew stares and expressions of disbelief from those who considered it an Unidentified Flying Object. To indigenous residents who'd populated the area east of there centuries and even millennia before—the Havasupai, Wiipukepaya, and countless others—Ignatius would be recognized as one of the "ant people" and welcomed warmly, whereas those he was about to meet would regard him with suspicion and thinly veiled disdain.

If they'd depart from their vicious, self-destructive ways, they could earn membership in the Hostii Intergalactic Organization and avoid these inspections, which were a bother to them as much as Ignatius and his fellow officers. But clearly that wasn't going to happen anytime soon, though at least the backward world's warring factions hadn't set off any additional nuclear devices for over twenty of their planet's orbital cycles. Such tests were what drew the HIO to that area in the first place, alerting them to the urgent need to monitor the situation.

He checked in with Rapcon as the ship skimmed the top of Tikapoo Peak, even though the personnel in Radar Approach Control should have been previously alerted to his scheduled arrival. They glided over Freedom Ridge, now only a few hundred meters above ground level, and seconds later over clusters of familiar hangars, antennae, and metal buildings. Ignatius set down in his usual spot where he waited for them to open the mountainside hangar where the *Volition* would remain for the duration of his visit.

These inspections were scheduled to last forty-eight Terran hours, though sometimes they took less, others more. Of particular concern was the distress call he'd received a few days before. While he didn't know the details, it sounded suspicious, placing his senses on full alert.

A 'troid, a *flora peda telepathis,* and a human pre-adult female, all from different worlds, being held captive... How could such a thing occur in the first place? Except for a few select locations, this world was off-limits for most intragalactic traffic, except for dire emergencies. Which, other than pilot error while recharging or entering a portal, was why so many interstellar vehicles crashed. That was probably the case here, but it still didn't sound right that such an unlikely trio would be traveling together in this galactic sector or anywhere else.

If only the unfortunate group had the means to travel to a more secure pickup point, for their own safety. A mere thousand kilometers to the east, indigenous populations occupied their own lands, where such as himself were not only welcome along with the other "star people," but safe from military intervention. On the positive side, it broke the boredom of another inspection run, so complaining wasn't justified.

While he waited for them to open Bay-3, he considered alerting Thyron, his contact for the rescue operation. Something told him not to, however. His insectoid instincts were strong and not to be trifled with. If for any reason the pickup was cancelled, he felt certain he would have been told. Unless something unfortunate had happened to them, which was possible, based on the ominous psignals he was picking up.

The hangar door crawled to the left, revealing a cavernous opening blasted out from the mountain. Ignatius set the controls for auto and the vehicle eased into the bunker, doors rumbling closed behind it.

While he waited for his crew to join him, the usual party of humans gathered at the exit ramp, *i.e.*, the base commander, whom Ignatius barely tolerated; the deputy base commander; his chief of security; and the Foreign Technology Officer.

Mutual distrust reverberated against his antennae like cosmic rays. One of the reasons Ignatius was assigned to these jaunts was his superior intuition, which flushed out secrets the Terrans were wont to hide— for example, any extraterrestrials they were collaborating with illegally to advance their scientific knowledge and application. If used peacefully, it was acceptable, but this world could not be trusted in that regard. Any technology with munitions potential was always exploited for that purpose above all others, no matter how much its peaceful application would benefit their people.

"Welcome, Captain," the base commander greeted him as he and his crew egressed, then reached the ground, but the words reeked insincerity. He was no more welcome than an asteroid collision, maybe less so. Ignatius caught an unfamiliar psibration hidden in the man's aura that he recognized as an Aurigan device, a psi-band amplifier implanted in his spinal cord. Only someone with something to hide or illegally spying on others would have an interest in such an unethical device, which was also available in a surveillance model.

Ignatius scrutinized the three men with his shiny compound eyes, smiling internally at the intimidating effect it always had. When upright, he was a meter taller than any of them and a thousand times stronger, to say nothing of his natural body armor and superior mental skills.

Ignatius knew there were already two beings at this location, one organic, one mechanical, who wanted off this planet, which wasn't surprising with Watkins involved. Asking directly could put the captives at risk, so he'd have to act as if he didn't suspect anything while he conducted what was supposed to be a routine site inspection. Fortunately, Ignatius had a secure, private psi-band he and his crew used for internal communications, with which he conveyed his suspicions to his landing party, advising them to be prepared for a confrontation.

It seemed ironic that he and his crew were backed by vehicles with far superior weapons to enforce HIO regulations regarding peace than the Terrans possessed for pursuing war, especially when the most common violations related to munitions development and deployment. As always, much of their time would be spent on the facility's second level which, for some reason unknown to him, they referred to as "Alice's Floor."

But holding extraterrestrials against their will was contrary to their treaty, and going in unprepared was nothing short of stupid. As was any Terran who even considered going up against the HIO.

Why couldn't humans cooperate with one another like his own species? For two galactic credits, he'd flatten the entire facility and return everyone to their rightful planets.

CHAPTER FORTY

Subterranean Level 4/Containment Cell 3
Nellis TMR
Restricted Area 51
Rachel, Nevada
August 20, 1978
1040 PDT/1740 GMT

So far, Thyron wasn't sure what to make of the situation. By his standards, Watkins was no more than an obnoxious bully who had to augment his psi abilities with an artificial device. At this point, being confined in his habitat was more comfort than punishment, since his environmental needs were met. As far as being confined, while he hadn't teleported since that first time, he didn't doubt he could do it again, to anywhere he wanted. Like wherever they were holding Gabe.

He thought about his human friend and psi-sought his location, finding him sitting on a tiny bed, elbows on his knees, face in his hands, and emanating a considerable state of distress. He scoped out the cell for electronic devices, finding audio and video sensors concealed amidst a network of pipes and conduits. At first he was surprised there was no guard outside the door. Then again, why would there be? Even if he escaped, evaded the surveillance systems, and found his way out of the labyrinth of tunnels, kilometers of harsh terrain surrounded the base, all of which was electronically monitored.

He pinged AG4MI on the microwave channel. It took a few attempts to awaken her from standby; then he had to listen to a volley of complaints before finally telling her to dummy up, tone conveying its meaning as he instructed her to jam not only the colonel's device, but video and audio in Gabe's location as well. Since she didn't know where that was, he networked her into his psi-net, enjoying how impressed she was with his natural abilities.

Little does she know, he thought, and prepared to make the jump to Gabe's cell.

Much to his consternation, it didn't work. He made it outside the habitat, but was still inside the room, which was similar to Gabe's, but otherwise empty. Unsuccessful, he decided to at least put the jam to good use and check in with Brad.

Brad, this is your mentor. The colonel's receiver is currently jammed so we can talk.

I really can't right now, his protégé replied. *The base is being inspected by some insectoid EBEs for treaty compliance and I'm escorting them around EVO&RE.*

Thyron's boughs bristled with renewed optimism. *Where are they from? The HIO?*

I believe so. Some galactic organization that tries to keep us Earthlings in line. Ha. Good luck with that!

Brad! They're our ride off this rock! We're supposed to meet them in two days somewhere southwest of here, but we've all been locked up, so won't be able to get to the rendezvous point.

Is that so? Brad replied, anger sparking his response.

Think you can help?

Probably. Their vehicle's in the hangar next to mine. There's a network of tunnels that connect them to most areas. Get here, and I'll help. Where are you?

In a room on the level below where you gave your presentation. Gabe's about a hundred meters beyond that, and the 'troid's confined in a storage compartment in a different section, but on the same level as the meeting rooms.

Need to go. Watkins is scratching the back of his neck, probably wondering why his implant isn't working. Over and out.

Thyron advised the 'troid to release the jam, then sighed with relief. So far so good. He was still outside his habitat, so decided to check the door—it was locked, as expected, but electronic locks were as easy to pick as human brains. He hailed the 'troid on the microwave channel again.

|AG4MI. I psied Brad. He can probably help us get to the HIO ship, which is already here, conducting an inspection. But we'll need to get there on our own.|

|My mechanical/structural assessment function and electronic sensors should be sufficient to figure out how to escape this level of confinement.|

|I was counting on that. The network of tunnels connecting this area to the hangars should be on the maps I gave you. Can you find your way?|

|Of course I can, chlorophyll breath. You, of all people, should know my capabilities, don't you think?|

|Right,| he replied, missing the insult. |So, we have two days before the HIO ship departs. This is a serious operation that's not going to be a piece of cake.|

|A piece of what?|

|Cake. A human food used to celebrate their annual life cycles.|

|So how does that relate to our plan?|

|It doesn't. It's a figure of speech.|

|A *what?*|

|Something you need to be more than an AI dingbat to understand—a comparison, an analogy, an expression to make a point. And the point here is that you need to get yourself to the *Volition.* Then be prepared to assist as required to make sure our escape succeeds. Which reminds me, add Brad and Ignatius, the HIO vessel captain, to your authorized user list. I'll get back to you in a while to do some jamming so I can contact Gabe and clue him into the plan.|

|He's going with us?|

|We can't leave him here. Watkins is filing conspiracy charges against him, based on security oath violations. The punishment for treason around here tends to be fatal.|

|You seem to have forgotten one very important problem—Terrans aren't allowed onboard HIO ships.|

|Hopefully, they'll negotiate.|

|If they won't?|
|Gabe's as good as dead.|

CHAPTER FORTY-ONE

Subterranean Level 4/Containment Cell 3
Nellis TMR
Restricted Area 51
Rachel, Nevada
August 20, 1978
1101 PDT/1801 GMT

It didn't seem that difficult, at least in theory, for each of them to find their way to either Galileo Bay-4, where Brad promised to help, or Bay-3, where the HIO ship was berthed. But Thyron knew he had one rather difficult problem: He was approximately a kilometer plus three highly secured levels away, and at the rate he moved, it would take him twenty-seven hours, forty-six minutes and thirty-eight seconds to get there, assuming no obstacles along the way. Wandering Area 51 tunnels for that length of time with motion sensors every few meters wasn't conducive to success. True, he could deactivate each one as he came into range, but it would be impossible to hide from any foot traffic. His only option was to try teleporting again.

Sensing a twinge of sadness impinging on his own natural optimism, Thyron tuned into Gabe's emotional state in read-only mode, finding him even more depressed than before—not just about the situation, but grieving, as if his fate were already determined.

Thyron's multi-dimensional intuition spread across time and space, through which he sensed that he and the 'troid would escape; Gabe's future, however, was fuzzy, as if it were fading in and out. Of course, being imprisoned on a secret base with a formidable level of security was enough to jeopardize anyone's future.

Uncomforted, he returned to the present. He had to talk to him, find out what was wrong. Either the man was cloaking his thoughts or in a deep, unreadable funk, which tended to be a very bad place to be—thoughts interacted in the cosmic soup, eventually morphing to reality. More than likely the man's fears brought him there.

He had to ping AG4MI four times before she came out of standby and followed his request to jam the colonel and surveillance equipment in Gabe's cell so he could make contact.

Gabe. What's wrong?

The man's response was a sardonic laugh.

Listen, Doc. We'll get out of here somehow. I know we will. The HIO ship is already here and I'm working with the 'troid and Brad to figure out how to get to the hangar. I can get us out of here. And we have more than a day to figure it all out.

Another laugh, more bitter than the first. *It doesn't matter. One way or the other, my life is over. I have nothing to live for. It doesn't matter what they do. They may as well kill me. Why not? All is lost.*

What are you talking about? Thyron asked, unable to comprehend how he could be so despondent. They hadn't even tried to escape yet.

They're gone, he replied, words saturated in dull chords of grief.

Thyron started to ask what, then caught a vision of the seed pods Gabe had saved. So that was it. He tuned into their psibrations, which were permanently linked to his via quantum entanglement at the DNA level. He found them secured within a heavily reinforced safe in the base commander's outpost, along with lab notes, journals, photos, and other documentation Gabe generated when Thyron was coming out of dormancy.

Gabe had told him repeatedly how their time together constituted his life's work and that the experience could never be met, much less exceeded, by any other. Thyron emitted a botanical sigh, adding one more task to be included in their departure plan.

Somewhere in the data, quotes, and colloquialisms Thyron had assimilated from the planet, a saying came to mind that seemed appropriate.

Don't worry, Gabe, he psaid. *It's not over 'til the fat lady sings.*

Subterranean Level 4/Containment Cell 3
Nellis TMR
Restricted Area 51
Rachel, Nevada
August 20, 1978
1201 PDT/1901 GMT

The realization that a day might not be long enough to plan their escape from their new circumstances hit Thyron like a figurative frost. His ability to access all dimensions, some of which were timeless, tended to make him pay little attention to such limitations. But the HIO ship's departure loomed with no telling how long it would be before the next one arrived—much less one with a psi-sensitive captain willing to push the limits of his assignment and possibly authority.

He still hadn't gotten in touch with Creena, which was another concern. Since he could determine her location, there was always the option of landing, then sending AG4MI to retrieve her, though that would definitely violate HIO regs such that Ignatius would probably never agree. He probed her emotional state and found its energy level low, much like Gabe's. His own energy level dropped in empathic response.

Holy guacamole, he thought. *Do I have to do everything around here?*

He pinged the 'troid hard, jolting her to full awareness on the first try.

|Ouch! That nearly fried my receiver! Was that amplitude really necessary, you obnoxious organic CO2 breather?| she replied.

|If you paid better attention, I wouldn't have to,| Thyron snapped. |And you know what else, AG4? You need to ditch the attitude.|

|And you need to show more respect. My preferred reference is Aggie, not my model number. Use it, or I'll start calling you Veggie.|

|All right, fair enough. Let's call a truce, at least until we get out of here.|

|Agreed. So why'd you wake me up?|

|You need to find out when that asteroid fungus colonel sleeps and jam him up good. We need to get our strategy together if we want to get off this rock.|

|Okay. Stand by.|

She pinged him back a few minutes later. |According to his usual schedule, he should be starting a sleep cycle in two hours fifty two minutes. The implant allows him to get by with only four hours per rotational cycle.|

Thyron felt a brief surge of panic as his defenses reacted to the time restraint. He had to figure it out by the time Watkins went nighty-night. Wanting to show his sincerity for the truce, he forced himself to thank her, then got to work.

He knew releasing the locks to Aggie's, Gabe's, and his own cell wasn't a problem. Just to make sure, he ran a test on his own. It took a few moments to find the correct frequency and codes, plus silence the alarm, but found nothing to worry about. Deactivating the motion sensors would be a bit more complicated, mainly since he couldn't take them all down at once, which would undoubtedly be noticed. Rather, he'd need to trip them, one by one, as each of them proceeded to Bay-3. He and the 'troid had maps, but someone would have to coach Gabe.

Actually, Aggie could do that, plus trip the sensors, making his own task less complicated. Yes, that was a good job for Aggie. Make her feel useful and less inclined to get in his way. He had enough to worry about.

If they arrived at different times, they'd be less likely to be caught. Thus, Brad needed to be on alert to provide a safe haven.

No. Bad idea. He couldn't risk getting Brad in trouble and wind up like Gabe.

If they could get to the EVO&RE hangar in Bay-4 through the tunnels, then they could undoubtedly get directly to Bay-3 by a similar route. If possible, leaving Brad entirely out of the loop was the right thing to do.

Right now, he and Gabe were detained on the fourth level; Aggie in storage on the third; Watkins's command post on the second; and vehicle bays on the first.

The 'troid could undoubtedly get there on her own. Her mobile capability had few limitations, at least in the way of speed, plus she had all sorts of defenses at her disposal, so he considered it a safe bet she could get there without intervention. If there was one thing he knew intimately at this point it was Aggie's capabilities. He'd briefed her on them and assumed she didn't need training or practice prior to implementation.

His cytoplasm rippled with humor at how the 'troid would respond if he had to help her out. Based on how she'd reacted when he beat her at the Miran game, tysa, on the way to Terra, she'd be impossible to tolerate. Her and that 'troid AI ego. He snickered. Which was exactly why he'd coded her with that *Chill-out/Shutdown* command.

The fact he moved so slowly and getting Gabe to safety were the biggest problems. Teleporting to his first destination would drain his reserves. Then what? If he could get to an elevator that could take him to the first level, he could always contact Ignatius, or even Brad; the engineer could always claim he found him wandering about to avoid being considered part of the escape plan.

So, that was a start; but there were still too many details they'd need to work out. Details that would determine whether they succeeded or failed.

CHAPTER FORTY-TWO

Subterranean Level 4/Containment Cell 3
Nellis TMR
Restricted Area 51
Rachel, Nevada
August 20, 1978
1613 PDT/2313 GMT

Thyron thought back to the two times he'd teleported. The first, he'd only intended to get out of his habitat, no farther. The second, that was as far as he got, even though his intended destination was Gabe's cell. Was there something about base security at the quantum level he'd missed? Granted, they were more advanced scientifically at Area 51 than most of the planet, thanks to reverse engineering alien craft with the misfortune of landing there, much like his own. But none should be beyond his comprehension of all frequencies in the electro-magnetic spectrum as well as the quantum psi-web.

No, that couldn't be it. He was missing something, doing something wrong. His mind played back that first experience and how he'd explained it to Gabe:

I gathered up my energy
In fullness of pure synergy.
Focused on the target spot
A bright flash later, there I got.

For his last attempt, he hadn't put nearly as much preparation into it. Instead, he'd casually duplicated his initial effort. Maybe that was it. Each time he wanted a different result, he'd have to put as much energy into defining it as he had that first time. Confidence only went so far. It was a major energy exchange at the quantum level that required more input, both mentally and physically, for proper entanglement and delivery to the correct location. That certainly made sense. So how could he test it?

He psi-scanned the tunnel outside his cell, then the remainder of the containment area, which he found clear for a radius of at least fifty meters. There weren't any motion sensors right outside his door, so if he landed as expected, no problem there. Thus, he focused on the door, releasing the lock, just in case. Next, he turned full concentration to what he intended to do, like the first time. He felt an encouraging jolt as it all came together, as it had before. Good. He shifted his mind to the tunnel, concentrating... harder...harder—

—Phoof!!

A blinding burst and he was there. *Holy guacamole!*

His energy, however, had drained like a fully discharged battery, lighting in the tunnel too dim for a quick photosynthetic fix. Deciding not to waste his energy attempting to teleport back, he shuffled to the door, wedged an articulating branch between it and the frame, and pulled—stuck fast.

Huh? He knew he'd felt the lock release. What happened?

Rootlets beneath his peduncles alerted him to subtle vibrations he recognized as footsteps, cadence indicating at least two beings. Hopefully he had enough energy to release the lock again; maybe it had timed out. He focused on the mechanism, willed the gears to turn, the bolt to fall...

Whew! Success!

He nudged the door open and waddled back inside, closing it just as two MPs stepped around the bend.

His boughs tipped upward in a botanical smile at his success. In theory, distance made no difference. If it went as planned, it would be his only stop on the way to Bay-3, but from there he'd have to find an elevator. All except one on Level 2, known to the locals as *Alice's Floor*, went to Galileo Bay, which was good. Unfortunately, all three were a substantial distance from the target area.

That could be a problem. A big problem. He might have to ask the 'troid to meet him after he made his pick-up. Or be on call, if for some reason teleporting failed entirely. At least Aggie's current location was only one floor away from either his detention area, which was one level below hers, or teleport destination, one level above. Even if he teleported successfully, if the 'troid wasn't available after that, the elevator he needed was approximately fifty meters away, which, at his pitiful glacial speed, would take him over an hour.

Gabe would have a far greater problem getting from Level 4 to Galileo Bay. The one elevator that went to all four subterranean floors was buried deep within the confines of S-4's many laboratories; all of which were in the midst of multitudes of workers. Thus, Gabe would have to use at least two, maybe three, to get up there.

The biggest problem all around was timing. Annoying and unfamiliar as it was, he'd just have to deal with it. As humans were prone to say, *Timing is Everything.* Not in his world, but thus it was.

Speaking of which, he jumped the habitat's timer and increased both the energy level and duration of the lighting by fifteen percent and matched it with increased CO2, hoping for the best.

Subterranean Level 4/Containment Cell 3
Nellis TMR
Restricted Area 51
Rachel, Nevada
August 20, 1978
1617 PDT/2317 GMT

Their tag-up started seventeen seconds after Thyron confirmed Watkins' brainwaves were stable in delta phase. Aggie started to jam the implant regardless, just to make sure, then realized that could affect the sleep cycle, so left it active; hopefully, the sleep phase blocked other input. The 'troid expressed confidence she could escape on her own. When they tied in Ignatius, he was pleased with the new plan versus dealing with the rendezvous point.

Gabe was still despondent and refused to join them, not wanting to jeopardize their safety and escape, even though Ignatius said under the circumstances he was welcome aboard for a lift, wherever he wanted to go. As it turned out, the restriction against Terrans on HIO vessels derived from Earth and since the insectoid was less than happy about something, he had no problem ignoring the directive. Thyron perceived Ignatius's opinion of the matter in the insectoid's native language, which translated roughly to welcoming any excuse to eviscerate Watkins in a rather unpleasant manner.

Listen, Gabe, Thyron psaid. *I know why you're upset and I'm working on it.*

What can you possibly do? It's hopeless. They're gone.

Not exactly. I know where they are.

Gabe's aura brightened by an order of magnitude. *Seriously? You do?*

Would I lie to you?

I hope not. Can you get to them?

I believe so. Don't give up. I've got this.

A cloud of confusion formed as everyone else had no clue what they were talking about.

Whatever you have in mind isn't going to jeopardize our mission, I hope, Aggie interjected. *I don't care to spend the remainder of my service life on this hideous rock.*

For what it's worth, I don't, either, Thyron replied, but left it at that.

They worked through the timing of their final plan, which would begin in just over twenty-four hours. Thyron had yet to contact Creena, but all agreed they'd deal with that as required, if he didn't reach her prior to their arrival.

Aggie would be the first to head out. On her way, she'd go by Gabe's cell to drop off a tracking device as well as another badge, for access as well as if he ran into anyone, both of which she'd manufacture using her new 3D printer.

Excellent idea, Aggie, Gabe replied. *Thank you so much. Make sure the badge is good for all levels, especially the elevators.*

Of course. I'll use Watkins's as the template. That should get you everywhere you need to go.

Great, Gabe replied. *While you're at it, could you fix me up with a new passport, too?*

No problem, the 'troid agreed, a flash of pride brightening her response. *What information should I include?*

Gabriel Francis Greenley, born May 16, 1925, Grady Gulch, Oklahoma.

Consider it done, Aggie replied.

After dropping everything off, she'd proceed to Bay-3, where Ignatius would admit her onboard the ship.

Gabe was up next, Thyron picking the lock to his cell remotely, then handing off to Aggie. The 'troid would monitor his location and douse the motion sensors along the way as he proceeded to safety. To make sure he didn't get lost, she would tweak the lights to indicate when and which way to turn; otherwise he was to go straight.

Thyron hadn't revealed what he was planning to do, in spite of feeling prickles of curiosity from the others, mostly because he didn't want anyone to inadvertently reveal his plan, to say nothing of assuring plausible deniability if he were to fail. The only reason he'd hinted intervention to Gabe was to dissipate his funk; otherwise the man might not have agreed to leave. Rather, he probably would have just sat there and experienced a very unpleasant and potentially permanent fate.

Subterranean Level 4/Containment Cell 3
Nellis TMR
Restricted Area 51
Rachel, Nevada
August 20, 1978
2240 PDT/0640 GMT

Later that evening, as Thyron ruminated on their plan and its likelihood of success, he realized he still hadn't reached Creena. He sought her out once again and tried to make contact. This time he connected to her psibration frequency, but found she was asleep. Too bad, this couldn't wait.

Creena! Creena, wake up. To his surprise, she did so with no additional promptings.

Thyron? Where on Earth have you been? she psaid.

Trying to penetrate the densest field of negative energies I've ever encountered, Thyron responded defensively. Worn out and stressed himself, his usual patience had departed. *What was the matter with you, anyway?* he went on. *Finding a ship wasn't easy. I finally had to interrupt an HIO caucus for outside help.*

Why are you talking in normal sentences again? she asked.

Thyron had nearly forgotten the days he'd spoken in rhyme.

I'm out of my environmental chamber, he said, then added, *for observation.* Initially, that had been the case, so it was good enough for now.

The girl asked some questions regarding one of her unsettling experiences, which he answered truthfully, based on what he'd observed of a dark and sinister entity seeking her in the quantum web. *Why didn't you come that night? I thought we agreed.*

I never said I'd be there that first week. Putting motor-mouth together was a challenge, even for me. Thyron debated what else to tell her since her aura indicated she was still distraught about something. Deciding that justified a fib or two, he added. *I'd no sooner get part of her assembled and the Earthlings would dismantle her again the next day. But that doesn't matter now. I've arranged for a ship. We'll pick you up tonight at twenty-one fifty-two sidereal time, at the place we made contact before.*

Tonight? What time is that here?

Yes, tonight. About one-fifteen, local time. And if you hadn't changed your thinking when you did, it would have been a long, long time before the next one. He wilted slightly, realizing the promise was contingent on their successful escape. He had some reservations, primarily regarding Gabe, but knew positive thinking was essential.

So you got us a ship, you really did, Creena psaid.

Of course.

And it'll get us to Mira III?

Most certainly. Of that much he was sure. There was also a good chance that since she was Miran, Ignatius would pick her up, whether or not he and the 'troid made it out. He frowned when he sensed hesitation tinged with sadness. *What's wrong?*

Nothing. I'm surprised, that's all. See you tonight.

Be ready.

I will.

Thyron sighed with relief. At least now he had one less thing to worry about.

CHAPTER FORTY-THREE

When departure time arrived, the first thing Aggie did was freeze the surveillance video before using her repurposed lasers to remove those annoying chains. Too bad she couldn't wrap them around that obnoxious base commander's skinny neck. To think he called her ugly! She may not be pretty, but she was certainly functional.

Next, she scanned the locking mechanism on her storage cell using the function that analyzed and produced electromagnetic signals. She determined the cipher lock's combination and code, then released it, deactivating its alarm as well. She secured Gabe's new badge and passport in a compartment just above her roloped assembly along with the tracking device, then telescoped her tubular body down to its lowest configuration so she was just under a half meter in height.

She partially extended one of her four arms to double-check the motion sensors' angular range, confirming she was low enough not to be detected, then used her lifeform scanner to check the tunnel for occupants. A human and another lifeform were heading her way. She waited until they passed, not proceeding until they'd turned down another passageway in a different direction from her destination.

The door to Greenley's cell should be of similar design to her own, which indicated she wouldn't be able to slip the badge and passport, much less the tracking device, beneath it. Thus, she'd have to release the lock and deactivate the alarm, as she had her own, which shouldn't be a problem. Elevator S-4/3-4J was 215 meters away, between the conference and residential area, which would take her down to Level 4. After that, it was 720 meters to Gabe's location, so at top speed of twenty meters per second, she'd arrive in a little under forty-seven seconds, not counting if she had to wait for the elevator. She sent this information to Thyron, scanned for occupants one more time, then rolled out into the tunnel, door latching behind her.

After turning to the right, she hit top speed within two seconds, the needed path conveniently straight most of the way. The whir of her rolopeds echoed softly, dropping in pitch as she slowed for the tight left turn that took her to the elevator. She hacked the access device, the door opened four seconds later, and she rolled inside. Selecting the only option, she arrived on Level 4 and rolled into the detainment area, surrounded by cement.

She sped the rest of the way to Gabe's cell where she deactivated the alarm and released the bolt, the botanist cracking the door open a moment later. Since she wasn't her usual height, it took him a moment to look down and retrieve the documents and tracking device. He thanked her profusely and wished her Godspeed, which was exactly what she intended to attain as she took off on the convoluted path necessary to get up to Bay-3.

She returned to the elevator without incident, got back to Level 3, then took the shortest calculated route to Elevator S-4/1-3B, which would take her to Galileo Bay. She zoomed past several intersections, so quickly she probably wouldn't have been noticed, but slowed before the one where she needed to turn. Detecting two lifeforms approaching, she skidded to a halt a meter short of the intersection and activated the mechanisms that controlled her survival strategy suite, just in case. If they turned her way, they'd be face to face; if they turned the other, she'd be behind them, giving her the advantage; if they went straight, no problem, she'd wait for them to leave, probably via the same elevator she wanted. Logic gates fired as she decided whether or not to knock them out, regardless of which way they turned.

Since she was the first to make the run, causing any sort of disturbance could alert security and destroy their plans. She assessed her options and the probability that they would turn her way. The cadence of their footfalls generated different sound patterns, which indicated one was human, the other not, most likely what the humans referred to as a small grey. The pair arrived at the intersection. Aggie poised to strike.

The pair turned right, directly into her path. She emitted a cloud of gas that would induce momentary disorientation, followed by amnesia, which would result in little more than a mysterious pause in their conversation. The grey blinked its black, almond-shaped eyes while the soldier stopped, shook his head, and looked around, Aggie whipping past them, around a bend, and into the elevator by the time the pair resumed their trek.

She arrived at the mandoor to Bay-3 and analyzed the lock while she hailed Ignatius on the ship's emergency channel. By the time she got through the door, he'd lowered the vehicle's ramp, allowing her to wheel inside to safety, hoping the others would be equally successful. Now her job was to release the lock to Gabe's cell again, deactivate the motion sensors along the route based on the location provided by the tracking device, and blink the lights at any intersections so he'd know which way to turn, if at all.

For a moment she considered why she hadn't taken Gabe with her in the first place. Of course she would have had to slow down and the encounter with the grey and soldier would have been far more complicated. No, this was the correct action, plus she was available to provide assistance as needed.

Simple.

Anything could be achieved with a well-orchestrated plan.

CHAPTER FORTY-FOUR

Subterranean Level 4/Detention Cell 5
Nellis TMR
Restricted Area 51
Rachel, Nevada
August 21, 1978
1712 PDT/0012 GMT

Gabe tried to brush the wrinkles out of his lab coat from being stuffed into the gunny sack, grateful that he'd folded it up neatly the day before. That had helped a little, but he still looked pretty scruffy, plus he hadn't trimmed his beard in days. Lack of sleep and not eating for over forty-eight hours weren't helping his nerves. They'd brought him K-rations, disgusting for any diet, much less his. He knew he needed to eat something, but couldn't, his stomach inside out since discovering his most precious possession was confiscated. Bad coffee and water were all he consumed, his entire gut in knots. Low blood sugar increased the nausea, combining with stress to make him light-headed and dizzy, adrenaline doing its best to compensate.

His hands were shaky as he examined the new badge Aggie had manufactured. This one was mostly white with a holographic gleam. Hopefully it was the correct version to get him where he had to go. He shrugged and clipped it to his collar, then examined the passport with a smile. She'd even included customs stamps for arrivals and departures to Los Angeles, Dallas, Rome, London, Rio de Janeiro, and Brisbane. *Perfect.*

He slipped it into the white coat's inside breast pocket with the tracking device, then gave both a pat for luck. He inhaled deeply, held it a moment, then let it out through pursed lips. Now he just needed to get to his destination without incident. Otherwise, he was toast.

The lock whirled, then clicked, indicating Aggie had released it, right on time. He took another breath and opened the door a crack, looking both ways before stepping out. The tunnel wasn't straight, which didn't help, but he assumed the robot wouldn't have released it if there'd been anyone around, based on the motion sensors.

He turned left and walked fifteen feet to where the tunnel branched to the right. He stopped, alert for activity—nothing besides the low frequency groan of the ventilation system. With another deep breath, he proceeded at an easy pace. The next fifty yards were the riskiest part of the trek, since there was no legitimate reason for a scientist to be in the detention area.

During their tag-up, Thyron had explained that the far side of Level 4, known as the *Aquarius* sector, housed a profusion of labs, but they were in a separate subterranean structure several hundred yards away which was connected to this end by a single tunnel. The lab section had its own elevator, good news because it was unlikely anyone would be in the area. Furthermore it was late afternoon, just past day shift shut down. Janet flights had just started arriving with the night shift, and resident workers, whether civilian or military, were on dinner break.

Fortunately, it was a straight shot to the elevator, no direction required; just long, dark, spooky, and smelly. When he got there he removed the badge, hesitating before slipping it into the reader. Now he'd find out, one way or another, if it was coded correctly; heaven help him, if it wasn't.

And realized Aggie hadn't told him the access code that went with it! *Holy guacamole, now what?*

Panic flared, then he sighed—he could contact her telepathically. But before he did, five numbers came into his head in the 'troid's throaty voice.

Three-one-seven-six-nine.

He smiled, certain she had a Brooklyn accent, as he entered the numbers with bated breath. When the reader blinked green he sighed heavily, the elevator arriving seconds later.

Okay, one level down—or rather, up—two to go. At least on the next two he wouldn't stand out so much.

The doors opened in a familiar location, the passage between the conference room complex and residential area. Through a layer of heavy glass the latter looked like a five-star hotel. Who stayed, much less lived there? Did he want to know? Probably not.

Now to get to Level 1. An unsecured door within the elevator alcove opened directly into a tunnel, the first intersection twenty-five yards ahead. No one in sight. So far so good.

After the intersection, the tunnel made an oblique turn where it met another incoming passage. No prompts, no flashing light; he continued straight. At the next one a caged light above winked, beckoning him to the right. As he recalled, he was to follow this one for approximately a half-mile.

A half-mile. Twice around a quarter-mile track.

It felt farther than a marathon, something he used to do regularly in younger days. Too bad he'd quit; now he was definitely out of shape. Too much work, not enough living, but that was how it was when you loved what you did for a living; married to his job and proud of it.

At a comfortable pace of around three miles per hour, it would take roughly ten minutes. A span that would slip away unnoticed when immersed in normal activity. Now it could determine his entire future, perhaps his life. Once he got to the next intersection, he'd make a hairpin turn to the right, then continue a dozen yards or so to elevator S-4/1-3B, which would take him all the way up to Galileo Bay. Once there, his renegade compadres would be expecting him and he'd be relatively safe.

The tunnel walls varied from random combinations of natural rock accented with cement, wide enough to walk four abreast like where he was now, to others of corrugated metal twenty yards across. Conduits with electrical wiring and copper pipes, probably water, wandered along the ceiling, most likely built during atomic testing in the '40s and '50s.

The persistent damp, earthy odor, undoubtedly loaded with mold spores, irritated his nostrils and he sneezed, muffling it the best he could. He didn't know if the surveillance system included audio; hopefully not. Motion-triggered cameras were bad enough. So far it appeared Aggie was deactivating them, as promised.

He glanced at his watch. Two minutes had passed.

Crap.

He'd always been an optimist, an *If life gives you lemons make lemonade* type, and he tried to envision a fortunate outcome to this catastrophic turn of events. He had to admit that no matter how it turned out, the experience was well worth it. If he never got to publish his findings or share it with another living soul, it was still the highlight of his career as well as his life.

But as a scientist, he was also a realist. Sometimes Murphy's Law preempted his attempt at positivity with a reminder that things were never so bad they couldn't get worse. So far, this appeared to be one of those times.

Sadness shadowed his thoughts as he considered what he may *not* get to do. Aggie had noted the odds of everyone making it out safely were in the vicinity of one out of eight hundred six. *Not bad, if you were buying a lotto ticket, but not good for a life or death situation.* He smiled at the thought of taking the 'troid to Vegas to win back some of what he'd lost a few years back at The Sands.

His thoughts wandered back through the past few months, savoring the experience at both a professional and personal level. It had been so fortunate that Thyron drove himself into dormancy, allowing him to witness his entire life cycle. His heart jumped when he thought of Thyron's latest promise, to retrieve the seed pods. The fact the attempt could prove fatal to the vegemal and possibly himself loomed, eclipsing past joys of hope and discovery.

A Y-intersection came into view up ahead; he checked his watch. Three minutes, right on time. He smiled when the lights dimmed in the passageway to the right. So far so good.

Eventually, the tunnel curved to the left, leading him to another cross tunnel. This one was easy, just proceed straight ahead. Elapsed time, five and a half minutes. The hair on the back of his neck stood up; he paused, listening. Footsteps? He held his breath; couldn't be sure. Remembering an old trick he'd learned as a kid playing cowboys and Indians, he got down on hands and knees, closed his eyes, and placed his ear to the cold, rough floor. Rhythmic reverberations rewarded his efforts, coming from the left.

Crap. Now what?

Mind reeling, undecided what to do, he opened his eyes, finding two pairs of military boots inches from his face.

He swallowed a gasp, heart slamming into his throat.

"Are you all right?" a male voice asked, extending a hand to help him up.

"Uh, yeah. Thanks," he said hoarsely, taking the guy's hand and standing up, then brushing himself off, avoiding eye contact.

"I, uh, thought I saw something sparkling on the wall," he said. "I have a minor in geology and wanted to check it out." He laughed, cautiously meeting their eyes, one then the other, hoping they'd just think he was another eccentric scientist as opposed to a bad liar. One was a sergeant, the other a corporal, both with sidearms.

The sergeant narrowed his eyes. "Don't I know you?" he asked, reaching out to check Gabe's badge.

Gabe froze, heartrate in the megahertz range.

"Yeah! Right!" the man replied. "I never forget a face. You were there for Inglehardt's pitch the other night."

"Yes, I was," he admitted, forcing a smile. "What did you think?"

"Pretty impressive. Hey, we won't hold you up. I'm sure you have somewhere to be."

"Yes. Actually, I do. Have a good day."

"Thanks."

Whew!

The pair cut around him on opposite sides and continued down the passageway. He wanted to check if they were definitely leaving versus radioing in the encounter, yet knew it would look suspicious if they saw him turn. He listened, footsteps fading. They were gone.

He sighed and took a few steps into the intersection, grateful his unfortunate status hadn't been broadcast to the entire base.

Then realized silence had ominous implications as well.

Panic struck; the tunnel blurred, spinning in a grey, vomit-inducing blur. He closed his eyes and reached for the wall, grateful his stomach was empty. He braced himself, heart pounding, until the vertigo faded. Slowly he opened his eyes.

All was quiet. *Good.*

He sighed again, relieved, and prepared to resume his trek. Except he had one rather serious problem—all four tunnels looked identical.

Holy guacamole. Which way?

He turned slowly, gasping with relief to see one of the fluorescent lights blinking straight ahead. He started toward it. Then noticed one in the perpendicular passage, unsteady as well. One was failing, the other Aggie's signal. He checked each for any tell-tale buzzing; both silent.

Which was which?

He shrugged, considered hailing Aggie, then decided to continue for a while first, relieved to see an elevator ahead on the right. Glancing around, he deposited his badge in the slot and carefully entered the code. It flashed green, elevator arriving moments later. Like the previous one, it headed up on its own, door sliding open on the next floor. Gabe stepped out, a tunnel like the others yawning before him. Expecting some indication he'd arrived in Galileo Bay, he proceeded forward, looking for clues; none apparent.

Something felt strange, as if he'd stepped into a time warp or another dimension. Was it nerves? Blood sugar? No, this felt different. Mental as opposed to physical. Having psychic abilities, he was sensitive to things others never felt. Often his impressions were unexplained or irrelevant; others, critical. Considering his precarious situation, paying attention was advised. Then again, the sensation could be the combination of vital sign levels off the chart.

If there was one thing he couldn't do, it was panic.

At the first intersection he paused to look both ways. An identical tunnel faded in distant perspective in either direction. He couldn't risk wandering around blindly, so he queried Aggie for directions. She didn't respond. In fact, it felt empty, as if she weren't there.

Uh-oh.

What could be wrong? She'd supposedly made it to Bay-3. Psi wasn't constrained by material barriers, so even if for some reason his location was lead-lined, she should have picked it up. Something was wrong and he had no clue which way to go.

He stood there and listened—hard—using his ears as well as his mind and intuition. Something was coming from the left. A disturbance of sorts, not audible, but energetic. He turned toward it. It swelled around him, distorting his perceptions. The tunnel appeared to pulsate, the impression eerie, otherworldly.

What were they doing over there? Messing with time and space? Was that why he couldn't contact Aggie? Or was it him, losing it?

Not liking what he felt at all and suspecting it was a subconscious warning, he turned the other way. He sensed nothing in that direction, at least nothing ominous; apparently whatever it was wasn't in his head. This entire sector known as S-4 was creepy.

Nothing would look more suspicious than standing there like a sitting duck. Thus, he sighed with resignation and walked cautiously away from the discomfiting energy field, hoping the motion sensors wouldn't betray him.

CHAPTER FORTY-FIVE

Subterranean Level 4/Detention Cell 3
Nellis TMR
Restricted Area 51
Rachel, Nevada
August 21, 1978
1718 PDT/0018 GMT

Thyron scoped out Watkins's office, taking careful note of everything's location to assure a safe arrival. The last thing he needed was to land somewhere in a position that tangled his branches or, even worse, got stuck or broke any. Furthermore, the commander's quarters were connected to his office, so any noise could awaken him. Hopefully, his implant still had him zoned out in the deepest phases of sleep.

As he summoned his energy in preparation to teleport, the farthest he'd ever attempted, something didn't feel right. In theory, distance made no difference. Was doing this a mistake?

He tuned into Watkins's brainwaves again. They were still in delta range, fast asleep. Of course there was no guarantee how long that would last, but for now all seemed clear. Aggie was dealing with the sensors and alarms, so he could concentrate on his mission. He shuddered, as if to cast off the bad feeling.

It was probably only nervousness because success meant so much to Gabe. Or maybe he was picking up on the man's anxiety as he made his way to the hangar. He psied him out, finding him still on his way to Bay-3. He got ready to report he was ready to make the jump when he realized the man's location was all wrong.

Somehow he'd wound up on Level 2 instead of Galileo Bay and was heading directly toward Watkins's office.

Gabe! Turn around! he psaid. *Turn around and go back to where the paths cross. Turn right, then left. That will take you to the elevator to Bay-3!*

The man's response was surprise followed by momentary panic; then, to his relief, the human did as directed.

Thyron sighed with relief and rebundled his energy. He felt the usual jolt when he maxed out, concentrated on the colonel's office, and a brilliant flash later, arrived.

He'd no sooner gotten his bearings when the alarm system exploded in ear-splitting decibel regalia. He'd never thought his sudden burst of energy would affect Aggie's efforts to suppress the security system, but that was the only explanation.

Holy guacamole! This is really, really, really bad!

Subterranean Level 3/Location 3398
Nellis TMR
Restricted Area 51
Rachel, Nevada
August 21, 1978
17:19:10 PDT/00:19:10 GMT

Klaxon alarms reverberated through the tunnels, amplified to a shockwave that hit Gabe like a nuclear blast. His heartrate tripled as he wondered who'd set it off. Had he, by his mistake? Very possible, since Aggie was muting the alarms along his intended path, not this one. Was the tracker not working? Had he lost it? No, there it was, still in his pocket.

While Thyron hadn't revealed exactly where he was going to retrieve the lost items, intuition told him they were in Watkins's office. Was the vegemal already there? It felt as if he was. Who'd triggered the alarm? Him? Or Thyron?

Holy Guacamole! It really didn't matter who or what, something had gone horribly wrong.

Paralyzed with indecision, Gabe just stood there, mouth agape. Should he still try to make it to Bay-3? Or help Thyron? His feelings for the *flora peda telepathis,* with whom he'd bonded as if Thy were the child he never had, prevailed. If anything happened he could have prevented, he would never forgive himself.

So where was the vegemal? He took a few calming breaths and tuned into his intuition until he felt it pulling him toward the direction he'd been heading when Thyron told him to turn around.

Jaw set, he executed a clean about-face worthy of the most valiant Marine then, like a parent saving his child from a burning building, plunged headlong into the chaos unfolding before him.

Satellite Command Post
Subterranean Level 3/Room SP3826
Nellis TMR
Restricted Area 51
Rachel, Nevada
August 21, 1978
17:19:12 PDT/00:19:12 GMT

Watkins woke up standing beside his bed, service revolver in hand.
What the hell?

He shook his head, trying to dispel the shades of heavy sleep, noting there was an unusual amount of chatter on the psi band. Something was definitely amiss. He checked the chambers of his .45; all were occupied.

Commanding a DUMB had considerably different logistical challenges than other installations. A Deep Underground Military Base was typically covert, Cheyenne Mountain an obvious exception. Threats didn't come from above, alerted by NORAD, but from within. Being the first USAF commander of a top secret base formerly managed by the CIA complicated things even further. It wasn't an assignment for just anyone. The competition had been stiff and when he won the coveted position, he vowed to perform his duties by-the-book. Done right, he'd get his stars from this assignment, a general at last, and fulfill his life's ambition.

There was no room for emotion in the military, especially with National Security at stake. He was accountable for everything that happened under his command. He reported directly to Majic-12, his own clearance higher than the Joint Chiefs or even the president, further multiplying his culpability. He was responsible—*period*—and screw-ups wouldn't be tolerated.

He especially detested the contractors and scientists who infested the base like vermin. Lacking the discipline of career military officers, they didn't take such things seriously enough, often thinking the public had some inane "right to know" in spite of signing security oaths; the violation of which was cause for execution. Such men who did so deserved their fate. Traitors, in every sense of the word. Yet he had no more immunity than anyone else if something went south.

The wail of sirens that blared prior to vehicle tests classified higher than Top Secret were familiar enough that he slept through them; the same ones used during thermonuclear testing until the early 60s and, in their own way, music to his ears. The strident pitch and cadence indicated it was an intrusion alarm coming from his office.

Why would anyone...

He answered his own question, remembering what had been secured in his safe a few days before. Was that treasonous scientist or one of his cronies insane enough to try to recover them? Apparently so. Fury surged as he recalled the man taunting him by reciting "The Star Spangled Banner", which had been the *coup de grace*. Such mockery was intolerable.

Clothed in drab olive skivvies and matching t-shirt, he stepped to the door of his satellite command post, reached forward with his left hand, and slowly depressed the handle.

Galileo Bay-3
Nellis TMR
Restricted Area 51, Sector S-4
Rachel, Nevada
August 21, 1978
17:19:15 PDT/00:19:15 GMT

It took Aggie precious seconds to realize her alarm suppression activities had failed. As a robot designed primarily for agricultural duties, she'd never witnessed, much less analyzed, a teleportation event, its effect unfamiliar, to say nothing of unexpected. The 'troid paused to absorb and assess the input, noting it included a huge spike that matched Thyron's psignature. Somehow, he and the anomalous situation were related. Certainly not a surprise.

Her neural network cycled back to the cryptic dialog between the vegemal and Greenley, which hadn't specified what their plan entailed. She replayed the conversation four times, trying unsuccessfully to deduce what it was. So far, what little evidence she had implicated Thyron, one way or the other.

After hailing the plant on the microwave channel to no avail, she reviewed her instructions versus the status quo.

Greenley was off-course, unauthorized access alarms active in his current location. Watkins was awake, psi-active and ambulatory. And Thyron wasn't responding.

Multiple anomalies related to her command queue activated a failure analysis routine associated with her artificial intelligence circuits. The result indicated she was 60% at fault. She emitted an electronic cry of horror followed by a digital expletive.

Where was that infernal plant? Undoubtedly, this was all his doing, one way or another. She'd never liked nor trusted him as a deviously talented organic lifeform who clearly held similar sentiments toward her. Truce or not, if his antics resulted in her spending the remainder of her service life on this rock, much less this hideous military outpost with its despicable commander, she'd trim him down to size, literally and figuratively.

Meanwhile, more seconds elapsed. It was her responsibility to intervene, by whatever means necessary, to rectify her mistakes and do everything possible to assure a successful mission. Thus, she continued analyzing the unexpected situation.

Again, she hailed Thyron to no avail.

One thing was clear. Her reputation was shot and Greenley was in serious trouble. The only way to redeem herself was to do everything possible to compensate for her failed command queue.

⚜ ⚜ ⚜

Galileo Bay-3
Nellis TMR
Restricted Area 51, Sector S-4
Rachel, Nevada
August 21, 1978
17:19:16 PDT/00:19:16 GMT

Ignatius rose to his full height, instincts on full alert. The insectoid knew intuitively that something had gone seriously wrong. The base was on lockdown and the fact that those he was there to rescue were currently staging an escape attempt was more than coincidence. Ironically, he had no legal obligation to any of the parties at risk. Their association with a girl somewhere else on the planet who came from Mira III was the only reason for official HIO involvement. However, now that he'd become familiar with the individuals involved, to say nothing of the results of his inspection that revealed unauthorized tampering with the space-time continuum, his commitment to their success had set like cooled volcanic lava.

His vehicle was primarily a research vessel, not a warship. Its defensive weaponry could only be deployed if the ship came under attack, which so far was not the case. He shifted his gaze to the 'troid, who at this point was the only one who'd made it to safety within the confines of the *Volition.* Her randomly blinking photoreceptors in a full spectrum of colors indicated she was as confused as he was.

The only one he knew he could establish communications with was Thyron. Somehow he was at the heart of the situation. Would contacting him exacerbate the crisis? Maybe. But without knowing more, there was no way he could lend assistance.

Thyron. Report status, he psaid.

No response.

Thyron. Report.

Nothing.

CHAPTER FORTY-SIX

Subterranean Level 2/Location 2387
Nellis TMR
Restricted Area 51, Sector S-4
Rachel, Nevada
August 21, 1978
17:19:17 PDT/00:19:17 GMT

Gabe stopped, unsure which way to go when the tunnel ended in a "T", all directions bathed in flashing red lights beating time with screaming alarms. With nothing better to guide him, he followed his instincts and turned right, running until he reached a heavy metal door with the stenciled words, SATELLITE COMMAND POST, COLONEL FRANKLIN B. WATKINS, BASE COMMANDER. He leaned against the opposing wall to catch his breath, having no idea what he should do, only that this was where he belonged.

His breath caught in his throat when the door opened a crack, then swung inward slowly on creaky hinges. He crept a few steps to his right, getting out of view, jaw dropping when he saw a familiar leafy branch snake its way into the hall, followed by an extremely unpleasant odor.

"Thyron!" he said aloud, words overcome by the ongoing din. "Are you okay?"

Of course. But we probably shouldn't hang around. Here, take this, he stated, revealing an accordion folder secured within his limbs, bulging with Gabe's notebooks, lab notes and a small fabric bag.

You did it! Gabe psaid with a grin, picking up the bag to kiss it before placing it back in the folder. He tucked the priceless cache under one arm, Thyron beneath the other, glanced both ways, then headed back the way he'd come, turning left at the first tunnel.

No, no, no! Thyron protested. *That way's crawling with MPs, all heading this way. Go straight.*

Not knowing enough to argue, he did as instructed, hoping Thyron was right.

Galileo Bay-3
Nellis TMR
Restricted Area 51, Sector S-4
Rachel, Nevada
August 21, 1978
17:19:47 PDT/00:19:47 GMT

Aggie debated on whether or not to disable all alarms, based on the human rationale "better late than never." Logic dictated that doing so at this point could reveal her illegal involvement to base authorities, who were undoubtedly monitoring the security systems. Could she make it look like an unexplained anomaly or drill? Maybe. All the racket was annoying and distracting, tying up circuits she needed to assess the situation. Then she realized she was on the *Volition*, neutral intergalactic territory. What could the Earthlings do to her? Nothing. She shut them down.

Gabe's tracker indicated he was on the move. She deactivated all motion sensors along his current trajectory, then compiled data from multiple tunnels, which indicated the passage of several troops converging on where he'd gone off course; he'd taken the wrong elevator from Level 3, winding up on Level 2 instead of Galileo Bay. How did he manage that? How did she miss it? Why hadn't he contacted her? Maybe it had something to do with that strange disturbance in the spacetime continuum on the *Alice Floor*. At this point it didn't matter, just needed to be fixed.

Further analysis of S-4's security system showed activity concentrated in the vicinity of the commander's quarters and command post. She checked Watkins's implant for location, finding him in his office, disoriented, and emitting random bursts of pstatic. She jammed it, assuming there would be loop chatter by her cohorts that he didn't need to hear.

Further assessment indicated alarm activation had deployed security barriers every twenty meters along all passageways within a hundred meter radius of the colonel's outpost. According to Gabe's tracker, he'd encounter one within twenty-three seconds.

⸸ ⸸ ⸸

Subterranean Level 2/Location 2308
Nellis TMR
Restricted Area 51, Sector S-4
Rachel, Nevada
August 21, 1978
17:20:01 PDT/00:20:01 GMT

Now that it was quiet, implying the situation was somewhat under control, Thyron responded to Ignatius.

I'm with Gabe, heading your way. What's the status down there?

Not good, the insectoid replied. *Heavily armed MPs everywhere. Base is on lockdown. Are you okay?*

So far. Can't say the same for the colonel, though.

Oh, no, Ignatius replied. *What happened?*

The best way to sum it up is that nature took its course.

Explain, Thyron.

My defensive response kicked in. Couldn't help it. His own fault for scaring me like that. Knocked him out, at least long enough for me to collect what rightfully belongs to me. Luckily, Gabe was waiting outside to give me a ride.

Did you kill Watkins?

No, I don't think so. Blinded, maybe. After the initial burst, I cut it off and left.

So he's conscious, but compromised.

Probably. Sure was yelling a lot. So what's the situation there?

Bay-3's blockaded. The 'troid is here, assessing everyone's status so we can come up with an alternate plan.

As Thyron conversed with Ignatius, Gabe stepped around a bend, then stopped short, confronted by solid metal a few meters away.

You need to hurry, Thyron psaid. *We're stuck. Just encountered a security barrier and can't go any farther. And I have a bad feeling about—*

An explosion finished the sentence, punctuated by a pinging sound. Gabe hit the wall, then fell to the ground. Thyron landed in a disheveled heap a short distance away. What was that? Some sort of shockwave? Getting his bearings, he realized it was far worse.

Thyron shifted his peduncles beneath himself and got up, then shuffled over to Gabe's still form, crumpled on his side on the stone floor. The back of his left shoulder had a small hole from which a viscous red fluid was leaking. On his other side, a profusion of crimson had saturated the ragged edges of a hole in the front of his lab coat.

He pushed it aside with one of his sturdier limbs, finding torn flesh, shattered bone, and ravaged muscle. Thyron gasped, shocked at what a human body had inside; nothing like what he'd seen on television, much less the tidy morphology of a plant. A dark pool that contained the essence of human life crept outward from beneath the fallen man, spreading at an alarming rate.

The violent death of living cells created an energy void that empathically sucked the life from Thyron as well, even more so due to their psi-entangled connection. He fought hard against the inclination to wilt, knowing he had to do something to stop any more blood from escaping. Following his instincts, he ripped off his right visual sensor and pressed it into the wound, willing its cytoplasm to mutate to human platelets, help the blood coagulate, and stop the flow. For now, that was all he could do.

By the yelling and footsteps approaching from behind, it was apparent their attacker was closing fast. Shaky and disoriented, Thyron nonetheless turned to face his foe.

Galileo Bay-3
Nellis TMR
Restricted Area 51, Sector S-4
Rachel, Nevada
August 21, 1978
17:20:40 PDT/00:20:40 GMT

Aggie's logic circuits cycled, seeking the best possible intervention when Watkins continued to move. Not only was the base commander in the same tunnel as Thyron and Gabe, but within a dozen meters. For some reason, Gabe's tracker had quit, plus a security barrier had been deployed, which prevented them from proceeding.

Perhaps she could open it long enough for them to get through, then close it again, isolating Watkins on the other side. Already familiar with the motion sensors, which were part of the same network, it didn't take long to find the circuit for the release mechanism. With the colonel's implant still jammed, she psied her plan.

Thyron, she psaid, *I'll open the security barrier long enough for you and Gabe to pass through. Do you copy?*

No response.

She tried again. Still nothing, though she sensed the vegemal's psimissions, modulated in a manner she'd never detected before.

Subterranean Level 2/Location 2343
Nellis TMR
Restricted Area 51, Sector S-4
Rachel, Nevada
August 21, 1978
17:21:04 PDT/00:21:04 GMT

Thyron shuffled toward their adversary, weakened but determined to place as much distance as possible between him and Gabe. He immediately noticed his depth perception was compromised by having only one eye. It wouldn't take long before a new one would grow back, but for now that was all he had.

Another shot rang out, again ricocheting off the walls and whistling past Thyron's single eye.

"I'll get you, Greenley, if it's the last thing I do!" the colonel snarled, voice hoarse and slightly muffled as it echoed through the tunnel. "That perverted plant, too! No way you're gettin' away with this! No way! Not on my watch!"

The tirade was followed by a string of expletives related to excrement and various other human biological functions that Thyron had never heard before, were out of context, and he could only barely begin to translate; but their murderous intent was clear.

Triggered by fear and fury, defenses stirred again within his primary bulb and burned through every limb. This time there would be no restraint, but he held back, knowing he was still too close to Gabe. He plodded forward, shuffling one peduncle forward, then the other, pressure building.

As he finally waddled around the tunnel's bend, more shots rang out, direct this time, nicking some branches, but otherwise unharmed.

Not an easy target, am I, Watkins? he snarled, bristling with botanical fury.

The colonel held a gas mask to his face with one hand, his weapon with the other. Seeing Thyron, he dropped the mask, took another step forward, then gripped the gun with both hands, leveling it toward his primary bulb.

No longer able to restrain the toxic buildup, Thyron let fly with a cloud of gaseous sulfuric acid, fanning it in the commander's direction. The man screamed, dropped his weapon, and covered his face with his hands. He fell to his knees and tried to reach the mask, but failed. Moments later, gasping for air, he tipped over sideways into a fetal position and lay still.

Thyron! Report! Ignatius psaid.

Thyron closed his eye, photosystems straining for CO_2 and needing more light. Depleted and wilting fast, he couldn't quit; he still had work to do.

Gabe's hurt, he responded weakly. *Rather badly, judging by how much blood is escaping.*

What happened?

He was hit by a projectile from the colonel's weapon.

Where's the colonel now?

Unconscious. This time maybe dead.

Dead? How?

Never mind. It doesn't matter. I can't move Gabe alone. I need help.

Thyron used the last of his reserves to waddle back to his human, bounty he'd retrieved from Watkins's office scattered across the stone floor. He swept everything back in the folder, wrapped some shoots around it, then draped his boughs over Gabe's still form.

Vegemals lived forever, provided they had viable seeds and bulbils. Death that was permanent and irreversible was incomprehensible. Fear, grief, and sadness he'd never experienced before coursed through his protoplasm as unfamiliar moisture transpired from his leaves and dampened the items held snugly between them.

Drained physically and emotionally, the lid of his remaining eye flickered closed, what little energy remained quickly draining through empathic entanglement.

CHAPTER FORTY-SEVEN

Subterranean Level 2/Location 2343
Nellis TMR
Restricted Area 51, Sector S-4
Rachel, Nevada
August 21, 1978
17:23:08 PDT/00:23:08 GMT

*H*ey! *Thyron! What's going on? Is that Code Red racket related to you?*

Thyron awoke slowly and shook off the unexplained moisture. Why was he covered with dew? *Brad? Is that you?* he answered.

Yeah, it's me. Are you okay?

Mostly, yes; I'll be okay. But Gabe isn't. He's leaking blood and unconscious.

Oh, my God. What happened?

Watkins shot him, Thyron psaid.

Oh, no! Where's the colonel now?

Knocked out, a few meters away.

Where are you?

In the tunnel, east of Watkins's office. But there's a wall. We're trapped.

Not good, Brad replied. *Only MPs can release the security barriers.*

Not exactly who I had in mind, Thyron responded. *Can you get to Bay-3?*

I don't know. Last time, I was under escort. Why?

Aggie should be there with Ignatius. If she can't help, maybe he can.

The robot. Right, Brad psaid. *Hmmmph. Shooting an unarmed NASA scientist sounds like an HIO violation to me. Stand by. I'll see what I can do.*

Thyron brushed a tender branch across Gabe's hair, leaves weeping with another surge of moisture. He didn't comprehend pain, his biosystems lacking nociceptors, which transmitted that sensation to an animal's brain. Empathically, however, he understood mortality as never before.

Hang on, Gabe, he psaid. *Help is on the way. I hope.*

⸙ ⸙ ⸙

Subterranean Level 1/Room GB4-1006
Nellis TMR
Restricted Area 51, Sector S-4
Rachel, Nevada
August 21, 1978
17:24:32 PDT/00:24:32 GMT

Brad sat fuming in his cramped office in Bay-4 as he absorbed the implications of his conversation with Thyron. He'd been working at Area 51 for just over two years and been perfectly happy—until Watkins came along. He'd never trusted the man and knew it was mutual. Whatever Thyron had done, the colonel deserved it. About then a bad feeling hit his gut, reminding him he'd taken security oaths he was about to violate, big time. No telling what the price might be; from what he'd heard, it would be bad. Placing him between the proverbial rock and a hard place.

He took off his glasses and rubbed his face with both hands, then sighed heavily as he replaced them. Thyron had done more for his career than anyone else—except, perhaps his uncle, whose connections at Lockheed's Skunk Works got him onboard in the first place upon completing his Master's in aeronautical design engineering at Caltech.

Watkins had done nothing other than issue veiled threats and open invectives, not only to him, but all the contractors on base. Until his breakthrough, thanks to Thyron, which had forced the colonel to admit his worth. His jaw hardened as less positive incidents, too numerous to mention, flashed through memory. That slimy bastard had definitely earned his place at the top of his list of people he wouldn't piss on if they were in flames.

The recent inspection tour with that insectoid Thyron called Ignatius came to mind. The alien towered over his own six-foot three-inch frame, yet projected vibes more benevolent than some of his own kind. Especially Watkins. Since there were clear HIO violations involved, he was confident the ant could help, maybe give him asylum, too.

He smiled at the thought, then focused back on the present, wondering how badly Greenley was hurt; Watkins carried a .45, most others a 9 millimeter. The difference between the damage each inflicted spawned memories of previous experiences with gunshot wounds. Timely medical attention was crucial to the man's survival; which had now fallen to him.

His security oaths loomed again, but he shoved them aside, switching to auto-pilot like he'd done during firefights when live ammo was so close overhead that a sneeze could make him the next one down, but someone out there needed help. Emergencies were like that. You acted first, worried later—if you survived.

He got up, removed the first aid kit from the wall, checked its contents, then stepped over to a supply cabinet where he added an I.V. pack and a bag of Ringer's. He unlocked the compartment where they kept the morphine, grabbed a couple vials and a syringe, then stuffed it all inside his backpack, grateful such medications were on hand for contingencies, whether workplace accidents or emergency landings of the UFO kind.

Ready.

But how would he get to Bay-3? With the base on lockdown, the last thing he needed was attention, which as a civilian was inevitable.

He stepped from his office into the voluminous hangar, checking the maze of gantries and catwalks to make sure no one was around. Fortunately, his team was usually gone at this hour, either off-duty or on dinner break. The operator platform to the heavy lift crane was vacant; likewise untended were the banks of electronic equipment that surrounded the UFO his team was back-engineering. He paused, sighing as he gazed upon the huge, wedge-shaped vehicle with renewed awe.

Damn, I love this work.

The hangar door was open, lockdown concentrated on interior tunnels. Since being promoted to lead engineer, he'd been issued a new badge. It was purple before, now it had the addition of a holographic background. Maybe now he could get into areas he couldn't before. He walked past the vehicle, out onto the sprawling dirt landing strip, turning left toward Bay-3. Not surprisingly, its massive door was closed. But every hangar had a man-door to the outside, as well as one within that led into the labyrinth of tunnels that connected every section of the base.

He eyed the red status light on the cipher lock, heart pounding, as he unclipped his badge from his collar. Then, holding his breath, he inserted it in the slot and punched in his code.

The light blinked green, tumblers turned, and the door yielded to his touch.

Subterranean Level 2/Location 2340
Nellis TMR
Restricted Area 51, Sector S-4
Rachel, Nevada
August 21, 1978
17:34:12 PDT/00:34:12 GMT

Thyron wasn't sure how much time had elapsed, but a while later the security barrier rumbled downward on arched tracks and disappeared beneath the floor, its only visible evidence diagonal yellow stripes along its leading edge. Moments later, he sensed vibrations. It drew closer, sounding like Aggie's rolopeds, but at a faster pace than expected. He peered down the tunnel, which curved out of view another twenty meters away, hoping it wasn't one of the electric carts delivering hostile intent.

What rounded the bend at an incredible speed was indeed the 'troid, two appendages collapsed to form a platform above her rolopeds. The other two extended forward from opposite sides of her cylindrical neck, his protégé gripping them with white-knuckled hands. Aggie jolted to a stop, Brad stumbling off in an awkward display of what humans referred to as Newton's First Law. He caught his balance, then stumbled back to remove a large bag hanging from one of the 'troid's articulated arms.

"Wow! What's that smell?" he asked, wrinkling his nose.

My defense system, Thyron replied.

"That's what you used to take out Watkins?"

Yes.

Brad's reaction projected surprise, but oddly enough, approval. "Good thing these tunnels have a good ventilation system," was all he said, not looking up as he set the bag on the floor, opened it, then removed a large box from which he pulled on a pair of rubber gloves. Thyron slipped into his thoughts, finding the man's mind awash in bloody memories that were oddly familiar. Where had he seen such things before?

Are you a hawkeye? Thyron asked.

Brad paused a moment to give him a questioning look. "Do you mean Hawkeye at the 4077th MASH, on TV?"

"Yes."

"No, I'm not a doctor," he said with a smile. "But I worked with men like Hawkeye. I was a medic in Vietnam, then worked my way through grad school as an EMT. I've dealt with injuries like this before, more than I care to recall. Last thing I thought I'd be doing here, though."

He rolled Gabe to his back with gentle hands, cutting away his lab coat and shirt with a pair of scissors. His jaw dropped when he saw what was attached to the exit wound.

I did what I could, Thyron explained.

Brad removed it gently, eyes widening in disbelief. "The bleeding's stopped." He closed his eyes and sighed heavily. *Thank God.*

Thyron brightened at the man's second reference to his divinity, watching as he cleaned and bandaged the wound, then placed the affected arm in a sling. After that, he inserted a thin tube in Gabe's other arm which was connected to a clear bag that contained a mixture he detected as sodium chloride, sodium lactate, potassium chloride, and calcium chloride in water.

Then Brad gathered up the bloody clothes with Thyron's severed photoreceptor, and placed them in a plastic bag beside him. He looked around on the floor, then got up to examine the walls, Thyron about to ask what he was looking for when Brad pulled out his pocket knife and removed something from the cement wall.

"Here's the bullet," he said, holding it up triumphantly before dropping it in a small container that he put back in the medical supply box. "With this, there'll be no doubt who shot him. You undoubtedly saved his life," he said. "How'd you know to do that?"

Thyron responded with a leafy shrug, further explanation halted when Gabe's eyes flickered open.

"Lie still. You're going to be okay," Brad told him, resting his hand on his good shoulder. "Hold on while we load you up." Gabe groaned, eyes closing again.

Aggie's arms configured into a platform onto which Brad carefully lifted his patient. Once secure, the surfaces adjusted into a makeshift recliner, placing Gabe in a secure position. Brad tucked a lightweight silver blanket under his head, another around him, expression grim. "He's pretty shocky, but should be okay. I suppose I should go check on the colonel."

A volley of footsteps, then voices, echoed from the direction of Watkins's office, followed by urgent shouts as converging MPs apparently discovered their downed commander. Brad glanced in that direction, psimissions a mix of anger and satisfaction.

"Forget that. C'mon, let's go," he said, picking up the plastic bag with one hand, Thyron with the other. "Whoa, you're heavier than you look!" he commented, shifting the vegemal to the crook of his arm.

"C'mon, let's get past that barrier and get it up again. Can you do that, Aggie?"

"Of course," she replied, rolling forward obediently. It clunked into place, muting shouts of protest from those on the other side.

"All right, let's roll," Brad said, then led the way to an elevator that took them up to Level 1. They exited to find a tunnel network that sprawled from the hub like a giant spider, each numbered arm leading to one of the hangars in Galileo Bay. A hundred meters or so down the one leading to Bay-3, scratchy radio transmissions mixed with the metallic clang of weaponry indicated they were almost there.

"Wait here while I see what's going on," Brad stated, setting Thyron on the floor.

Several minutes passed before he returned, face solemn but lacking any hint of additional trouble. "Watkins is in the infirmary in critical condition, pending airlift to Vegas. He's alive, but blinded, perhaps permanently, and on a ventilator. His lungs are severely damaged, one collapsed. The only orders he'll be giving anytime soon will be to the bedpan nurse at the VA Hospital." His mouth quivered, as if stifling a smile. *Karma's a bitch, ain't she, Watkins?*

Who's Karma? Thyron and Aggie asked in unison.

Brad laughed. "Never mind. I forgot you could read my thoughts." He grinned at the 'troid. "You, too, eh?"

What about Gabe? Thyron asked.

"And us?" Aggie added.

"When I got there, the deputy base commander and Ignatius were discussing the situation. They don't want it to escalate into an interstellar incident, which could get messy. *Real* messy. So, it sounds as if you can collect your belongings, then all of you are free to go."

CHAPTER FORTY-EIGHT

Onboard HIO Intragalactic Starship **Volition**
Nellis TMR
Restricted Area 51, Galileo Bay-3
Rachel, Nevada
August 21, 1978
1947 PDT/0247 GMT

Gabe lounged back in Ignatius's command chair, feeling weak and a bit loopy from the pain shot Brad had given him, but smiling nonetheless. "I don't know how I can ever thank you," he said, his gaze lingering affectionately on each of the unusual individuals gathered around, all bathing his psyche with vibes of caring and concern.

"Likewise," Brad stated, reaching out to take Gabe's extended hand. "Thyron definitely gave my career a quantum boost. But I really think I've had it with this place. I talked to my former boss at the Skunk Works a few weeks ago. He's been trying to get me to come back. I've decided to take him up on it. They have some cool new projects where I think I can make a real difference."

"That's great," Gabe replied. "I definitely don't plan on ever coming back. As long as Watkins is alive, I'm at risk, so I'm gone, too."

"Probably a good idea," Brad stated. "I'll have to come back for testing time to time, but I can tolerate that, especially with Watkins gone. I wish all of you nothing but the best. It's been an amazing experience, all around. I'll get out of your way so you can take off." He shook Gabe's hand, gave Aggie an awkward hug, and ran affectionate fingers along Thyron's extended bough. "Have a safe trip." He laughed. "We certainly don't need another Roswell."

Ignatius activated the ship's ramp so Brad could depart, the engineer giving them one final wave before stepping off into Bay-3's cavernous depths where he activated the hangar door. It rumbled open slowly, setting sun dusting the distant mountains and desert that stretched for miles around with orange shadows. The *Volition* lifted silently, folded its landing struts, and drifted into the open, where it engaged its anti-gravity drive and seconds later shot beyond low earth orbit to an altitude of five hundred kilometers, then headed south-southeast.

Galileo Bay-3
Nellis TMR
Restricted Area 51, MH4
Rachel, Nevada
August 21, 1978
1952 PDT/0252 GMT

As soon as the *Volition* departed, Brad prepared to leave the hangar, relieved all had ended well, even better than expected. He was particularly grateful that Ignatius had insisted that he be granted immunity for his actions, given it was a life-threatening situation. The deputy base commander had stated there was no reason for it to be on his record or anywhere else, since the incident officially never happened, putting him completely in the clear.

After the door rumbled closed, he turned to head back to the base interior. When he got to the door, he noticed the plastic bag that contained Gabe's bloody shirt and lab coat where he'd tossed it on the floor. He picked it up and walked outside through the mandoor to the Dumpster, the contents of which would eventually be incinerated. He tore open the bag and grabbed the ripped and soiled garments, intending to toss them inside. He stopped, noticing something in the lab coat's inside pocket—a passport drenched in blood as well as a small electronic device, which he examined closely for a moment, then dropped in his shirt pocket. After that, he proceeded to wad up everything else and toss it in the bin. Something heavy fell to the ground—that strange organic sphere which Thyron had placed in the wound. Part of his bulb or some sort of fruit, perhaps?

He picked it up, cringing when he fully realized it had been one of the vegemal's eyes. He examined it closely, marveling that it had worked so effectively as a coagulant. Oddly enough, there was no blood on it, dried or otherwise, and except for the dust it had just picked up, it looked pristine. It certainly had fascinating medical implications.

He brushed off the dust, pondering again how Thyron would have known to do such a thing, then scrutinized it again, deciding it definitely resembled some sort of bulb or seed pod.

Maybe he should plant it. Yes, that's what he'd do. As soon as he got back to Burbank, he'd pick up a ceramic pot at the Mexican market and give it a shot at life. If nothing else, it would remind him of the off-world mentor he could never talk about who'd given his career a stellar boost, literally and figuratively.

No telling what it might become.

***Onboard HIO Intragalactic Starship* Volition**
Low Earth Orbit
Altitude: 350 Kilometers
August 21, 1978
0301 GMT

Thyron pondered what they'd accomplished the past few days, absently watching Ignatius set the ship on autopilot, then summon a hover-litter to transport Gabe to the infirmary. While he and Brad had provided excellent first aid, the bullet had done significant damage. Brad had even commented that at such close range, if it had been a direct hit instead of a ricochet, it would have probably taken Gabe's arm off. The HIO ship had the benefit of medical advances from multiple worlds that held promise for rebuilding cartilage, bone, and anything else that had been destroyed beyond the limits of normal healing.

"Aggie, I'm going to need a new passport," Gabe mentioned while they waited for the med tech. "Let's use different information this time, just to be safe: Gabriel Francisco Maria Fernandes, May 16, 1925, Manaus, Brazil."

The 'troid complied, printing it out and handing it to him just as an insectoid arrived with the litter. The giant ant helped Gabe get onboard, then followed as it glided out of the piloting suite.

That 3D printer has certainly come in handy lately, hasn't it? Thyron commented.

Aggie's photoreceptors blinked stand-by for a long moment before she responded. *Yes, it did,* she finally admitted. *I'm impressed with that and the other mods you made. I suppose I should thank you.*

Thyron's branches tilted to his equivalent of a satisfied smile. *That would be most appropriate,* he psaid back.

Doesn't mean I will. Only that I should, she responded.

That's fine. Ignatius, do you happen to have a tysa game onboard?

The ship's captain eyed them both, mystified by their cryptic conversation. *It is likely available for download in the Miran database component,* he psaid.

Point taken, Aggie admitted, photoreceptors blushing red as they focused on Thyron. *Thank you. Satisfied?*

The vegemal's branches lifted a little more as he remembered the *Shut down/Chill-out* command he'd also added. *Yes,* he replied, amazed he and the 'troid had gotten along as well as they had, showing even adversaries could work together for a common cause.

The three of them chatted about the past few days, filling in Ignatius on the details of their escape, until Gabe returned an hour or so later.

Could they help? Thyron asked.

Actually, yes. A lot, Gabe replied. *The med techs were impressed with what a good job you and Brad did. It had already started to heal. They replaced the torn up cartilage and bone tissue, set a new matrix for muscle to rebuild upon, and even covered it all with artificial skin that'll be absorbed as my own replaces it. Pretty nifty.* He moved his arm to demonstrate, wincing only slightly.

"So how are we going to do this?" Gabe asked, turning to Ignatius. "It's not like you can just land this thing at the Manaus airport. Can you?" he added, eyebrows raised.

"No, not procedure. Would cause serious upset," Ignatius replied, voice crackling through his translator as he spoke aloud. "Fly-overs common. Delivery of passenger create major incident. Will land authorized area. South Nazca. Deploy there small drone as looks of jet-powered Terran aircraft you call Lear. Will you deliver to airport of Manaus, then auto-return Nazca. No question, no controversy."

"That's quite a distance. I'd guess over three thousand miles. How long will it take? Will it make any stops?"

"Drones travel fast. Travel time, twenty-four minutes."

"Holy guacamole!"

"Contact required with persons below?"

"No, that won't be necessary. I have relatives in the area. It'll be fun to surprise them."

"Area is familiar?"

"Absolutely! I've done a lot of work in the Amazon. Actually, I was born there. Didn't leave until I was eleven. My mother was born there as well. My father was an American anthropologist, working with indigenous cultures. They met, fell in love, and got married."

"Why did leave?"

"Eventually, we returned to the States after a political uprising in '35," Gabe explained. "Good thing they left, Vargas came into power in '37. Unfortunately, we arrived in Oklahoma right in the middle of the Dust Bowl, but it wasn't quite as bad in the north part of the state, where we were. Tough times, nonetheless. Luckily, my parents made sure I was fluent in both languages, but it's been a while since I've spoken Portuguese, other than a few times with my niece, Francesca. As far as anyone knows, I was born at home in Oklahoma, but the last passport Aggie generated is correct. Other than the fact it's my mother's maiden name." He chuckled. "I would've never gotten a Q-level clearance if they'd known I wasn't born in the States."

Ignatius nodded his humongous head, apparently relieved that this segment of his trip promised so far to be uneventful.

"One of my cousins has been trying to get me down here to consult for his *fazenda,* a coffee farm, hit hard by the black frost in '75," Gabe went on. "They lost acres of plants that had to be replaced. They want me to help develop a variety that's more frost-hardy. It's in Minas Gerais, but I can do most of the work from Manaus. They'll be thrilled to see me. Everything happens for a reason. There's no such thing as a coincidence. *Não há coincidências."*

CHAPTER FORTY-NINE

HIO Remote Subterranean Outpost
Nazca, Peru
August 21, 1978
2213 Peru Time/0313 GMT

The *Volition* soared toward its destination, Thyron marveling at the world below, diversity of the terrain far exceeding his expectations. Barren areas reminded him of Sapphira, then abruptly changed to mountain peaks that pierced the clouds as they crossed Mexico. An influx of multiple botanical species followed, similar to what he'd encountered on Verdaris. He'd barely tuned into the luxuriously verdant emanations when they left it behind for a stretch of ocean, water teeming with life beyond anything he'd ever imagined. He sensed intelligence residing therein, almost wishing he could prolong his stay, his assessment of Terra a welcome distraction from the difficult moment yet to come.

Sky and land darkened quickly as their trajectory shifted eastward. A coastline came into view among the shadows, a continental landmass stretching to the horizon in one direction, an ocean of salt water toward the other, a gibbous Moon tipping its waves with silver light.

More mountains, a barren plain, then odd markings highlighted by moonlight, hundreds of kilometers below. A profusion of spiral designs and figures Gabe pointed out as a hummingbird, monkey, spider, and other creatures all grew larger as the vehicle descended, eventually less than a hundred meters above ground. The craft glided above a perfectly symmetrical geoglyph, its hypnotic pattern comprised of interwoven squares, circles, triangles, and dots. The mandala-like design beckoned, attention drawn to its innermost square, in which a circle was inscribed. Several radial lines within suddenly came to life, each blinking a rainbow of color. The square divided into four sections marked by wisps of rising dust, barely visible in the moon's subtle glow. Each square split diagonally, inner section folding inward to reveal a gaping cavity.

Until then, the lightshow had remained suspended above the opening horizontally, but now each beam began to move, breaking from the center and elevating toward the *Volition.* A chime sounded and yellow indicators flashed on the ship's control panel, beeping while Ignatius adjusted their position until indicators switched to green. Another chime of a different pitch and the ship descended, settling softly on the subterranean surface far below.

Landing lights revealed the cavernous area extended as far as they could see in every direction. Vehicles in a variety of sizes and models lay before them in silent repose, quantity cloaked by darkness. A short distance away, a relatively small craft awaited, ramp deployed, interior illuminated.

"Holy guacamole!" Gabe exclaimed. "Last thing I expected way out here!"

"Been here over thousand Terran years," Ignatius stated in his translator's monotone pitch. "Delivery vehicle programmed for journey. Flight plan set to Manaus, who expect arrival."

"Really? That's it? It doesn't look anything like a Lear," Gabe commented. "Looks more like a miniature version of the *Volition.*"

"Yes, will appear as small jet-powered aircraft known to Terrans as Lear. Off-worlders helped design."

"It will? But where are the wings? Tail? Or engines?"

"Such features hamper non-atmospheric hypersonic flight," Ignatius explained. "Lear features deploy after deceleration and entry, when destination arrived."

"Ahhh, makes sense," Gabe replied, then chuckled. "As much as any of this does, anyway." He took a deep breath and released it in a sigh as Thyron rested the gaze of his remaining eye upon him, the man's expression switching from sheer excitement to melancholy. The man was easier to read now that he'd ditched the beard, which came in handy since he'd become so adept at cloaking his thoughts.

How long will it take for a new eye to grow back? Gabe psaid.

It won't be long before I see
the world again in stereoscopy.
I'd give you both at any time
or anything you need that's mine.

Gabe's emotional mix was too complicated to express, but he knew that Thy could feel it. *Thank you for saving my life,* he psaid. *And making it joyful again. I wish you'd come with me.*

To stay with you on this strange land
is simply not the cosmic plan.
Our lives have crossed by destiny
must now diverge indefinitely.

You're waxing poetic again, Gabe noted with a smile. *Space travel becomes you.*

Atmospheres and populations
inhibit my interpolations.
Since it's lacking interference
The void of space makes quite a difference.

Gabe nodded, wondering what it would be like to get away from pollution in all its forms and allow Earth to heal, as she surely would, free of human intervention.

At that point, words failed them both, an empathic exchange of deep affection taking their place. Thyron noted the unexplained dampness transpiring on his leaves and that Gabe had a similar track on his cheeks.

"I'd best be going," Gabe said, wiping his eyes and switching to audio as he got up from his seat. "Thank you, Ignatius, for more than I can say. I never dreamed I'd have a ride as spectacular as this. And Aggie, thank you as well," he said, patting one of her arms. "Thyron, may your visit to our planet always hold a place of esteem in your infinite memory. You will forever live in mine." *Your progeny will be well cared for,* he promised silently, hand over his heart, where, beneath his shirt and secured around his neck, lay a drawstring bag of seedpods.

The ramp whined as it lowered to the ground, drone waiting a few dozen meters away for its sole occupant. Thyron shuffled to the exit and watched him go, lifting a branch when his forever friend turned at the bottom and waved a final farewell, again placing his hand over his heart. Gabe lingered a moment, blinked hard, then turned and proceeded slowly to the craft where he climbed inside, door easing down behind him.

When the ramp closed and sealed with a hiss, Ignatius carried Thyron back to his position by the window strip. Consumed by unfamiliar feelings, he watched the ground retreat, as the *Volition* lifted effortlessly, then hovered a few hundred meters above ground, night somehow darker than it had been before. The drone deployed, then assumed a southeast trajectory against a background of stars toward its destination. Moments later, the gaping opening eased closed, the only witness to its existence a few persistent dust devils.

At Thyron's request, they monitored the drone until its safe arrival, then swept across magnificent rain forests and steamy jungles. Undaunted by darkness, Thyron immersed his psyche in their botanical splendor, feeling an unanticipated bond with one particular region as they soared northward.

If they didn't have an appointment to retrieve Creena, he would have asked Ignatius to explore the planet some more, though he suspected the HIO wouldn't approve, much less the ship's captain who'd undoubtedly resist any additional deviations, of which there had already been too many.

CHAPTER FIFTY

Benson Mountain Fresh Dairy Farm
Northern Cache Valley, Utah
August 22, 1978
0115 MDT/0715 GMT

The *Volition* arrived in the appointed place, clear skies alive with stars belonging to one of the galaxy's spiral arms. A few meteors slashed the celestial dome, moon high above the eastern mountains. A town glowed to the south, houses mostly dark in the post-midnight hour. Ignatius had insisted that such landings could only occur at such times, except for life or death emergencies.

Thyron connected with the girl's psi channel, startled to discover she wasn't alone. Ignatius also noted the anomaly and was uncomfortable. Did the other person expect to join her? Thyron tuned into the conversation, assaulted by the girl's emotions, which duplicated his own recent experience. For a stay that began simply to obtain transportation to Mira III, it had become unexpectedly difficult to leave.

Having had enough drama for a lifetime or more, Thyron shoved the emotional overload aside, ready to proceed as planned and deal with it later. No telling what could go wrong if they hung around longer than necessary.

C'mon, Creena! Don't delay
Board the ship or simply stay.

She lingered a bit longer, then finally boarded. They ascended as soon as she'd reached the flight deck and settled into an acceleration seat, joining him and Aggie. The ship hovered above one of the valley's many fields of ripening grain for a moment to draw energy from the planet's magnetic field, disrupting the area's power grid and extinguishing the town's lights. The ship departed at last, engaging the warp drive upon leaving the solar system. Creena's long, dark hair hid her expression as she got up to gaze out the window, but her aura revealed she was still distraught. Curious about her experience, he pinged her to see if it was anything like his own.

What is wrong?
What did they do?
You should be glad
and not so blue.

"You were wrong, Thyron," she said, voice unsteady. "The humans there aren't bad at all. Well, at least most of them."

"Are you out of orbit?" Aggie screeched. "They stole our ship, tore me apart, wouldn't let us go..."

Humor tickled Thyron's protoplasm as Creena waved her to silence. "I know you can't understand, but at least try to believe me. They weren't all bad, they really weren't, at least not where I was. They really weren't."

The girl's brown eyes swam in an abundance of moisture, much as Gabe's had, and Thyron noticed his leaves were transpiring again, understanding the phenomenon at last. He trembled with a sense of emptiness, loneliness an emotion he'd never comprehended before, much less experienced. He pondered the irony of this link he'd developed with humans, beings he'd previously categorized as evil. While that designation fit Watkins, it certainly didn't apply to Gabe or Brad. Apparently Creena's experience had been similar.

The Sapphirans came to mind, deeds he'd witnessed that he considered no more than a hunting expedition. He wilted with the horrifying revelation that while he accused Aggie of murder for annihilating plants which were marginally sentient, he was guilty as well. Perhaps even more so, having not only condoned the pygmies' cannibalistic jaunts, but facilitated them. He shuddered with guilt, recalling how he felt when he thought Gabe was going to die.

The past couldn't be rectified, but in the future the pygmies' horrific practice needed to stop. Someday he would return to Sapphira to make it happen. Teach them how to find other means of sustenance by culturing native plants, then eventually embrace a diet similar to Gabe's.

He'd left Sapphira to pursue enlightenment, never suspecting it could arrive so painfully, much less through an emergency landing on a backward planet. Gabe was right: *Não há coincidências.* His desire to expand his wisdom to pass on to his progeny had been achieved. He'd gained knowledge, but in addition he discovered new vistas of understanding and emotion; which, at the moment, were exhilarating as well as agonizing, much like thrusting forth his first shoots upon his initial awakening. He sighed as words he'd heard a multitude of times came to mind, making sense at last: *Like sands through the hourglass, so are the days of our lives.*

EPILOGUE

Manaus, Brazil
Rio Negro River
11 November 1981
0445 Atlantic Standard Time/0845 GMT

Gabe knew it was time. How he knew, he wasn't sure, but Francesca had suggested the Full Moon on the 11th, and somehow it felt right. Where he needed to go, he *did* know. It would be a long, insect-infested journey, but he owed Thyron as much. After all, the vegemal had not only saved his life, but enriched it beyond measure.

His feelings were mixed about what lay ahead. In the past three years, a mere four percent of the seeds had germinated under his care, only a few dozen remaining as viable baby plants, now about six inches high. Whatever growing conditions existed on Sapphira, he'd apparently failed to duplicate them to their satisfaction. They grew slowly and he wanted to make sure they were strong enough to be on their own before releasing them.

While he'd retained a select few to mentor personally, the rest had the right to be free and wild as Thyron, nature, and the cosmos intended. But it still hurt to let them go, knowing without proper protection they'd face a multitude of dangers. Their mobility gave them the means to find all sorts of trouble. He chuckled, understanding how a mother felt sending her child off to kindergarten.

He got up before sunrise, savoring his coffee as well as the view from his high-rise apartment's balcony, overlooking water in all visible directions. Manaus was situated on a promontory where the

Rio Negro's dark waters to his right merged with the muddy Rio Solimões fifteen kilometers to his left, their combined flow creating the mighty Amazon. The bird's eye view never failed to leave him breathless, reminding him of the *Volition*, soaring at unheard of speeds high above the planet he called home.

The Moon sank slowly, disappearing into the Rio Negro, dawn breaking in the opposite direction moments later, moonlit water yielding to the Sun's brilliance on a new day. He'd never been much of an astronomer, but he couldn't help noticing that he felt a metaphorical connection, as if one phase had culminated, another about to begin.

As the moment's magic faded, he went inside and dressed in his favorite pair of khaki shorts and short-sleeved plaid shirt, then had a leisurely breakfast. After that, he retrieved the seedlings from their nursery in his spare bedroom, sending them reassurance as he ceremoniously placed them in a metal toolbox in which he'd punched a few air holes, bottom softened with a layer of native soil. He secured the latch and placed it in a canvas shoulder bag, then sprayed himself with a generous coating of deet-based insect repellant.

As ready as he'd ever be, he grabbed the bag and his straw hat, then left, taking the elevator to the ground floor. He walked to his car, where he set his precious cargo on the passenger side, placing the bag's strap around the seat back for additional security. He wished he could have brought Lupe along, but hadn't figured out how to explain what he was doing, much less why. He'd met her at the local garden supply mart a few months before, her love of gardening a more powerful attractant than pheromones. Maybe someday he'd tell her.

His blue Fiat left the paved thoroughfares of the metro area when he reached the side of town tourists seldom saw. The small car bucked through ruts and potholes in troubled dirt roads that snaked between boxy shacks with dilapidated tin-roofs. Twenty minutes later, he reached his destination, a remote marina on the shores of Rio Negro.

Only a few minutes past seven o'clock, it was nonetheless hot and muggy, air saturated with the eclectic scent of algae, fish, and mold, with an afterthought of diesel and sewage; the antithesis of Nevada's dry mountain air. He parked at a clearing fifty meters from the water's edge, gathered his bag, and walked to a crude dock where he explained where he wanted to go to a private guide named Pedro. Clearly of native descent, the man appeared to be in his late twenties, shaggy black hair framing dark almond eyes and a smile that revealed a few missing teeth. A short dialog revealed he was exactly what he was looking for, someone familiar with the target area.

Pedro grabbed an extra can of gasoline from a nearby shed, then they stepped aboard a motorized canoe the same color as the water and headed south toward the opposite shore, four kilometers away. It was but the first leg of their journey to the Ariau River, one of many tributaries, the mouth of which lay another fifty kilometers upriver to the west.

A dozen meters out, Pedro opened up the motor to full throttle, hull slapping the waves in ambitious rhythm. The Sun shone hot on Gabe's back, casting golden rays across rippled water, stirring memories of childhood excursions with his father to the same location.

A few minutes later, a playful river dolphin joined them, its perpetual smile hinting that it knew Gabe's secret. As it chirped and clicked, he reached out telepathically in friendly greeting. The animal danced on its tail beside the small boat and for a moment he feared it would jump inside, its antics already alarming Pedro.

Não, não faça isso! he psaid, relieved when the animal took his advice not to do it, spun once more, then dove into the green depths and raced ahead, as if leading the way.

When the boat reached a few hundred meters short of the opposite shore, Pedro veered right to head upriver. Versus where they'd embarked, the river's width doubled at a small bend, then narrowed again when they approached a finger of land.

His guide continued westward, following the southern shoreline, waving to a similar boat heading the opposite way, stern-mounted green, yellow, and blue Brasilian flag flapping stiffly in the breeze. As they passed the small peninsula, the river widened again, spreading to the horizon in all directions other than the heavily wooded land to their left, now a few hundred meters away. The rainy season would begin soon, during which islands currently visible as anonymous mounds would disappear beneath rising water.

Just over two hours later, they rounded another point and hung a tight turn into the Ariau. While Rio Negro commonly reached over twenty kilometers wide, the Ariau in places was a mere ten meters or less, the rainforest's canopy looming overhead, obstructing the sky. Vegetation clung to its banks, the growl of the small outboard joined by the cacophony of jungle birds, insects, and howler monkeys. It was still a little over eight kilometers as the crow flies (or perhaps parrot was more appropriate) to where he had in mind, the water calmer but progress slower as Pedro maneuvered around sundry branches and other obstacles; hopefully no crocodiles.

Caboclos, who were of mixed heritage between indigenous Brasilians and Europeans, lived in small villages throughout the area, which suited his goal not to release the seedlings too far from a human settlement. Knowing Thyron's beginnings were with primitive cultures, it seemed fitting for his progeny to have a similar opportunity. He recalled that on one of his boyhood visits, his father had hinted that his maternal great-grandmother had been a member of the tribe. The idea he might have cousins there was an odd but cozy thought.

He pointed out the designated *igarapé*, a small channel which would lead to his intended destination. Pedro navigated accordingly, the ongoing jungle symphony replacing the outboard's roar when he killed the motor and tipped it out of the water before the prop got hopelessly entangled in vines and organic debris. Rhythmic dipping of the paddle and water lapping the sides of the boat joined the rainforest refrain, the relaxing, hypnotic sound nearly lulling Gabe to sleep. He opened his eyes at the chatter of a family of otters as they scattered and dove beneath the surface, a frenzied chorus of monkeys announcing either their presence or something less friendly, perhaps a jaguar.

Eventually, voices and other sounds related to human activity swelled ahead, a cluster of natives visible as they rounded the next bend. Clothed in an incongruous mix of western and traditional dress, three men were busy hauling ashore their catch for the day. Another, still in a canoe, grinned with pride as he held up a very respectable-sized flounder.

Gabe waved in friendly fashion, wondering how anyone could eat such a thing, as the canoe coasted to shore and Pedro executed an expert jump to dry ground, barely rocking their vessel. Gabe leapt past the water's edge, nonetheless sinking in mud that covered his well-worn hiking boots. While Pedro finished beaching the boat, he plodded ashore and sought the tribe's leader, whom he found in a dome-shaped hut wearing native garb, including the traditional necklace of jaguar teeth, feathered headdress, and body paint in hues of yellow, orange, and green.

"Mais exaltado líder," he said. *"Precisamos da sua ajuda com uma importante missão."*

Following his respectful greeting and request for assistance, he explained that a plant species he'd found needed a safe location to assure its survival. Not only did it have important medicinal qualities, but possessed previously unseen mobility. Furthermore, ancient legends claimed the plants could talk to those who communicated with spirits.

The chief immediately summoned the tribe's shaman, to whom Gabe repeated his request along with its explanation.

"Seria uma honra," the shaman replied, bowing. *"Eu sei o lugar. Me siga."*

As expected, the man said that he was honored, adding he knew the perfect place. Leaving Pedro eyeing scantily clad native girls, Gabe followed the two natives through a narrow, vegetation-strewn trail, besieged by days past. He swatted away mosquitoes undeterred by deet while trying to watch where he stepped, barely missing a hairy tarantula that scampered across the path. Was it his imagination or did he feel welcomed by the surrounding vegetation? Or was it extended toward the seedlings?

The chosen spot was sheltered by towering trees and protected on all sides by boulders, some the size of his car, which formed what appeared to be an ancient site similar to a henge. The shaman explained it was a sacred area where the gods promised a miracle would someday occur that would unite all living things.

Gabe shivered, startled by a sudden flash of déjà-vu that raised gooseflesh on his arms, sultry heat notwithstanding. He slipped the canvas bag from his shoulder and set it on the ground, wincing with a twinge of pain that had never entirely retreated, in spite of the high-tech intervention onboard the *Volition*.

He hunkered down and opened the flap, removed the toolbox, then unlatched and lifted the lid, seedlings inside stirring restlessly as they reached toward the light. The rainforest grew quiet as he picked each one up, kissed it gently, and set it on the ground, watching the shaman and chief for their reaction when the tiny plants shuffled about on budding peduncles, investigating their new home.

Wonder caressed the natives' features, starting with their dark eyes, then igniting their countenances with broad, joyful smiles. The natives helped him move a few more rocks, filling the gaps to keep them contained a while longer, all realizing that in time they'd find their way out into the world. When they'd finished, the chief and shaman knelt carefully to avoid injuring any of their tribe's newest members, then lifted their hands skyward as they chanted praises in an unfamiliar language. Gabe bowed his head and likewise thanked the heavens for this fateful moment. The natives rose, and as if on cue, wild sounds resumed, jungle residents spreading the word.

Knowing that Thyron's progeny were where they belonged, Gabe returned to the village, where Pedro was still flirting with the girls. Just behind the guide, he noticed a young native boy about the age he'd been when he'd first visited the area. The youth held a basket of açai, one of his favorites, so he dug several *cruzeiros* from his pocket and offered them in exchange for filling his now-empty bag. Truly one of the many joys of returning to Brasil had been the vast variety of fresh fruit available year-round.

He motioned to Pedro that he was ready to leave and both climbed onboard the canoe. Gabe waved goodbye, promising to return, then winking at the boy with the açai, watching until the village faded in the distance. They reached the first bend where dense tangles of tropical growth and the call of birds swallowed all evidence of human presence. When they reached the Ariau, Pedro topped off the tank, then it took a few sharp pulls to restart the motor. As soon as they turned onto Rio Negro, Pedro opened up the throttle, tracing a wake of green foam as the bow bumped a random beat across the waves, the river's flow now in their favor.

Gabe leaned back, elbows propped on the seat behind him, and closed his eyes, sun overhead hot against his face. With his mission accomplished—which had gone even better than expected—he pondered his next step.

He grinned as potential titles for his submission to the highly ranked professional journal, *Plant Physiology,* played through his mind. Often finding a catchy yet suitably dry title, using the appropriate scientific nomenclature acceptable to academia, was more difficult than writing the paper itself.

"New Plant Species Discovered in Amazon Rainforest." Nope, not nearly unique enough; that happened daily. *"Exotic Wood Sorrel Species Found in Rainforest."* No. *Booor-inng.* How about *"Exotic Sentient Oxalis Species has 317 IQ."* He chuckled to himself, knowing even though it was probably accurate, it nonetheless wouldn't fly; but he could tell he was getting closer.

"Exotic Rainforest Oxalis Species Exhibits Sentience and Mobility." Maybe that would work, though *sentience* was a trigger word in botanical circles that could get it zapped. Perhaps his niece, Francesca, would have some suggestions. Now married and back in Brasil, she'd be thrilled to be coauthor on what would be her first post-doc publication.

The *Phytochemical Society's* journal was on the list, too. *"Mechanism for Defensive H2SO4 Emissions in Exotic Oxalis Species"* would certainly gain some serious attention.

Then came the anthropology journals. *"Amazonian Caboclos Tribe Declares Sentient Plant Fulfillment of Ancient Prophecy."* He smiled, knowing his father would approve. Whether or not Thyron could hear him, he didn't know, but he psaid it anyway.

Thanks again for saving my life, Thyron. Our children are in the best of hands.

He reclined the rest of the way, resting his shoulders on the aft seat, and stretched his arms wide, embracing the moment as one of satisfying completion, then folded them across his chest, content.

He'd kept his promise. Life was good.

He'd nearly fallen asleep when a familiar voice touched his mind.

When we met I thought you fierce
When my limb you went to pierce.
But in time you proved your worth
To set my seed on planet Earth.

His eyes flew open, mouth agape as he struggled to sit back up, precariously rocking the canoe. Pedro yelled, struggling to right the craft before it capsized in piranha-infested waters while Gabe's favorite expression echoed across Rio Negro to the tangled jungle beyond.

A refrain of monkeys and tropical birds sent back a primitive reply, one that he would swear for years to come included a parrot echoing his words:

"Holy Guacamole!"

THE END

*This episode of Thyron's story began in the chapter entitled "HE/927-652-A" in **A Dark of Endless Days**, Volume II of the Star Trails Tetralogy. Don't miss **The Sapphiran Agenda**, Thyron's backstory from **Beyond the Hidden Sky**.*

www.StarTrailsSaga.com

AUTHOR'S NOTE

Thyron barged in, uninvited, when I was writing *Beyond the Hidden Sky*. I didn't design him, I didn't create him. The *flora peda telepathis* just walked on-stage, after which he revealed himself and his various quirks. I had no idea there was such a thing as thylakoids when I named him, but now that I think about it, he named himself. Various other characters in *Star Trails* have just appeared as well, but Thyron is by far the most unique. My readers are never neutral, they either love him or hate him. Either way, his popularity motivated me to write *The Sapphiran Agenda*, a short story that explains his cultural roots as well as why he and the Sapphirans were on Verdaris where they met up with Creena. Since completing the tetralogy, I've known the story of what happened when Thyron and Aggie were at Area 51 needed to be written, too.

As soon as I started to put this story together, Gabe appeared. Since I'm a physicist, not a botanist, research was required (100+ webpage bookmarks' worth) as well as picking the brains of people better versed in biology. I'd especially like to thank my medical guru, James Mitchell, for suggesting the discovery of neurons in Thyron's leaves. In addition, much appreciation goes to my beta readers, Maria Lenartowicz, Lisa Klaes, and Jeanne Foguth, for their patience and input slogging through earlier versions of this story. I also want to thank my fans for wanting more about Thyron; my son, Gary Fox, for the Portuguese translations; and especially the grand pooh-bah of all editors, Stephen Geez of Fresh Ink Group, who did a superb job making me realize with due humility that I didn't know the English language nearly as well as I thought. I'll forever also be grateful to those who have speculated upon or defined plant sentience, as well as Wikipedia, Google, and Google Earth, which have made book research a breeze compared to what it was in the "old days". Thank you, one and all, for your valuable contributions.

I needed a plant to use as a model. I can't remember how I discovered oxalis, probably searching on photosynthesis when it popped up. What really blew me away was that situations related to oxalis's properties developed in the story *before* I knew they even existed, specifically its medicinal applications. So, to a point, much of that is serendipitously accurate. The parts involving sulfuric acid, however, are made up, though plants transmutating phosphorus to sulfur has been suggested. And of course, Thyron is a fictitious character. However, if he were real, I believe he'd approve of being related to oxalis. It's a very cool and interesting plant. I was planning to plant some when I noticed some had already sprung up among the catnip and mint beside my bay tree.

Holy guacamole! You just never know...

ABOUT THE AUTHOR

Marcha Fox is a science fiction fan and author who has always been fascinated by space and time. She's an old-time *Star Wars* nut whose favorite movies also include *Back to the Future* and *Deja-vu*. Her life-long love of astronomy eventually drove her to obtain a Bachelor of Science Degree in physics from Utah State University, followed by a career of over 21 years at NASA's Johnson Space Center in Houston, Texas, where she held a variety of positions including technical writer, engineer, and eventually manager. Needless to say, during that time she got to see all sorts of very cool NASA stuff in other locations that included Florida, California, Alabama, and Washington, D.C., as well as the European Space Agency in The Netherlands.

Her physics training allowed her to "do the math" regarding various elements in her books, especially Cyraria's starsystem, orbital dynamics, and resulting seasons in *A Dark of Endless Days*, to assure reasonable accuracy along with hoping to instill an interest in science and engineering to her fans by showing its relevance in an entertaining way. More detailed information as well as a discussion guide for parents and educators are included on her website, *www.StarTrailsSaga.com.*

She's the mother of six grown children, seventeen grandchildren, and so far, five great-grandchildren, though she denies being old enough to have such an expansive progeny.

CONNECT VIA SOCIAL MEDIA

Facebook
https://www.facebook.com/marchafoxauthor

Website
http://www.StarTrailsSaga.com

Twitter
https://twitter.com/startrailsIV

Blog
http://marcha2014.wordpress.com/